Praise for *The Fighter*

'Like living language, literary modes have both a formal and a demotic form. What we call "noir" is high tragedy brought down to the forgotten and disavowed – the fallen, who can do little but go on falling. Ours to witness the beauty and power of their fall. With *The Fighter*, cleaving to tradition, Michael Farris Smith brings that tradition brilliantly into the present' – **James Sallis**

'Smith's fiction is full of hard people in tough situations, but his obvious love of language and innately rhythmic prose lift his stories to a higher level' –*Big Issue*

'Equal parts brutal and beautiful and harrowing, it's left me totally bereft' – **Chris Whitaker, author of *Tall Oaks* and *All The Wicked Girls***

'Crisply written tale of thwarted lives and raw-boned courage' – *Booklist*

'This resourceful writer weds violence, despair, and glimmers of hope during a few tense days in the life of a once-legendary bareknuckle fighter… A gifted storyteller who parses battered dreams and the legacies of abandonment with a harsh realism that is both saddening and engaging' – *Kirkus* **(starred review)**

'Smith's great talent here is writing about ancient, universal concerns – parents and children, aging, and place – in a setting so vivid and specific that the book practically tracks mud up onto your doorstep. His vision of the Delta is powerful and lingering' – *New York Journal of Books*

'A novel that takes hold of your heart in a tight vice, *The Fighter*… is also written with diamond-like care and has a visceral impact, although not always for the faint-hearted' – *Crime Time*

Praise for *Blackwood*

'*Blackwood* is a fine and captivating novel with a sturdy
Faulknerian theme – past and present are never exactly separated,
and actions in the present are provoked by words or deeds
from long ago. Michael Farris Smith's prose is calm yet full of
feeling for this place and these people, and he handles scenes of
introspection and scenes of hostility with equal skill. In Smith's
hands, pages keep turning' – **Daniel Woodrell,** *New York
Times* **bestselling author of** *Winter's Bone*

'In Smith's haunting, engrossing latest (after *The Fighter*),
strangers awaken an evil force lurking… Smith's meditation on
the darkness of the human heart offers a moving update to the
Southern gothic tradition' – ***Publishers Weekly***

'Lurking over *Blackwood* is a family of itinerant grifters – a
version of Faulkner's Snopes clan, forces of chaos, human kudzu
except for the youngest of them, a mysterious boy in whom
Colburn sees his young self. As in the best noir, a soul-strangling
inevitability hangs over Red Bluff, yet somehow Smith gives his
doomed characters a dignity in the face of forces well beyond
their control' – ***Booklist*** **(starred review)**

'Unsettling, heartbreaking, and frequently astonishing, this
Southern gothic never runs out of revelations… A gleaming,
dark masterpiece by one of Southern fiction's leading voices'
– ***Kirkus*** **(starred review)**

'Call it Southern Noir or Southern Gothic or the legacy of Larry
Brown but the reality is Michael Farris Smith is writing with one
of the most powerful and distinctive voices in current fiction'
– **Square Books**

NICK

Michael Farris Smith

NO EXIT PRESS

This paperback edition published in the UK in 2021
by No Exit Press
an imprint of Oldcastle Books
Harpenden, UK

www.noexit.co.uk

A CIP catalogue record for this book is available from the British Library.

ISBN
978-0-85730-453-7 (paperback)
978-0-85730-455-1 (epub)

2 4 6 8 10 9 7 5 3 1

Typeset in 12.5 on 15.6pt Garamond MT
by Avocet Typeset, Bideford, Devon, EX39 2BP
Printed and bound by Clays Ltd, Elcograf S.p.A.

Sign up for our newsletter: noexit.co.uk/newsletter

Twitter @noexitpress

Facebook fb.com/noexitpress

Instagram instagram.com/noexitpress

For Sabrea

Hiraeth (n.): *a homesickness for a home to which you cannot return, a home which maybe never was; the nostalgia, the yearning, the grief for the lost places of your past.*

THE END OF THE MENACING ROAD

A Foreword
by
Michael Farris Smith

I had read *The Great Gatsby* a couple of times during my twenties. The first time I read it, I was in college and my reaction was almost no reaction. I was a bored and uninterested student and I'm not sure anything less than a lightning bolt striking the classroom would have caught my attention. I even remember thinking, what's the big deal?

The second time I read it, I was living in Geneva, Switzerland, in the midst of spending an unexpected few years as an expatriate. It was a brave new world, one that I loved right away, one that I embraced, one that I wanted to hold onto and never let go, though I knew a return home to Mississippi was inevitable in the near future. On this second reading, in my late twenties, I began to notice things in Nick Carraway, the story's narrator, that I found in myself. Uncertainty about where he belonged, but trying to figure it out. Shifting ideas about notions of home and country. A curiosity about the people who surrounded him that often fell into confusion and vagueness. Was it possible I could relate to Nick Carraway?

Fast forward another fourteen years to the next time I picked up *The Great Gatsby*. I'm not even sure why I picked it up, other than I was looking for something shorter to read and I saw it there on my shelf, and I had mostly forgotten about it. So I decided to sit down and see if it awakened anything in me that might have been lost over the years.

It was one of the most surreal reading experiences of my life. It seemed as if there was something on every page that spoke to me, that related to my own experiences, that spoke to my own, and still very alive, thirst for the unknown. The further I moved into the novel, the more at home I felt in it. And then getting closer to the end, I came across this line:

'I was thirty. Before me stretched the portentous menacing road of a new decade.'

Only a few lines earlier, Nick has just remembered that it is his birthday. As if to remind himself that he exists. That he is alive. The 'portentous menacing road of a new decade' rang in my head again and again. I closed the book right there and put it down and could only think about my own life when I was close to turning thirty.

I was twentynine years old when I came home from Europe. And I came back to a home town I did not recognize. My parents no longer lived there. My sisters were gone and starting families and careers in other places. During the time I had been gone, my friends had done things like get married, have children, buy houses, get jobs, get promotions. And here I was, sleeping on somebody's couch, with all I owned stuffed into a couple of duffle bags. It was strange, not just because of what they had all become, but because of what I had become. Somewhere along the way, I had decided I wanted to try and write. I had spent years reading as I sat in the cafes in France, as I sat in my apartment in Geneva, as I traveled on the train from one country to another, and something had moved inside of me. It's difficult to explain or define, all I knew was that when I got back to Mississippi, I was going to write. I wasn't really sure what that even meant.

So there I was. Twentynine years old. On the verge of turning thirty, with the uncertainty of a new decade before me, with my attitudes about self and place drastically different than they had been when the decade of my twenties began, with this urge to try and write, with home and the people I knew all colored in different shades. It felt as though I was standing on the edge of a canyon, a strong wind at my back, and that if I stepped over the edge, I would either be crushed on the jagged rock below or I would be lifted and carried by the wind. It was indeed a menacing road before me, full of doubt.

As I sat there with *Gatsby* closed, thinking about Nick's notions of turning thirty, the decade of my own thirties ran through my mind. I did begin to write and it was difficult. I got married. I enrolled in and finished a writing program. I began submitting stories and received a pile of rejections until I finally published a few stories. We moved. I kept writing. I kept getting rejected. My wife got pregnant. I tried to write a novel and it didn't work. I tried to write another one and it didn't work. I wrote a novella. We had a baby girl. We moved again. I got depressed. I kept writing. I got depressed again. My wife got pregnant again. I started another novel. Nobody wanted any of it. I kept writing. We had another baby girl. I was going to be turning forty soon. I kept writing and kept getting rejected and kept getting depressed and tried to keep my head above water, waiting for something to happen.

It did. But not until I was forty. My novella was accepted. A year later, my first novel was accepted. I realized then that the decade of my thirties had to be an evolution. It had to be the metamorphosis. I didn't know it while I was going through it. But Nick Carraway had known what it was going to be like. He had known it was going to be unpredictable, an emotional whirlwind, a decade of challenge.

I opened *Gatsby* again and finished it. But from that moment, the character of Nick Carraway lived in my imagination and I began to consider him from different angles. But he admits almost nothing about himself in *Gatsby*. I realized I only knew three things about him. He fought in the Great War, he was from the Midwest, and he was turning thirty. That was it. For someone who I thought I found great comradery with, I didn't know anything about him at all. The thought occurred to me – it would be interesting if someone were to write his story.

Almost before I could finish the thought, I knew that someone would be me. I shared his feelings of isolation, of bewilderment. I had lived the expatriate life like Fitzgerald and the other writers of the Lost Generation, all of who had a profound impact on both my writing life and emotional life. I was a writer, filled with an idea that excited me and propelled me, which is really the only criteria I have for a project I want to work on. I realized the gravity of it all, the weight of its literary heft, but I could not stop thinking about it, which meant I had to write it. So I did.

It's impossible to know what is going to grab hold of you. I think back to the first time I read *The Great Gatsby* and I only shrugged my shoulders. I think back to the second time I read it and I began to feel its emotion and truth. And then I think about the third time I read it and how it changed me. How it became a part of me. How it made me realize that you can face a 'portentous menacing road of a new decade' and you can survive and come out on the other end of it reborn. Because the edge of a new decade means you are alive. It means you are on the edge of experiences and emotions you cannot yet understand. It may be a 'decade of loneliness' as Nick predicts. But that loneliness may also manifest itself into the wind that carries.

I

1

A HEAVY MORNING FOG DRAPED across Paris and there was the corner café. The wicker chairs and the flowers on each table and the small man with the small eyes who sang while he worked. The chairs next to the window where Nick sat each morning and drank espresso and watched the hours of his leave tick away and on the days when the sun filtered through the trees and fell upon the cathedral across the street it seemed to him that there could be no killing. There could be no war. There could be no way that one man could drive a bayonet through the skin and bone of another until the tip of the blade dug into the earth underneath. On the days when the children began to appear in the park in front of the cathedral and climb and tumble and chase and the sun came full and the small man sang a long and turning song, then he felt the strange calmness of belonging in such a moment, so far from home, so close to going back to the front, the assurance of the Parisian day warming him so much that sometimes he had to unbutton the top button of his uniform and allow the warmth to escape before it became something else.

The morning of the fog, there was no light slashing across the statues of saints and there were no children. Only him and her and the singing man. She sat with him with her legs crossed and her hands flat on the table waiting for Nick to touch them and she said I want to see you in the morning when you wake. She had said this to him before he slept each of the last seven nights, the only seven nights he had known her, the longest he had ever spent time with any woman. His days spent walking with her and trying to understand her elementary English and her trying to teach him words on street signs and in shop windows. Trying to make his mouth make the correct pronunciation by squeezing his cheeks and lips and him slapping her hand playfully and then walking more. Stopping to sit on a bench in a park. Stopping in a café for an afternoon lunch. Ignoring his own reflection in windows because it reminded him of the uniform he wore and what was waiting. Winding through Montmartre and smoking cigarettes and watching an Italian paint the sun as he sat with his back against a tree and squinted through the tree branches toward the yellow sky. Walking along the river in the twilight when the lights first appear and there is both sadness and promise in that wonderful vagueness of day when time holds and anything seems possible.

And then those seven days and nights were gone and they sat together in the café and stared at one another and then stared out into the fog. Her hands waiting. His train ticket was stuck in the breast pocket of his uniform and she said I want to see you in the morning when you wake. She said it every few minutes, no other words between them, as if it were part of the mechanical workings of time. It was a sentence they practiced together and she said it perfectly and when it was time he grabbed her hands and held them and felt her knuckles and then her nails as if he had never seen a hand before. Then he stood and he left without saying a word because he didn't know what else to do. Something pulsed in him and scared him and kept him from saying whatever it was he wanted to say to her. And he wanted to tell her that I will come back if they don't kill me and I am damn near certain and scared as hell that they will kill me and you cannot imagine what it is to feel the earth shake with man's destruction and see the blanket of blood across the countryside and to never be certain if there will again be the sunrise. Each morning that it comes I stare at the horizon and try and draw it inside and hold it. So much that he wanted to say to her but he could not as if there were chains attached to his words and he was sentenced to a life of introspection.

He walked along the sidewalk and the fog swallowed him as he trudged with his pack across his back and his insides splitting and he listened for her voice to call for him. He listened for her to be the one to reach out and to somehow know all it was he wanted to say. He walked slowly and listened and waited for her voice to cut through the gray day but it did not come and then he was too far away from her to turn back. As he approached the train station he saw the other uniforms summoned to return and he heard the engines and the whistles and he was certain that he was going to die in this war. And when he did who would be at his funeral to truly mourn? There would be a coffin in the front of the sanctuary of the white-framed Episcopal church and his family and friends of his family and dedicated customers of his father's store and friends from the neighborhood and friends from school and an entire church filled with those who had some weightless attachment to him. They would sit on the pews and sniff into handkerchiefs and hug and shake hands and his name would give them all some strange purpose. And they would be there to share in a sadness but who would be there to mourn? To gasp and pray and hurt and hope for his soul? Did anyone truly love him and did he love anyone and the answers to all of his questions were clear and that was when he stopped and turned around and headed back for the café, walking first and then running. The pack heavy on his back and his mouth open in panic and the fog thick and like a curtain that hid her from him.

He ran and he saw lights of the café through the gray and he called for her and believed that he would have someone to mourn and someone to mourn him when the day finally came to lie down and leave the world to all the others. He called out to her as he ran and when he reached the café he stepped inside and he wiped his eyes and looked to their table. But she was gone.

The small man was wiping the bar and humming. He stopped and looked at Nick and then he pointed toward the door she had walked through. He clapped his hands and said *Vite, vite* and when Nick stood still he slapped the bar and shouted as if to wake him.

Nick dropped his pack and shoved it in the corner of the café and ran out, so little time between now and the train's departure and he ran along the sidewalk toward Boulevard de Clichy where they had walked so often in the last days. Several blocks and at each turn he expected to see her ahead, to catch her and say those things to her but she was never there. He wondered if he had run past her in the fog or missed her at another café and the fog seemed to thicken with his anxiety and he turned and called and searched but she was not there. He listened for her voice and he ran again and he began to grab at strangers though he knew they were strangers but he grabbed with the fraught hope that her face would be on the unfamiliar figure. They screamed and slapped when the frantic man in an American uniform pulled at them and said where is she and then he gave up on their help. He snatched a café chair and stood on it as if it might lift and carry him to her but there was only the fog in every direction and nothing magical about the chair.

He could not miss his train. He would not. It was not what he had been trained to do. He called again. And again and again. A waiter stood next to him and fussed and then Nick stepped down from the chair. He retraced his steps to the café with his eyes searching no more but only straight ahead at the ground before him and when he reached the café the small man said something to him in French that he both understood and did not understand. He lifted the pack from the floor and stuck his arms through the loops and he marched toward Gare Saint-Lazare as if he were already there in the mud and blood. He arrived at the station as the porter made the final call and he climbed into a car but he did not sit down. He stood in the aisle and looked across the heads of the passengers, out onto the platform, pretending to see her.

2

THEY EXPECTED THE COUNTER ATTACK at daybreak. The guns rat tat tatted all through the night, white flashes across a clouded landscape that might have been brilliant starbursts in a more imaginative and peaceful place. Flares spiraled, red and yellow arcs of light that kept their eyes open and toward the sky. At sunrise the mist hung low across the land and rose out of the craters like a great mob of spirits ascending and then they heard the planes and it began.

Grenades and shellfire threw the earth toward the sky and then came the roar of thousands of hungry men going for the throats of thousands of other hungry men. The rifles fired and once they were emptied the bayonets and once they were broken off in the rib cages out came the knives and the hands and knees and fists and whatever else could be used to kill. The constant explosions around them and they began to separate, the living and the dead and those somewhere in between. Men and pieces of men. Some walked through the battle, inattentive, looking for arms and hands. Another held the back of his head together with both hands. Some ran away and some played dead and others had long been void of humanity and ripped and shredded like barbarians that needed blood to survive.

They had gained nearly two hundred yards the day before but the counter attack drove them backward. The voice of retreat spread between the shellfire and screams and they turned and they were forced to cross back over the trenches that they had taken the day before. The planes rained down and gave them an escape. Those that were too slow or hobbled or simply dazed took bayonets into their spines and necks and the backs of their heads and those that were still on two feet joined the retreat, unable to save anyone but themselves.

When they reached the dugout they thought they had left for good two days ago, they tossed down their rifles. Gasped for air. Checked themselves for cuts or wounds that adrenaline had overcome. Some vomited. Some talked to themselves in loud voices of fear and hate or called out to people they loved. Others lay back and stared into the smoky sky. Still others bled until they couldn't bleed anymore.

The planes chased and fired and circled and fired again until the enemy was pushed away. The two armies settled in for recovery, hoping for rations, waiting for what was next. In an hour's time the dust settled and revealed a cloudless sky all around them. A pale blue. Pure and clean.

Artillery fire echoed in the distance and in the trenches those who were still alive helped with the wounded. A carnival of recovery. Men screamed from missing legs or feet and some fought to breathe against the bullet holes in their stomachs and chests. Stretchers carried out some but others only wrapped their wounds and waited for medics who had no chance of doing all that was needed. In time the screaming would cease. The bleeding would stop. And they all looked around to see who was left.

Random shell explosions came closer and recreated a low lying cloud of smoke and dust. But the sun settled and a ribbon of pink cut through the haze and lay across the horizon. Flocks of blackbirds passed between the shellfire and from one side of the sky to the other the blue transformed from light to dark.

And this was the worst time of day. After the fight and after the recovery and before nightfall. Those who remained waited for the sounds and they came, the voices from no man's land. The calls for help. The strained cries of dying. The sounds of pain and desperation and begging and pleading. Voices so close but so far away. There could be no help and the voices were already in their graves and they knew it. They knew it because they had sat and listened to the same cries. The same pleas. At the same time of day. There was nothing that could be done for them now but wait for the end but that never kept the voices from crying out until the fall of day, into the earliest of night, through the dark.

Nick unbuttoned his coat. He reached in and took out a rag and wiped the sweat and blood and dirt from his face and neck. He checked himself for cuts or holes and then he felt around in his pockets and found half a cigarette. He didn't have a match and didn't feel like asking. He sat on his helmet and leaned against the trench. There was thirst but the water went first to the wounded so he licked his lips and tried to gather a mouthful of spit. Then he swallowed.

A sergeant passed through and a new face was the only one who rose to attention and the sergeant told him to look around. You don't see nobody else saluting do you? We don't bother with that on the line. Save your getting up and getting down for the bad guys. Nick took the cigarette from his mouth and handed it to the newbie and he took it and he said I never done that. I never done what I just did.

'None of us have,' Nick said.

'But you been here and done it already and I swear to God

I don't see how nobody's alive. I don't even smoke and here I am about to smoke. I never done that.'

'Sit down.'

'How long you been here?'

'I don't know.'

The newbie sat down. He looked at his hands and then touched them to his neck and ran them along his legs and around his stomach.

'You're not hit or you'd know it.'

'I don't believe it. How come? That shit's flying everywhere.'

'Don't think about it.'

'I don't even know if we won or lost.'

'Me neither.'

'Then what the hell are we doing?'

'Trying to win or lose.'

'I can't do this. I can't. I got to go.'

'You'd better stay down.'

'I can't. I can't stay here. I got to go.'

'There is nowhere to go.'

'Bullshit. I'm going home,' he said and he stood and put on his helmet. Picked up his rifle. He turned in a circle as if looking for something else.

'You'd better stay down,' Nick said again. 'If your head pops up above that trench you'll get it.'

'I ain't going that way,' he said. 'I'm going back the way I came.'

The sergeant passed back through and the newbie saluted again and the sergeant said I told you not to do that shit.

'We'll get rations soon and you'll feel better,' Nick said. 'Find a light for that cigarette.'

'Do we have to do this again tomorrow?'

'Probably. And the next day too.'

'Then I won't feel no better. I got to go.'

'Okay,' Nick said. 'But keep your head down. And give me back the cigarette.'

The newbie gave the cigarette back to Nick. He looked around nervously. The sky nearly dark and lanterns glowing along the trench.

'The flares will begin soon,' Nick said. 'If you wait those will make you an easy target.'

'I never done nothing like this. I can't stay here. Don't tell nobody.'

Nick nodded and then told him to go west. Or south.

'Which way is that?'

'Like you said, the way you came from.'

'I ain't a coward.'

'You don't have to explain.'

'I ain't.'

'You'd better keep your head down.'

The newbie pulled his chin strap tight and then stepped past Nick and he crept along the trench as if anticipating an ambush from his own kind. The others noticed him and had seen this before and someone called out to give momma a big hug. I should have told him, Nick thought. If nothing else you will be alive for another day if you stay here. If you keep your head down. As soon as you climb up and out, you are dead. As soon as you are alone, you are dead.

3

THE RATIONS CAME IN THE morning. Tins of sardines and pressed ham. Bricklike bread. Water and cigarettes. They ate with their filthy hands, allowed more per man today than they would have received the day before. The planes returned but there seemed to be a pause. No orders had been passed along, no command to get up and go. Though it could come any second.

Nick's right hand shook uncontrollably. He sat on it. Held it folded under his arm. Talked to it. The shaking had started in the night and only stopped when he fell into a brief and fidgeting sleep. When his eyes opened, the shaking returned and it had not stopped. He ate with his left hand hoping that any type of nourishment might return some strength and settle his hand and his nerves.

He wanted desperately to take a walk. To climb up and out of the dugout and to walk across the countryside and touch the wildflowers and find a butterfly and lie down in the grass and feel the breeze. He wanted to be alone, to have to see no one and talk to no one. He wanted the constant pops of the shells and the hum of the planes overhead to go away. Silence. Only a simple silence and a walk and he felt like he could be human again. But that wasn't going to happen. He ate and took slow and heavy breaths and finally the shaking slowed and then stopped.

The men ate and settled in. Still no suggestion of a fight today. Down to his left a trio with Texas accents played cards and to his right a dozen men gathered and paid cigarettes and pennies for the chance to see photographs of naked French women that the trench entrepreneur had brought back from leave. Those who paid got to hold the photograph and had to fight off freeloaders peeking over and around their shoulders. Those who paid were allowed to hold the photograph for maybe a minute and then were forced to give it back. Pay up if you want a second look, the entrepreneur said. Those girls ain't cheap. The men with something to give happily bought a second look and those who didn't moved up and down the trench trying to borrow or steal some currency.

Nick held a stick and drew shapes in the dirt. A triangle, a square, a rectangle, a circle. Like the worksheet of a little boy. Then he tried to draw the head of a dog and it looked more like a horse. He then drew a pig face with some success and he gave it the body of a giraffe. He wrote his name. He wrote her name. He drew two stick figures standing next to one another. And then he fought the schoolboy impulse of drawing a heart around the stick figures and instead he only drew a line that connected the two names. Then he picked up a pebble and dropped it on the connecting line and he made the sound of a tiny explosion almost at the exact instant that a heavy explosion shook the earth and the men reached for helmets and rifles but then a lieutenant called for them all to sit tight. It ain't as close as it sounds. We're not going anywhere.

He drew long hair on her stick figure and then made scissors with his fingers and pretended to cut it off and he left the trench and was standing at the gates of Parc Monceau where they had found one another. He was watching the pigeons dance around the bust of Maupassant and a carousel turned and played a mechanical song while children sat atop ornamented horses and went up and down. Women stood together with strollers. A man slept on his back on a bench with a newspaper covering his face. Nick flicked a pebble and scattered the birds from Maupassant's shoulders and then across the pathway he had noticed her pushing a cart. She stopped at each bench and stopped people walking and she held picture frames toward them. Waved her hand across the frame and some nodded politely and kept going and some paused and touched or maybe held the frame but none bought. An older woman gave her a franc coin but didn't take a frame and she tried to give it back but the old woman wouldn't have it. She moved along with the cart and tried again and more rejection. Nick moved to keep watching her. She made a lap around the pond and behind the willows and sat down on the steps of a short bridge and nibbled at something she pulled from her pocket. Her hair was cut short and choppy and she wore no gloves and had a coat too big for her. Her skirt rose above her knees.

Nick had walked past as she sat on the steps and he looked into the cart. An assortment of handmade frames, decorated with red and black strips of lace and tulle and costume jewelry. A frame on top of the pile held the sepia photograph of a naked woman holding the neck of a bottle of absinthe in one hand and a short whip in the other.

'You like this one?'

'You speak English?'

'Of course. Do you?'

He lifted the frame that held the naked woman. He looked into the cart and the other frames were without the same allure.

'How much?' he asked.

'You do not want this one. It is only to make men look.

31

And some women. It is not so easy to sell an empty frame.'

'Do you make these?'

'Yes.'

'I can buy one?'

'If you want.'

He reached into the cart and took out a frame. Rudimentary and uneven but a red ruby at each rough corner.

'This would be good for my mother.'

'Is your mother alive?'

He cut his eyes at her. 'She would have to be.'

She stood from the steps. Brushed the flag on the shoulder of his uniform.

'Do you enjoy this war?'

He gave her a baffled look.

'I think some men find pleasure in a war,' she said. 'I cannot think of another reason to have one.'

'Neither can I.'

'But you do not enjoy it.'

'The only men who find pleasure in a war are the ones who get to decide that we have one.'

Another shell exploded and Nick jerked and his helmet fell off. Again they were told to sit tight. Again he returned to the park.

'Where is your home?' she had asked.

'It's getting difficult to remember,' he said. He then moved his eyes from hers and studied the frame. 'How much for this one?'

'Whatever you like to pay.'

'I would like to pay for that one,' he said and he pointed at the naked woman.

'That is not for your mother.'

'You are right.'

She took the frame from his hand and set it into the cart and said we can talk of this later. Right now I would like a coffee. If you would like a coffee also then come with me. He had noticed her eyes being somewhere between green and blue and her small mouth and nose set between sharp and drawn cheeks.

'Can we also eat?' he asked. 'I'm hungry.'

'Yes,' she answered. 'We will have a coffee and we will eat and we will walk if we like one another after everything.'

After everything they liked one another and stood to leave the café. She asked Nick to wait outside as she had to go to the toilet. He stood on the sidewalk with her cart and smoked but when he looked back through the café window he saw her not in the toilet but sliding from table to table and snatching fragments of bread and halfeaten pieces of meat and cheese and stuffing them into her coat pockets. She swiped cigarette butts from ashtrays and dropped them into another pocket. Nick turned away when she made for the door and hoped she hadn't caught him watching.

They walked and she pulled the cart and she sold two frames along the busy Boulevard des Batignolles. Nick noticed her careful tone when showing the frames. Her dirty fingernails gently handling her work. The artisan pride when she delivered. He thought she seemed like something out of a story and that their meeting and then eating and now walking felt like the product of someone's imagination but then as they moved along Boulevard de Clichy and up into Montmartre she seemed to merge into the physical world. He found himself bumping into her just to make contact or touching her arm or hand when helping her move the cart up the tall stairs that lifted them to the top of the city. She was a voice. A real voice on a moving body with eyes that gave him attention and kept his thoughts on right now instead of what lay ahead or behind.

'Do you want to know where we are going?' she asked when they reached the top of the steps.

'Not really,' he answered.

'I would like a drink and it is cheaper in Montmartre.'

'I would hope so as many stairs as we've climbed.'

'Have you been here?'

'No.'

'Then look.'

She took him by the shoulders and turned and faced him toward the city that fell below. Their steady ascension had taken them to the edge of Place du Tertre and Paris stretched out and sat quietly as if without engines or voices.

'If you stand here for a long time it is possible to believe that nothing is bad,' she had said.

'Nothing?'

'Rien.'

He turned to her. Her eyes across the Parisian sky but the life quickly drained from them and then her melancholy bled into him and he felt her solitude. He stared across the city and sensed not only her loneliness but the eternal loneliness that resides in us all and for the first time since he had felt the anxiousness of youth he realized that he wasn't alone. There are others like me, he thought. And she is one.

She sat down on the top step.

'Wait here,' he said.

He walked into a bar at the corner of the plaza. Two men stood at the doorway and argued in Spanish and he stepped between them. One called *Americano* but Nick kept his head down and moved to the bar. He bought a tall carafe of wine and he took two glasses and when he slid back between the two men they clinked their beer glasses to the wine glasses squeezed between his fingers.

He returned to her and she sat with her knees drawn against her chest and Nick poured. When the wine was gone the day began to fade and they walked back down the stairs. She asked him to help with the cart to where she stayed and they moved into Pigalle, a gritty series of streets scattered with dance halls and red lights. She walked more quickly through Pigalle and Nick hustled with the cart to keep pace. He was about to ask why she was racing when she pushed open the door of an empty building and they stepped inside. Nick paused and looked at the dustcovered windows and then back and forth along the street and she reached out and took him by the arm and pulled him inside. She closed the door and slid a cinderblock behind it to hold the door shut and told him to follow. They stepped through the remains of a job begun and then abandoned. Scraps of plywood and lumber and large chunks of plaster wall lay scattered across the floor and a giant coil of wire nestled in the corner like a copper tumbleweed.

Nick followed her to the back of the building and then she opened a door that led to the alley behind. She stuck her head out and looked both ways and then she motioned to him. They stepped across the alley and went into a door that was wedged open with a folded magazine and inside the door was a staircase. Once Nick had cleared the doorway she closed the door gently and the light of day disappeared.

The stairway was enclosed and windowless, the only way in or out the single door. She took out a matchbox and a halfsmoked cigarette. She stuck the butt in the corner of her mouth, struck a match, sucked hard to relight the butt. Then she held the match toward the staircase and nodded as if the gesture itself were some additional secret he should recognize.

She went up first. The match burned away and she tossed it and Nick followed her closely in the darkness, a steep and narrow rise. She didn't speak and he didn't ask and they kept going up and up until they reached the top floor. She asked if he was still there and he whispered yes. You don't have to whisper she told him and then she opened the door to the attic.

She dropped the butt from her mouth and squashed it with the toe of her boot and walked in first. The attic reached high above them and loose arms of plywood lay across the beams. Clothes racks filled with old costumes covered the attic floor space and she moved through the tight rows, turning her thin frame sideways. Nick trailed her, the costumes brushing against him and the evening light coming in the windows and shading everything in blue. He stopped in the middle and gazed at the cluster of dresses and suits and coats and the stacked boxes of hats and shoes.

'What is this place?' he asked.

But he saw on the other side of the costumes a chair and a thin mattress on the floor and an open suitcase. She crossed the attic floor and stopped at the windows. Evening lights had begun to shine and she emptied the cigarette butts and scraps of food from her pockets onto the windowsill.

Nick moved out of the costumes and noticed a shadeless lamp on the floor next to the mattress. He bent to turn it on and she said not yet. Scattered on the floor were newspapers and old magazines. Costume dresses lay piled on top of the mattress for warmth and comfort and in the windowsill with the butts and food lay stockings and a hairbrush and handheld mirror. On the floor beneath the window was her cut hair and a pair of scissors. Long and curvy locks of brown like cut strips of ribbon.

She opened the window. From the end of the block came the rhythm of a bass and a snare drum and an energetic clarinet twisted through the thumping beat like a tenor-toned snake. Solitary lights glowed across the rooftops. A horse and buggy clopped past underneath and the shrill laugh of a woman came from somewhere close. The Parisian sky was clear, the stars visible and the stovetop smoke from homes pushed in the breeze like earthfallen clouds.

She picked up the brush but set it back down and she ran her fingers through her choppy hair. She threw her head back and shook it in habit of having the length. Then she turned to him and said mine is more short than yours.

'It looks good,' he said.

'Men like long hair, I think.'

'Then why did you cut yours this way?'

'Maybe I do not want men to like me.'

'Do many men like you?'

'You must look around Paris. There is no such thing as many men. They are all somewhere else.'

'It's possible I have stood beside some of them. But they will come back.'

'And so my hair will come back.'

'I like it this way.'

'Then maybe you are not a man. Maybe you are something different,' she had said.

A litter of shellfire snapped him from the attic and he fell facedown in the dirt. Grabbed his helmet and he and the others hugged the earth and felt it coming. He told himself to think of her think of her think of her.

She had pulled the windows closed and turned around and

looked across the makeshift room. They stood together in the attic above Théâtre du Rêve, a small theater below that once thrived with dance and song but had stopped trying during the war. The attic was a place to store the production costumes, racks of discolored highnecked dresses and floorlength overcoats and mismatched suits and evening gowns. The clothes were bunched tightly on the racks and the racks filled the floor and wall space but for a slither of a pathway that led from the door to the window. Coming and going her shoulders brushed the forgotten costumes and she told him the touches seemed to her like a friendly welcome or the loving sadness of goodbye and there was a comfort in not being alone in the attic room but surrounded by the costumes that once had life. She had found the attic by accident, she told him. Wandering with all she owned in her suitcase and looking for any open door or any empty building to get into for a night or two or three. She had looked into the windows of the building under renovation and turned the knob and it opened and she sat there the first night. Waited for the morning and for the workers to return. But they hadn't. And so she had stayed another night and another and she realized no one was coming back. She had gone into the alley to piss and she had seen the back door of the theater and then found the staircase and then found the costumes. She felt safer up high. Warm among the costumes. Eyes across the city. She had a window to look out and wonder what was going to happen to her.

'You live here?'

'Until someone asks me to leave.'

'I don't think you need to worry about that. It looks like a costume graveyard.'

'What is this word? Graveyard.'

'It is the same thing as cemetery. Do you know the word cemetery?'

'I know this word. So you believe the costumes are dead. I believe they are alive.'

He nodded and picked up a wedding gown from a pile of dresses on the bed and he held it up as if to examine its craftsmanship. He touched the sequins around the waist and along the neck and then he folded it and laid it back on the pile.

'It does not matter. I will not be here long. Someone will come.'

'Where will you go?'

'I do not know.'

With me, he wanted to say. But he had nowhere to take her and no promise he could make.

'I am afraid most nights,' she said.

'So am I,' he answered. And as soon as it was out of his mouth he wanted to take it back. To hide this part of himself. But it was honest and quick like a heartbeat, nothing to be controlled. He folded his arms. Rolled his eyes to the ceiling. Tried to think of anything else.

'How do you make the frames?' he asked.

She opened the windows again and said come over here. They leaned out and she pointed. A scrap pile of wood lay in the alley several buildings away.

'A person who makes things out of wood leaves this,' she said.

'A carpenter,' Nick said.

'A carpenter,' she repeated. 'And then I take the pieces of cloth and the lace and buttons and many other things from the costumes. The glue I steal. I put them together like a child with a puzzle.'

'Tomorrow I will buy you a big bottle of glue.'

'Tomorrow you will no longer want to see me. Or tomorrow you will no longer want to leave me.'

'I think there is something in between that.'

'No. I think it is one or the other.'

She was blunt and beautiful and scratching and clawing and free and bound and she seeped inside of him. She is so different and I am scared of her and I keep finding new ways to be scared but not right now. Don't let it show right now.

'I have a room where you can come and stay,' he said. 'It is closer to the river. There is a nice café next door.'

'There are many nice cafés.'

'Not as nice as this one.'

'Does your room have four walls and a woman downstairs who asks for the key when you leave?'

'Yes.'

'Then I think this room is better and you can stay with me.' She closed the windows again. Several wine bottles with candles in their necks stood together in the corner and she lit them. Then she sat on the edge of the mattress and unlaced her boots. She took off the first one and held it up and felt the wobbly heel and touched the tender, worn sole. She took off the other and tossed them next to her suitcase that lay open with her few clothes spilled out onto the floor. She stood and unbuttoned her loosefitting coat and her loosefitting blouse and hung them on the back of the chair. She stepped out of her skirt and then rolled off her stockings and the cool night air sent chills along her arms and legs and she shuddered for an instant. And then she lay down on the mattress, sliding herself between the pile of costumes. And she waited.

This is not real, he had thought. You are not real and if you are what do you want and what will happen after this.

She waited.

You do not do this with someone. You do not walk across a park and find a woman who speaks to you with direct and maybe honest words and you do not go with her to a strange place and you do not do this. This is not real. This is some ploy or some trick and you cannot be there the way you are there and I don't know what you want. And I don't know why I am scared of her.

She waited.

His hand began to shake and he grabbed it quickly as if it might strike lightning if ignored.

She waited.

Maybe this is real. Maybe I can have this. The world is different now and you know that and maybe your world can be different too and you can have this and you can lie down with her and she doesn't want anything and she is not going to trick you and this is real. Maybe you can touch her and feel her and maybe the sky is still blue and the sirens reverberating outside across the city are not for you. Maybe this.

She stared at his hand. She moved onto her elbows and her chin rose above the fringe of the wedding gown and she said something in French. Whatever it was she said had drawn him to her and he went down to his knees beside the mattress.

He leaned up in the trench now. The murmur of men and the whistling above and he looked around. The wildeyed faces of strangers. And he was a stranger to them. So few remaining that he had begun this war with and he had stopped asking names or exchanging histories or gathering or giving anything personal with men who might not be there in an hour. But they were bound by this thing that had forced them all together, that forced them to do what even their nightmares could not have imagined. He sat with his knees pulled up and he anxiously listened for the next explosion that would propel them up and out and he wondered if this would be the time that he was shot through the chest before he could even make it out of the trench. If this would be the time that the grenade landed at his feet. If this would be the time that he would stumble and be stabbed before he could get back up. He dropped his head on his knees and listened and waited and tried to force something good into his thoughts and all he could think of were the words she had said that helped him across the room to her and how she had touched the tip of her finger to his restless hand and for the entirety of his life he would wonder what it was that she had said. The next explosion fell damn near on top of them and rose them all to attention, and then another and another and the same lieutenant who had told them to sit tight moments before now screamed for them to rise and attach your bayonets and form the line. Get your shit together and get ready to go and kill.

4

AFTER THE ATTACK, AFTER THE wounded were dragged away, after cigarettes, they peeked over the edge of the earth and watched the two Germans stagger toward their side. Mindless and confused and certain they were heading in the direction of safety. A rifle raised and settled to shoot them but another said hold on. Let's watch a minute and see what they do.

The two lost men held hands and swayed like drunks. One sang and the other rolled his head and every few steps they would both stop. Look around in all directions. Exchange in brief conversation. And then walk and sway and sing again as if strolling down some boulevard of promise.

The heads rose all along the dugout as word of entertainment spread and the unusual sound of laughter passed from one man to the next. The couple now swung their arms together and danced and skipped in a circle, the dust at their heels and their steps surprisingly careful around the craters and the song louder and when they turned their backs the Americans saw that one of the lost soldiers was missing part of his skull. That caused the laughter to grow and they pointed and began to heckle the gruesome sideshow as if it was part of the act.

Nick had dozed but another slapped at his arm and told him to get up. You got to see this. He rose to the noise. Climbed up and asked what was going on.

43

'Out yonder. Got two lollipops dancing around like schoolgirls. Looks like they got no idea where they are. Or who they are, don't seem like. Hope their pockets ain't filled with grenades.'

The two soldiers skipped and swayed. Stopped once and shared a long embrace and the jeers and whistles multiplied but the couple ignored. They held on to one another. Seemed to be making some kind of promise. And then they let go and made several more playful circles and then the one with the missing piece of his skull collapsed to his knees.

'Go ahead and gun 'em,' somebody called out.

But that was met with disagreement as the men wanted the show to go on.

'Shoot them,' Nick said.

'What for?' the soldier next to him said.

Nick looked at him. The grin on his face as he took in the spectacle. Something both grave and childlike in his expression. Nick didn't answer and he watched again.

The one who sang stopped singing and dropped to his knees with the other.

'Come on! Act two!' someone yelled.

'You ain't kissed yet!' yelled another and then there was laughter and then others joined in, trying to top one another.

Then the singing began again. Except that it was a different kind of song from before. It was not the circuslike song of their disillusioned playfulness, but the song of hurt. Long, extended words that rose and fell with the tone of despair or degradation. Maybe even hope. Something prayerful or meditative and the man sang with conviction as he held his companion underneath his arms. Holding him so that he would not fall to the ground but stay with him and it was easy to see with the slumping weight that the man with the missing piece of skull was not there anymore. But the other held him and sang to him and his voice seemed to stretch across the bloodstained land as if carried by birds.

The jeers and jokes ceased. The men watched quietly.

Nick slid down, not wanting to see anymore.

And then a single rifle shot splintered the moment and the song came to an end.

They had lain awake in the middle of the night in the attic and he told her that he was not certain anymore of his home. I don't believe that I can trust it. I don't believe I can trust my home or my country. Or this country. Or any other. It is a strange feeling. She lay with her head on his chest and his arm wrapped around her and he felt her back and the bones of her ribs.

'No one can trust so much at one time,' she said. 'But you have a place to go. That is something.'

'Maybe. Is Paris your place?'

She rolled off the mattress and lit a candle. Then she reached into the open suitcase and pulled out a folded piece of paper. She slid back underneath the costumes with him and she unfolded the newspaper ad and showed it to him in the candlelight.

It was a large advertisement with a dancing girl in the center. The dancing girl's skirt was hiked and she kicked a leg and exposed high stockings and the wide smile of something like lunacy covered her face. The dancing girl pranced on a stage and spotlights shined on her from each corner of the advertisement.

She pointed at the words and translated for him. A large script ran across the top of the ad and said the stage is yours in Paris. Running down each side of the girl's body were the promises. Showgirls needed. Shows nightly. Room and board and travel provided for performers. Best wages. Support our men. Across the bottom of the page, underneath the floating stage, was the name and address of the Red Brick Club on rue Pigalle. After the address was the instruction to write to us, describe yourself, and if we feel like you are ready for the lights, your train ticket will be mailed to you.

After she had read it all she folded the ad and tossed it on the floor.

'They do not tell you many other things,' she said. 'When you arrive you must pay for the train ticket. But I do not have money. So I take the room upstairs and I am fed but I must pay for every night I sleep and every bite I take. I am bought before I get here.'

'But you danced?'

'Never.'

Nick reached across the floor into his coat and pulled out a pack of cigarettes. He took one out and held it to her and said try a whole one. She put it in her mouth and Nick reached for the lit candle. They smoked and stared up at the attic beams where the faint candlelight disappeared.

The streets of Pigalle and Montmartre were filled with young women who had answered such ads. They came expecting chorus lines and flashy piano players and the heartbeat of a new direction only to find that these dance halls were places where women danced on makeshift stages with bottles swinging from their hands and men reaching for their calves as they stepped and slapped and cackled with each troll of fingers across their flesh.

'You have a choice to make,' she said. 'Serve drinks for almost nothing or become something else.'

'You could not go back home?'

'My home is no longer there. It is in the ground. So now I am an artist. Starving like an artist. Selling nothing that I make like an artist. Hiding like a mouse in an attic.'

'I saw you sell two frames.'

'Do you see how many remain in the cart?'

'I have never made anything.'

'You have. Only you do not remember. All children are artists.'

'I think I was born this way.'

'You are a poor boy. I think you have bigger eyes than you say.'

'I once thought to write.'

'Write what?'

'I never decided.'

She sat up, her bare back exposed. The orange tip of the cigarette blossomed as she smoked and then she let her head fall back and she blew the smoke straight up into the air and said you should not be so sad.

'I'm not sad.'

'You are something.'

'I have to go back to the front.'

'You do not have to. Does your captain know you are here in this room with me?'

He shook his head. They smoked. Nick turned on his side and faced her and said I have six more days. She lay back down and pulled the dresses across her and said you do not have six more days. We have six more days. I give my days to you and you give your days to me. And if we want more when those days are finished then we can take them.

5

REINFORCEMENTS ARRIVED AND NICK AND the others marched in a staggered line toward the relief camp. They walked for several miles along a dirtworn path and then they climbed into the backs of trucks that carried them the rest of the way.

The camp surrounded a village of what had once been a thousand residents but only a hundred or so had ignored the evacuation and remained. Tents for the men stretched out from the town center and a hospital had been set up in the storehouse of the local winery. The camp was a bustle of officers and the coming and going of battalions and Nick and the others climbed out of the trucks and were given permission, unless they had open wounds, to go directly to the chow line.

The day was hot and the air hung thick. Nick took a plate of beans and rice and bread and then he walked into the village square and sat in the shade of a slender alleyway. A clothesline hung across the alley, draped with towels and sheets. A military truck buzzed around the square and an old man with a wild gray beard smoked a pipe and sat in an open second floor window and watched the soldiers sitting and eating on the sidewalks of his home. Two nurses hurried across the square, one on each end of a stack of folded stretchers, and Nick waited for the whistles and calls that always chased but the nurses passed to silence as none were willing to stop chewing after an extended stay on the front. While they ate a private walked around with a box and handed out packs of cigarettes and matches and chocolate bars.

When Nick was done he set the tin plate on the cobblestone. Leaned back and unbuckled his belt and opened the button on his pants. He patted his stomach that had risen like a loaf of baked bread. Up above a woman with thick arms leaned out of the window and began to pull in the clothes from the line.

'Bonjour, l'américain.'

Nick raised his hand and gave a friendly wave.

'Fatigué?' she asked.

'Yes. Fatigué.'

She gathered the sheets and towels and disappeared inside the window. Nick's head fell back against the building and his eyes closed. He was almost out when she whistled. He looked up and she was leaning out of the window.

'Tenez, l'américain,' she said and she tossed a cigar down to him. It bounced off his hands but he picked it up. Smelled it.

'Merci,' he said.

'C'est bien, l'américain,' she said and then she tucked inside again.

Nick twirled the cigar. Set it next to his plate. The sun disappeared behind scattered clouds and across the square soldiers lay on their backs or on their sides and tried to find sleep. Birds gathered and danced around scraps of bread or rice and those who did not smoke swapped cigarettes for chocolate. Nick's hand began to tremble and he looked at it and said you don't have to do this right now. You are sitting in a little French town with your stomach full and a nice woman has given you a cigar to go along with your cigarettes and chocolate. So stop shaking and relax. Smoke your cigar.

But you've never smoked a cigar, he said, answering himself.

I never smoked cigarettes either but here I am. And sure I have smoked a cigar. I must have at some point. After Yale beat Harvard all the boys were smoking cigars and singing and swaying in the cold December sun.

Not you.

Well if I didn't then I'm sure I smoked one at Buddy Holland's wedding. He was handing them out to everyone. I remember champagne and the band with the guy who played the standup bass and his mustache curled on the ends.

You took it but you didn't smoke it. You said you didn't smoke when he handed it to you. Remember how funny he looked at you? Like you were missing the point. Which I think you did.

I'm sure I've smoked a cigar.

I'm sure you haven't.

Then I'll smoke this one.

You are supposed to have a special occasion for smoking a cigar. At least that's what you have always believed.

I've always believed a lot of things.

It's not the time for philosophy or politics. You need a special occasion to smoke that cigar.

No I don't.

Yes you do, l'américain.

Then I'll invent one.

Nick bit off the tip of the cigar and spit it out. Then he struck two matches at once and sucked on the cigar until it lit. He gagged at its strength and fell to the side with big coughs.

'That's a big boy cigarette,' a voice called from down the sidewalk.

The French woman stuck her head out of the window and asked something and he waved her off. Sat back up. Wiped his mouth. Moved the cigar to his lips. Inhaled and blew out the smoke with the same breath. The smoke was heavy and sat in front of his face in the stagnant summer air. Above more clouds had gathered and the low rumble of thunder or artillery fire or both came from the west.

So. What's the special occasion, he thought.

I live. I am alive.

Above him one of the shutters slammed shut. He casually looked up at the clothesline. Casually sucked on the cigar. The other shutter closed and it was then he heard the doors closing shut in his mind. First his mother closing the bedroom door and then his father closing the back door as he walked out onto the back porch. Never words of hate or resentment only the closing of doors and the stretching silence that followed. The empty stares or the turned backs or the creak of a house settling into silence.

6

IT WAS AS IF HE had lived a separate childhood. A life divided. A mind divided. Time divided by compartments of light and dark.

The dinner parties his mother hosted with the polished silverware and shined plates. The table in the corner stacked with wine bottles and fresh flowers in a crystal vase in the middle of the dining table. The guests moving about the house in calculated nods and handshakes as they shared the language of the expected. Nick sitting at the top of the stairs and watching and listening.

The spring days in the garden with his mother as she knelt on an old quilt to keep her knees clean as she clipped the dead left from winter. Nick piled the clippings and put them in the garbage can as she talked and talked of what she would plant this year and how much it had rained or snowed and she hoped against a false spring because there was nothing more cruel than a false spring. His father in the garage sharpening the shovel and hedge clippers and at the end of a day of pruning and trimming shrubs they sat on the porch and ate something with gravy. Always something with gravy in the first days of spring. After they ate his mother and father sat on the swing close to one another and he caught them smiling as he ran around in the front yard or tried to climb the neighbor's tree though his father told him to keep off the small branches or I'll end up having to replace something that God already made.

He lived in a neighborhood of sidewalks and shade trees. Houses were white with black or forest green shutters and window boxes hung from porch rails and first floor windows. Women swept the sidewalks wearing aprons and men in ties with coats slung over their arms picked up the newspaper from the front lawn as they got out of their cars in the late afternoon and went inside to see what was for supper. Children rode bicycles in the street and a busted nose from a bad hop in a stickball game or the anxiety of falling in love for the first time was the height of trouble. He learned from his father not to get too close or too far away from anyone or anything and was treated much like his father treated the family hardware business, with attention and concern to make sure he was functioning correctly.

Work. That was what his father talked about around the dinner table. In between flipping the pages of the sports section. This family has run on work for generations. And you'll do the same one day. You'll walk into my office and it will be your office and then it will be your son's office and so forth and so on. This is a fine business to learn. Runs itself. But you got to know what you're doing, how to talk to people, how to listen even if you're not really listening because you'll hear about it all. Not only how many lug nuts or quarts of oil they need but what a hassle it is to get the frame square or how much the rain has set everybody back or my wife has been nagging me for weeks to get this done. You'll hear it all and you got to listen.

Then getting a little older and his father offering him coffee. Nick feeling like a bigshot and getting up early for school and beating them down to the kitchen. Taking the white mugs from the counter and setting them on the table next to the sugar bowl. Taking the small bottle of milk from the icebox and setting it next to the sugar and waiting for them to come down. Calling. Come on. I got it ready. His mother and father coming into the kitchen with brushed hair and tied robes and his mother set the coffee to brew and they settled at the table with their son.

During these stretches of contentment he always noticed something in the eyes of his father when his father looked at his mother. Something almost mournful, a tenderness and a happiness but blended with the distance of loss. Sometimes she caught him looking at her and she would smile and maybe even blush but mostly Nick watched his father as he stared at her. His mother unaware as she washed dishes or read in her spot at the end of the sofa or wrote a thank you note to the host of some party or dinner they had attended the weekend before. His father's watchful and careful eyes settled on the placid nature of his mother and at times Nick sensed the wonder in his father's stare and other times he sensed desperation.

There was work and school and church. Birthdays and anniversaries. Cooked meals and blue blossoms in the yard and old leaves twirling in the chill wind and smoke from the chimney. The sunlight falling into the bay windows in the early morning and his father walking up the driveway at the same time each evening. The rhythm of being.

But these stretches were interrupted by other things. By a blackness that interrupted the periods of goodness and stayed with them for weeks. Months. Closed doors and the curtains pulled. The docile nature of an evening of conversation replaced by the lull of electric light or the clatter of dishes in the sink. His father downstairs and his mother upstairs in the bedroom. The bedroom door locked. The light off behind the door. Great spaces of solitude in the same house that was sometimes filled with the smiling faces of friends and family but during this blackness the house seemed to grow and the space seemed to stretch in height and spread in width and Nick was left to wonder where the voices had gone.

His mother disappeared during these times and he was left to his own in the afternoons after school. His aunts dropped by to check on him and sometimes took him for ice cream. But she's here, he wanted to say. You don't need to check on me. She's here. But she was only there behind the door and he knew that too. They left casseroles or leftover chicken and mashed potatoes for him and his father to eat for dinner. They left soup to take up to his mother as she would eat little else during this time. His father came home from work in the evening and walked into the silent house and pursed his lips and looked around. Looked past Nick as if he wasn't there.

Mom is upstairs, Nick would say though he hadn't been asked.

I know where your mother is. Have you seen her?

No.

Are you hungry?

Yes.

Do you have homework?

I finished it.

Did you call for her when you came home?

Yes.

What did you do?

I went to her door and knocked and asked if she was feeling better. I told her I was home and that if she needed anything to tell me. She said okay.

Did she say anything else?

Nick would shake his head.

At night Nick would go upstairs to his mother's room to tell her good night and she would let him in. Read with me, she said and Nick sat beside the bed with three or four books to pick from and he read to her as she lay propped on pillows and she held the blanket underneath her chin as if cold or scared. When he finished one book he would ask if he could read another and she would say yes until he had read everything he had brought with him. In the better times he was the one lying under the covers and she was the one at his bedside reading but during the blackness the roles reversed and when he was done reading he kissed her forehead and tucked the covers around her. Asked her if she wanted to say a prayer and she said no but be sure and say yours before you go to sleep. She carried heavy eyes and her color gone and sometimes her hair matted against the side of her head where she had been sleeping all the day long. Nick kissed her and held the books under his arm and then he would go back downstairs to find his father and most nights his father was not in the house but outside.

He had helped his father build a redbrick firepit in the backyard the summer he was ten and when his mother went behind the door his father had taken to standing in the dark and burning newspapers in the pit. He never kept them when she was part of their lives but when she was held by the blackness he stacked them next to his reading chair. Separated the sections and rolled them before he went to bed and wrapped rubber bands around the ends to give them the form of a baton. He kept the rolls stacked neatly on a shelf in the garage and each night after he and Nick had found something to eat and after they had exchanged what few words his father could muster, he told him to go upstairs and see his mother and then he took the rolls and wandered into the backyard like a messenger, slipping off into the night with news to deliver. His father stood at the edge of the firepit and stared at the stars or clouds or halfmoon or whatever there was to stare at in the sky and then he struck a match and lit the end of the first roll of newspaper.

Nick would come outside after reading with his mother and stand next to his father. The rolls burning methodically and his father never lit another until the one before was done. Bluegold flames twisted from the ends of the rolls and then bit by bit black pieces of the paper peeled away and drifted up and across the backyard, wrinkled and charred with hairlines of orange glowing on the burning edges. The stories and reports and promises of the daily news disintegrating in the night air and Nick would ask if he could light a roll and his father handed him the matchbox and he stood still with his hands in his pockets and his eyes fixed on the firepit as he waited for his son to take his turn to try and burn it away.

In the nights in the backyard or when they were in the house together or maybe taking an evening walk, Nick and his father said little. Nick fought to conjure up a story from the school day or to share some interesting tidbit he'd picked up in science or history and his father answered with polite nods or crossed arms that suggested disbelief or confusion. A man not cruel to a boy. Only unable to see him the way he needed to be seen as his mind was occupied with his own confusion and disbelief.

Nick took to lying awake at night. Listening for steps or movement or anything that told him his mother was still alive in that room. That she was in the blackness but she was safe and she would come out of it again like she had so many times before. And this time she would stay out of it and there would be a straight line in her life. In his life. In their

57

life. He began to make marks on his headboard, undetected beneath the edge of the mattress, counting the days that she was gone. Knowing the more marks he made the closer it was to being over. Tiny grooves in multiples of five that reached into twenty-five, thirty. Thirtyfive, forty. The highest being fifty-two before he came downstairs before school to find her sitting there with her makeup on and her hair down and clean and brushed. With eggs in the skillet and toast in the oven and a wink that said it is over for now. I am alive again. What do you want me to pack you for lunch today?

He would lie awake and listen and hear the footsteps in the hallway. Their room on the other end of the hall from the stairway and his father or maybe his mother crossing past the threshold of his bedroom, the creaks in the floor predictable and dependable and he would sit up. Hold his breath. Try and measure by the sound of the stairs the weight of the person going down. Heavy cracks and it was his father and soft squeaks said it was his mother. He then tiptoed across his bedroom and listened at his door. Sometimes there was muffled crying. Other times he waited to see if the back door would open and if it did he moved to his window and watched his father's silhouette shift back and forth across the yard, a cigarette folded underneath his hand in the same way that he smoked on the sidewalk in front of the store, not wanting to be so obvious. The red tip at his father's wrist and Nick watching it turn and wander as his father stepped in his slippers across the damp grass of the middle of the night.

If his father was outside Nick would put on socks and then open his door and creep out into the hallway. Go to the bedroom door that his father had left cracked open and he touched his hand to the door gently and pushed it open, just wide enough to slide through. In big quiet steps he moved to the edge of their bed and his mother breathed heavy in her sleep and he stood there and touched his fingertips to her hip and felt the rise and fall in her breathing. The room so black with the shades down and the curtains pulled. So black and he could see nothing but he imagined everything. Her dreams or maybe her nightmares and his father's eyes wide open as he lay there next to her and the doctor who sometimes came and talked to her for hours and what they might say to one another, their voices only murmurs as he and his father sat downstairs. He imagined creatures in the night slipping out from under her bed and out of the closet and slithering across the floor and up the bedposts, across the blankets and gathering between the sheets and then whispering to her all through the night that she should go deeper and deeper down. You are not there yet. Not quite yet. We can carry you deeper. Nick waved his hand when the creatures felt too real. He imagined everything in that black room where his mother lay buried and sometimes he whispered a prayer of resurrection like he had heard on the lips of the choir. He whispered promises to her that if she would trust him and his father then you will not go deeper but we will help you up and spend a day in the sunshine and that is all you need. One good day. Maybe it will be tomorrow.

Some nights he would slide along the edge of the wall in his sock feet and stand at the top of the stairs. He waited and sometimes a chair in the kitchen would slide and he knew his father was sitting there with his face in his hands or maybe having a drink or maybe both. And then he would go to find out.

On this certain night he made it down the stairs but not without sound and felt it was impossible that his father did not know he was there. But he moved on. At the base of the stairs he waited for the voice to tell him to go back up. You have no business being awake. A boy needs his sleep. But the voice did not come and he crept on like a thief in his own home. Stopping in the doorway between the kitchen and dining room. He spied his father in a chair with his back to Nick and no light but that from the moon that came through the window and gave blue shadows.

His father sat with his elbows on his knees and his face in his hands. Just the way Nick always imagined him sitting in the dark.

'She has never been the same,' his father mumbled and he sucked in his breath twice as if trying to catch it. Nick like a shadow. So still and listening to his father mumble in the dark.

'She has never been the same,' his father said again and he lifted his face from his hands and let his head fall back. Nick took a step back anticipating his father's rise but his father stayed in his chair.

She has never been the same since when, the boy wanted to ask. What was she like before whatever it is you're talking about. Before all this. Why does it come and go and why can't we stop it?

A short glass of bourbon sat on the table and his father wrapped his fingers around the glass and held it. Didn't raise it but only held it and he sat up straight in the chair. The wooden chair talking back with the movement of weight and the boy paralyzed and waiting.

A heavy sigh. Both hands around the glass now as if to protect it and then his father raised the glass and tilted it just enough so that the bourbon would meet his lips.

Keep talking, Nick wanted to say. Please keep talking.

His father set the glass down.

'Tell me what to do and I'll do it,' his father said. 'Tell me what to do.'

His father was something different now. In this solitary moment with the night surrounding them and his mother asleep and the world around them quiet and the moon glaring at them through the window his father became another thing. Not the stoic and certain man who taught him about handshakes and looking people in the eye and not the straightforward businessman who only missed a day of work if he was on the edge of his grave and not the man in the black suit who stood with his shoulders back as he sang from the hymnal. His father whispered and asked for mercy and seemed like a helpless thing on the verge of being crushed and Nick took a step back and slid behind the wall of the dining room and he bit his lip until it bled to keep from crying.

'Somebody tell me what to do and I'll do it.'

The glass raised and set again.

Nick moved across the dining room. He heard a match strike and then smelled the cigarette as he reached the first stair. He raised his foot to climb but not high enough and he stubbed his toe. A bump in the dark.

The chair in the kitchen slid and he heard the man stand. He heard the bottle pour into the glass. He waited for the voice. He would have given anything in that moment to have heard the voice and been called into the moment. To be asked to be a part of whatever his father was talking about and whoever he was talking to. Call me and I will come in there and sit with you. He wanted the voice and he wanted to sit in the chair next to his father and watch him in the moonlight and listen to him in the moonlight and be let inside of the things that kept them both awake at night and later he would blame himself for not doing something or saying something in the middle of that night. To try and make them both believe there was the possibility of something good and something closer between them. Between all of them. He waited and wished and only a word could have changed it all to the boy and he heard his father move but it was not toward him. Instead he moved across the kitchen to the door leading to the garage and it opened and closed behind him.

7

H<small>E HAD MARVELED AT THEIR</small> simplicity. Lying together naked underneath the costumes and without reasons attached to what they were doing or why they were doing it. Only that this is what two people wanted. He lost his anxiety and began to discover more about the body of a woman and there was a carefulness in the way he moved and he allowed himself to be guided and to learn.

On the third day she asked him why he kept looking at his watch. You are often looking at the time as if you are waiting to run away and he took it off and stuck it in his coat pocket. Along the river he sold the watch at a used jewelry kiosk and used the few francs he got for it to buy a pack of cigarettes and candy canes and they sat beneath Pont des Arts and alternately smoked and bit off the hard candy.

In the mornings after they explored one another they walked. They had coffee and bread at the café that looked out to Église de la Sainte-Trinité and the small man moved between the tables with a towel slung over his shoulder and a song on his lips. After coffee they drifted toward the river and stopped at Quai Voltaire. Few skiffs moved up and down the Seine and boys sat along the riverbank with long poles and long lines. She told him the regular boatsmen were all off fighting or dead in the war. Nick then told her that he had never been fishing and she bragged about the giant carp she

63

had caught with her grandfather in the small river that ran through her village. How she baited the hook with brown insects with bent legs that sang in the night. Crickets, he said. Crickets, she repeated. And she went back to the tall tales of catching carp as big as dogs with a single singing cricket and that her grandfather had once fished the Mediterranean until his boat sank because of the weight of his net. He was never allowed to go back because he took too many fish. She then told him of going to New Orleans with her father when she was very small and somewhere there was a photograph of him holding a large fish with one hand and her with the other and they were the same size. Nick shook his head and watched her eyes glow as she told the tall tales and he did not laugh or argue but let her travel as far as she would travel.

After they were done watching the fishing and the boats they would get a cold bottle of white wine and a strip of saucisson sec and walk along Saint-Germain to Jardin du Luxembourg. They sat underneath the trees and drank from the bottle and Nick cut the sausage with a pocketknife. Children chased after pigeons and some pushed sailboats in the fountain with wooden poles and then stood anxiously and waited for the breeze to return the boat so they could push it again. Old men walked with old women across the pebble pathways, arms wrapped together and their steps careful through the children. There was always a spot to lie in the grass or a café with cheap wine and cigarettes. Always a hand for him to hold and as the days passed he reached for it more often in the way that a child grows accustomed to reaching for and expecting help.

He helped her with the cart in the late afternoon and early evening and she talked him into holding the frame that held the photograph of the nude woman. You are a good advertisement.

Young strong American. We will sell one thousand. He didn't want to be an advertisement but he did it anyway, holding the frame and walking beside her, holding it forward to the men who could not help but look and to the women who could not help but look. He was embarrassed the first time she asked him to do it but that fell away and he carried the photograph with more salesmanship each time, raising it high and calling attention when no one seemed to care. Tugging at the frame with fake strength to show the durability of Ella's creations. Offering pricing deals that she did not authorize and she would tug at his arm and yank him close to her. Scold him and then snap the frame from his hands and put her mouth on his to shut him up. Somehow whatever they were doing together attracted more buyers to the cart and by the end of the week all the frames had been sold. As he had promised their first night together, Nick bought her a big bottle of glue. At an artists' den in Montmartre he bought several small cans of paint and brushes from a skinny Russian happy to have money for wine and as they strolled through the cobbled streets he made her promise to have new frames ready upon his return.

'You will return?' she asked.

'Of course I will,' he said. She looked at him as if she might believe it.

'But for you to return there must be a departure. And you have not yet departed.'

'No. I am still here. One more day.'

'Then you do not have to leave. There does not have to be a return.'

'I don't understand.'

'You don't have to.'

'You keep saying that,' Nick said and they stopped walking. Faced one another. She had been telling him each night that he didn't have to go back. Each night he had said I don't have a choice and he didn't want to say it again.

'It is simple,' she said.

'You know the answer. I know the answer.'

'Why must you return? To fill a hole in the ground? There are enough of those.'

'It's just the way it is.'

'Why?'

He didn't have a ready answer.

She sat down in the street. 'We can go,' she said as she looked at her feet. 'Somewhere together. Just go. Where it is safe for the both of us.'

'I can't do that.'

'Why do we have to do what we are told? Why do we have to do what the war makes us do? We did not choose.'

'But it chose us and I know what waits for me,' he said and he knelt beside her. 'There is nothing that scares me more.'

She stood. She gathered the bag that held the paint and brushes and she touched her hand to the back of his head and said you will not find me again and that should make you afraid or it should make you feel something.

'I will find you and I will return,' he said as he rose.

'We can go somewhere. And we can live. Somewhere safe for both of us.'

'Are you not safe here?'

She did not answer and began walking. He waited. Then followed her.

'I will come back as soon as I can,' he said.

'I know.'

'I don't want to.'

'We can leave now,' she said and she stopped and turned. Waited for him. 'We can leave.'

It was not what he had ever thought of or heard or imagined. Going where you want with who you want and to hell with the rest of it. He was as far removed from who he was and what he had known. In another country and with this woman and he felt himself awakening from a long dream as the hours with her seemed to both stand still and race by. He was in another country where he had been brought to kill and in the midst of that he had found this city and he had stepped away from the killing and the smell of the dead and she was some strange part of all that shrugging off. He tried twice to talk her out of the attic and into a room that he would pay for and each time she gave him a crooked look as if to say you still don't understand. After the second time he felt small and insulting and said nothing more. Only talked to her and touched her and listened to her as he tried to believe that this was somehow what he had been sent here for. He was far away from the man that he knew but not far enough. He said I have to go back and I don't know how to make it more simple. And then I will come back to you. She gave a halfsmile. Something patient and empty. And then she said it is not so simple.

8

Nick and his battalion were back and forth from the front for weeks. Seven weeks and two days according to the pebbles he kept in his pocket. Each a day that he survived. Each a day closer to returning to Paris. They were in the middle of relief time when the rest was cut short by the news that the battalion was not returning to the front. The men cheered and slapped one another on the back as if the war was over. The sergeant paused and let them have their moment of triumph before explaining that if you think it's bad at the front, you ain't seen nothing yet. We're going into the forest.

For weeks the Germans had been gathering more and more troops along the backside of a five-kilometer strip of forest on the northern side of the front. It had not been considered a threat at its inception but as the armies stood at a standstill, the forest had become a stronghold for both men and supplies and it was time to move them out as they had steadily crept both men and artillery farther into the woods. Closer to the battle. Several small battalions had been sent to shell the Germans out of the trees but they had been slaughtered. The effort needed more men and more force and Nick's battalion was going to be a part of the fearsome maneuver.

The men were told to eat and drink plenty of water and

restock your kits. We leave in an hour. When the hour was up they loaded into the trucks and drove across the countryside in the opposite direction of the front. The trucks eventually made two right turns and arrived two miles from the forest.

Get out, they were told. We walk the rest of the way.

As they walked a light rain began to fall and they watched the shells rain down on the land that they were marching toward. Scout balloons hung in the sky above the tree line and lightning crashed in the distance like some faint reminder of a natural world. The trench was a hundred yards away from the forest and the rain fell straight and steady as they reached the depleted regiments. Thousands of men were now hundreds and all that was standing in the way of the Germans spilling out of the woods and cornering the French and Americans at the front.

It rained through the night and knocked down the flares. There was no cover and no sleeping. They had expected to attack at daylight but the clouds stayed thick and the rain fell without cease and the orders changed. We will go in the dark. We will slide on our bellies in the cover of night. We will not give the machine guns hidden in the trees the benefit of the light of day. And so they waited and imagined the monsters in the trees.

When night came, they began. The earth between the trench and the forest had long been destroyed. Great caverns and craters and not a single step of flat ground. The rain formed puddles and ponds and created a slick and filthy terrain for the crawling army. One by one they sloughed across the broken earth. Inching through the darkness. Mud in their eyes and nostrils and ears. Mud in their mouths and some lapped at the puddles to quench thirst and the creeping army seemed to become part of the earth itself. Only whispers between them of when to hold and when to crawl again. The rain continued through the night and then an hour before daylight it stopped. By then they were so close to the forest that they could hear the foreign language and hear the clink of metal as machine guns were wiped and reloaded. A thousand men undetected.

The whistle blew and they rose like a burst of nature and delivered the surprise they had hoped for. Rifles fired and others were jammed with the muck but they were quickly on the first line of men and machine guns and they roared and shot and slashed. Their rage echoed through the forest and once they were past the German first line, the second line scattered them as the bullets came from invisible enemies, the flashes of gunfire coming from the still black woods and the trees splintered and limbs flew and men dropped quickly. They found trees and stumps to hide behind and found their grenades and lobbed them up and through the limbs. Orange blasts rended the dark canvas and gave them a chance. They advanced again and the gunfire shredded them but many continued on and then the Germans rose from their trenches on command and met them.

A storm of violence spread through the forest and in the middle of it all artillery fire began to erupt around them and no one knew who was firing and who it was intended for. The explosions took Americans and Germans and heightened the madness until both uniforms called for retreat and ran for cover. The fractured trees burned and the low limbs held the smoke close.

Bodies lay sprawled across bodies. Those remaining found cover behind fallen trees and in the muck of new craters and held tightly to the wet ground. Disoriented and seemingly lost and so many dead. An uncertainty of what was next. But they had done what they had been challenged to do. They had moved into the forest.

The wounded were dragged to the back of the line and then the others began to dig. Small spades were removed from their belts and they dug homes for themselves and those to come. The rain dripped from leaves and tapped on their helmets and heads as they worked. Exhausted and hungry they sat in their holes with their heads below and tried to realize that something good had been accomplished though that was never an answer that came to any of them until much later.

The water came around and Nick filled his canteen and then passed it over to the next hole. A sergeant he didn't recognize crawled between them and said drink up. They might be back before the end of the day. We done fucked them up. And we're not getting any reinforcements until morning so don't be looking over your shoulder for help.

The forest made him wish for the front. You could see at the front. You knew where you were supposed to be at the front. Everywhere he looked he saw a tree and behind every tree he imagined a grinning man with a rifle and a knife and a grenade.

He drank from the canteen and pulled a tin of some kind of meat from his kit. He had peeled back the lid and pinched a bite between his fingers when another soldier slid into his hole.

'Jesus Christ,' he said. 'Nobody said nothing about jungle warfare.'

Nick ate the bite. Held another toward the man who shook his head and took off his helmet. His hair was in a buzz cut and he bled from a tiny knot at his crown. He pulled a rag from his coat just as a trail trickled past his ear.

'I can't sit over there in that hole. I see Germans everydamnwhere out here. Jesus Christ. Trees standing and trees down and roots sticking up like broken bones.'

'I find myself missing the wide open spaces of killing.'

'Damn straight. If I'm gonna get my ass busted in two I'd at least like to know where it's coming from. Feel like I been shoved in a drum and pushed down a hill. I didn't sign up for this shit.'

'You signed up?'

'I didn't have nothing else to do.'

'I bet you can think of something now. So can I.'

'You signed up, too?'

Nick nodded. The man with the buzz cut laughed and said at least I got the excuse of being stuck out on a farm in east Tennessee. It's good most of the time and just pretty as hell. A creek ran through the hardwoods on the upper twenty acres. Can't see neighbors in no direction. And we got all seasons. Snowpowdered valleys and windswept leaves and pretty dogwood blossoms. Nick noticed the man's eyes drift as he described the place and he could see valleys and he imagined the sun on the dogwoods and he imagined a dry pair of pants.

But it gets damn lonely, the man kept on. It was just me and my dad. My momma died when I was born. I got two sisters. Millie and Addie. But they're older and both ran off with the first boy that come sniffing around. Just me and him in this four-room house my granddaddy built. Got a square porch that reaches out on all sides. We didn't have nothing but forty acres but we couldn't handle nothing more anyhow. Used to have about three hundred in the family but my granddaddy pissed it all away. Son of a bitch loved to gamble but he wasn't no good at it. My dad said he'd lost more in one little smoky room than most folks could lose if they lived twice over. Lost the deed to every single acre. Only decent thing he ever did was build that house and make a deal that me and daddy could stay on the land and try to make a living. Maybe if I had three hundred acres I wouldn't be sitting here. The man looked around and said I bet this could be a pretty place without all the shit.

Nick slid down in the hole some. Lay back.

'My dad told me not to come,' the man said.

'Mine too. I think now that was good advice.'

'Yep,' he said and he looked down at his mudcovered boots. His mudcovered knees. 'The hell of it is I did damn near every other thing he asked me to do my whole life. Never fussed none about the work. Never hardly got a hair out of place. I can't even remember now what made me want to volunteer. And I sure as hell can't remember why I wouldn't let him talk me out of it. But I wish I would have because we ain't getting outta here.'

'It could be worse,' Nick said.

'How the hell you figure that?'

'Have you ever seen them come around grabbing up guys for the tunnels?'

'Yep. They always get the new ones cause ain't nobody else dumb enough to go. Ain't nothing but a place to dump bodies.'

'Then see?'

'See what?'

'It could be worse.'

'I'd just as soon run out of this hole naked with nothing but rocks to throw as to go down in them tunnels. I'd have a better chance that way anyhow. I ain't never heard of nobody coming back after going under.'

'I don't think that many do.'

'But it seems damn near about the same in these woods. I can't see us getting outta here.'

'We might,' Nick said.

'Look around. I been lost in the woods before and it's scarier than scary. You ever been lost in the woods?'

'I can't remember a time I've been in the woods.'

'Then maybe that's why you don't look so spooked. Except for that hand of yours,' he said and he pointed.

Nick hadn't noticed. He'd come to accept that his hand was going to shake and he hoped that it would stop whenever he needed it.

'Don't be fooled. I'm spooked,' Nick said.

'I got lost in the woods when I was a boy and you don't forget that shit. I was out hunting and trying to track down a deer I shot. Followed the blood trail and quit looking where I was going. Next thing I knew the sun was getting low and I didn't know where the hell I was. I hollered but I was too far out. I kept on hollering though but that didn't keep it from getting dark and all kinds of shit moves in the dark. Stuff that's there and stuff that ain't there. It can be a rabbit or a squirrel shuffling around but when it's dark it sounds like a damn bear or something else willing to rip your guts out. All I could think about was falling asleep and waking up to a bunch of coyotes chewing at my stomach. It's crazy what your mind can do to you. I always thought it was supposed to be your friend but it'll give you up quick as anything. Especially when you can't see.'

Nick nodded. Being lost in the woods didn't sound much different to him from being lost at home. He put his shaking hand behind his head and rested on it.

'And we can't see,' Nick said.

'Hell I was more scared than I'd ever been and it was my

own woods. But that ain't nothing compared to this. I didn't have no choice that time but to gut it out through the night and soon as I could see I started running and hollering. Fired my gun. But my daddy and a bunch of men was looking for me and we figured it out. I didn't think I'd ever feel like that again but I was wrong. I can't believe you never been in the woods.'

'I'm in the woods now.'

'Yeah. We all are, ain't we? I just don't see many of us getting out.'

'Stop saying that. You're going to have to get out of this hole if that's what you want to talk about. I'm doing enough thinking about dying on my own without you reminding me of it.'

'Sorry, pal,' he said. Nick expected him to sit. To change the subject. But he was beyond that. He was beyond talking about anything that didn't concern living and dying and surviving a night in the woods.

'Talk about something else. You might not make it out of here and I might not either but it doesn't have anything to do with us. It's not about who is the best shot or who is the strongest or who has some special skill for cutting a man's throat. It's about good luck or bad luck and that's it. So there's no point in talking about it.'

'What you want to talk about then?'

'I don't give a damn. Talk about the rain. Or your goddamn fingernails. I don't care.'

They both looked around the hole. Up at the dripping trees.

'I don't want to talk about the rain.'

'Then don't,' Nick said. He felt around in his coat trying to find a cigarette though he knew he didn't have any.

'You think they're gonna hit us back today?' the man asked.

'Probably.'

'I can't think of nothing else to talk about.'

'Then let's don't talk.'

'If I don't I'm gonna go crazy.'

'Then talk. I don't care. Talk about whatever you want to talk about but I don't have to talk back.'

'Nope. You don't. You ain't a whole lot of fun.'

'I'm not trying to be fun.'

The man with the buzz cut opened his coat and held his hands inside.

'You got a girl?' he asked.

Nick picked up his helmet and set it on his head. Tilted it low across his eyes.

'I said you got a girl?'

'No.'

'I don't neither. And I'm glad about it.'

'Go ahead and tell me why.'

'Not with your attitude.'

'Go ahead. I know you can't keep from it.'

'I'm going back over there.'

Nick nodded and eased his helmet down farther.

'I thought you had to talk about something,' Nick said.

'I want to. But it takes two to talk.'

'It takes one to talk.'

'You ain't never been alone much. Have you?'

'Why is that?'

'Because if you'd spent as many days as I have out in the middle of goddamn nowhere trying to make a living off land that sometimes wanted to cooperate and sometimes didn't then you wouldn't mind having a conversation. No matter what it was about.'

'It's not the same thing.'

'What?'

'Before you said you were lonely. Now you're saying you were alone. It's not the same thing.'

The man huffed. Stuck his helmet on his head. 'You're kind of a smart guy. Aren't you?'

'No.'

'I bet you got a lot of school in you. And you probably read lots of words.'

'What else would I read besides words?'

'See what I mean? You're a smart one. At least you think it.'

'I don't think anything.'

'Then you're just a son of a bitch then.'

'It doesn't matter what I say to you.'

'Then don't say nothing.'

'That's what I've been trying to do.'

'Son of a bitch. I'll leave you in your little kingdom.'

The man crawled out of the hole and across the ground and he slid back down into his own hole. Moments later a big glob of mud sailed across from one hole to another and smacked Nick on top of the helmet. A pause and then another smacked on his shoulder and splattered his face.

Nick threw off his helmet and came up out of the hole like a madman. He went for the man with the buzz cut, diving down on him and punching and clawing at his face and the man yelled and punched and kicked but Nick was on him. The man's helmet came off and Nick shoved the back of his head into the mud and the man yelled he's killing me he's killing me. A handful of soldiers peeked up out of the surrounding holes and crawled over and down into the hole and tried to pull Nick off the man with the buzz cut and their movement and yelling triggered a smattering of machine gun fire from

the dark recesses of the woods that made them all forget
what they were doing and they dropped to their stomachs
and squeezed close to the earth.

9

I̶N SOLITARY MOMENTS HE TRIED to remember the things or people that had meant something to him. It began as a practice of reassurance. You have another life out there and these are the good things about it. But the habit eventually turned into a collage of memories that irritated him.

The train horn that echoed across his small town in the late night as the cargo passed from east to west and how on nights when he had trouble sleeping he would lie there and wait for it, its arrival a comfort and its horn like a single, simple lullaby. The straight and smooth sidewalks of his childhood and riding bikes in the summer with a baseball mitt hanging over the handlebars and half a dozen others trailing behind as they rode to the elementary school playground and started up a game that began with the goodnatured charm of boyhood but always ended in an argument.

The echoing halls of New Haven where professors lectured with authority and certainty and how he had taken some of their most heartfelt ideologies and passed them off as his own in what he saw now as juvenile editorials in the campus newspaper. The wide walkway separating the dorm and the library that was lined by lampposts where he walked in the night and his shadow splintered in random directions and as he moved he saw the varying degrees of shadow as varying degrees of himself and he wondered how many were truly inside.

The box of cowboys and Indians and horses under the bed in his room that he took out and played with by the moonlight once his mother and father were asleep. His hesitancy to let the cowboys always be good and the Indians always be bad and the way that he allowed everyone on the Western frontier of his mind to be a survivor.

A date he took to a football game and her thick and wavy blond hair that fell over the collar of her fur coat and her eyes that shined like polished dimes. When she spoke he could not decide if he was entranced or appalled as she only spoke of her family name and her family homes and the family she was planning after she graduated and no matter that there was no man involved at the moment because there would be one whenever she decided which one fit the way she and her family expected him to fit. Her shrill when a touchdown was scored and her condescending stare toward those less beautiful than her.

His mother licking her hand and flattening his cowlick before they walked into church and his father squeezing his shoulder as they moved down the aisle toward their usual Sunday morning pew and how their seat had never once been occupied by an unfamiliar face.

The books he read sitting on a concrete bench as he chewed on a sandwich and waited for his next class. *Notes from Underground* and *A Simple Heart* and *Fathers and Sons*. Stories that he thought he had understood then but he understood better now with the grime under his fingernails. The redhead from Philadelphia who sat next to him in American History and told him he didn't need to waste his time reading fiction as long as there were books published on politics and war but who later became one of the biggest liars Nick knew as they both rowed on the crew team and in the locker room the redhead bragged of sexual escapades that they all knew he had neither the looks nor courage nor grasp of the English language to pull off.

Nick sat with his memories in the way that others sat with photographs of wives or children, holding the worn edges and staring at the faces as if staring into an unanswerable question. Others read the same letters over and over again. Not reading, Nick thought. But reciting. The words engrained and beating like a heartbeat and giving nourishment. Some kept rings or pocketknives or lucky rocks tucked in the inside pockets of their coats and took them out and rested the trinkets in the palms of their hands as if feeling the need to touch something that would not fire or explode.

But Nick did not have any of these things. He felt the tinge of jealousy in the early days at not being the owner of such keepsakes but as the days and weeks and months had gone by he had lost the desire for anything physical that could be lost. He let himself be comforted or frustrated or broken or sustained by the thoughts and memories that he knew he could change if he wanted to and in his darkest moments he began to separate himself from the images, as if they belonged to someone else and he had overheard the stories. Overheard the descriptions of home or of faces and voices and it hurt less to remember the good and he laughed at the absurd and if he was certain that none of the others were in earshot, he described his own memories to himself aloud as if he had stepped out of his body and sat next to himself in the dirt and was educating this visitor about who he was and how he had come to be there.

10

NICK AND THE OTHERS WHO survived the forest were
rewarded with leave and there was no doubt where
he was going. On the train to Paris he imagined seeing her
from a distance. Watching her for a while before sitting down
next to her or calling her name and hiding behind a tree.
He imagined the frames in the new colors or the blends of
colors that she had created and he heard their footsteps as
they climbed the dark stairway into the attic and he saw the
sun in the open windows and a shadow across the curve of
her bare back. He moved his fingers and imagined them in
her short and soft hair and he heard her telling him that he
didn't have to go back and we can go somewhere and this
time he wasn't certain how he would answer.

He arrived in Paris at the Saint-Lazare train station in the
middle of an afternoon of sun and marched directly to the
last place he had seen her, the café at the end of rue de Clichy.
It was not a long walk and his pulse quickened as he moved
with stretching strides. The doors and windows of the café
were open and people sat at the outside tables and smoked
and he walked in and out three times as if he were certain she
was there and maybe hiding as part of some game. Back out
on the sidewalk he stood with his hands on his hips and was
nearly taken out by a bicycle. The small waiter recognized
Nick and scolded the bicycle for riding on the sidewalk and

MICHAEL FARRIS SMITH

then he took Nick's arm. He led him to a barstool and sat him
down and welcomed him with quick chatter that bounced
off the preoccupied soldier. Nick drank an espresso and then
nodded to the man and walked out. He thought to go to the
attic but he didn't believe she would be there in the light of
such a clear day.

He hurried to Parc Monceau. Crawling with children and
their busy shadows. The song of the carousel never ending.
He walked the pathways and looked for her and the cart but
saw neither. He ate a sandwich while leaning on the iron
gates of the front entrance of the park and then he wiped the
crumbs from his mouth and walked on. Up through the hills
and high steps. Back down and across the Tuileries and then
along the river. His eyes in and out of the cafés and scanning
the park benches but no sign of her as the afternoon trailed
away. He stood at Pont Neuf and scratched his head and then
his chin and then reminded himself that the quickest route
from A to B is a direct line. Go to the attic.

He moved north again toward Pigalle and sometimes he
walked and sometimes he quickened to a run. He crossed
streets without waiting and ignored the honks and shouts.
He imagined the attic at the forgotten Théâtre du Rêve and
the racks of costumes and he could see her sitting in the
windowsill as if she knew he were coming. He reached Pigalle
and moved in and out of side streets, trying to remember the
theater and the door of the abandoned building that she had
led him into and he felt stupid for not having written it down.
His forehead sweating and smacking his lips nervously as
he searched and then he recognized the building. Scraps of
wood and piles of plaster right where he remembered them as
he opened the door and walked through and into the alley. In
the alley the cats scattered and he opened the door that took

him into the black staircase. He started carefully but after the first flight he hustled, taking two steps at a time and then up above he saw the light from the space underneath the door and he tried to gain an extra step and he tripped and fell, smacking his shin and slamming his fist but not stopping. Shaking it off and making it to the top of the stairs. Standing at the door to the attic. Catching his breath and smoothing his hair and wiping the moisture from his top lip.

He opened the door and the light fell into the staircase. He stepped inside and moved between the costumes and he called her. There was no answer but a sour smell grabbed him and he saw a buzzing of flies. He called her again and she answered with an exasperated exhale and he pushed through the costumes and she was there. Lying on her side and sweating and her knees brought up to her stomach. Her arms wrapped around her knees and rocking a little and not the eyes he had known but replaced by the vacant stare of the sick.

The attic floor was splattered with vomit. Some there for days and some for hours. Nubs of candles stuck in bottle necks and her clothes and stockings and boots scattered as she lay in only her underwear with a silver evening dress underneath her folded body. Nick knelt and felt her forehead and she was hot and sweating. Her face pale and cheeks drawn and her color drained. A nearly empty bottle of whiskey sat on the floor next to the chair and wadded up next to the bottle was a costume shirt dotted with blood.

'Ella,' he said.

She did not lift her head. She lay and rocked and squeezed her legs. Her lips were dry and cracked and she whispered I did not want to.

'What is it? You need a doctor. Let me take you.'

'No,' she said. 'I cannot move.'

'What can I do?'

She only shook her head and touched her dry tongue to her dry lips.

He scanned the room. The vomit and the shirt spotted with blood. Cigarette butts and only an ounce left in the whiskey bottle. The smell of rot and the sound he now realized of flies. He stood and opened the windows. He picked up an old newspaper from the floor and waved it to move the putrid air. He moved back to her. On his knees and wanting to touch her but not knowing where. Wanting to help her but not knowing how.

'How long have you been like this?'

'You came back,' she whispered. 'You should not.'

'I told you I was. Now what can I do?'

It was a different room. No more mystique and no more sanctuary and no more enchantment. He touched her bare shoulder. Touched her back. Felt her breathing and then he looked around the room again and tried to figure out on his own what had happened. And then he thought about the pebbles he had kept in his pocket and how many there were when he was given leave and he had been gone for more than two months. He thought about what they had done together in this space during their seven days and then he moved his hand to her damp forehead.

'Ella,' he said as it occurred to him. 'Are you?'

She took several heavy breaths. Let go of her knees and gingerly moved her legs down. She folded her hands underneath the side of her head and closed her eyes.

'No more,' she said.

Nick moved his hand from her back. Sat back on the floor.

Across the room he noticed a brown bottle lying on its side. The cap off and the bottle empty.

The air left him. He sat with his mouth open and stared at the pill bottle. Moved his eyes to the bloodstained shirt and to the bluewhite sky outside and then back to her. She was so thin and white and he wanted to scream or stand and kick at the walls or rage at something. He wanted to throw blame at fate or the workings of time or luck or bad luck or himself or her. He wanted to do something other than hold it all in but she began to cry and he held it all in. Because the thing had already been done.

11

He SAT WITH HER DAY and night and wiped her face with a damp rag. She sipped from a bottle of laudanum when there was too much pain and then she slept for hours at a time. A deadened, motionless sleep. Sometimes she spoke out from dreams but it was always in French and Nick could not decipher what she was saying or who she might be talking to. He only hoped that it was a vision of them together behind her eyes and that the words she spoke were not of bitterness or guilt. Her voice was monotone and in fragments and he thought once he heard his name but later as he walked along the street below and smoked he knew she hadn't said Nick.

While she slept he cleaned up the attic. Scraped away the vomit and got rid of whatever she had used to wipe her mouth or wipe the blood. He kept the windows open and bought fresh flowers to help with the smell. He sat in the windowsill with a cigarette and blew the smoke back into the attic to fight the sourness and he had taken a bucket of rainwater and some rags and wiped down everything. The windowsills and chair and lamp. The floor and her brush and some books. He folded her clothes and stacked them neatly in her suitcase. He went down into the alley and gathered wood scraps from the carpenter's pile and stacked the scraps next to the unopened bottle of glue and paint cans. Across the tops of the cans he set the brushes and he fixed a wobbly wheel on the cart.

He had bought bread and bananas and slices of ham. Bottles of water and wine and the chocolate bars he knew she liked. During the first two days she took little but the laudanum and sips of water and wine but after two days he had gotten her to eat some. Sit up straight. Stand for a minute or two. When she was awake she said little and answered his questions with head nods or shakes and she did not look at Nick when she talked but instead out of the window. He was able to put together that she had gotten the pills to get rid of it from a girl at one of the Pigalle dance halls and that she had been alone and sick in the attic for a week. Maybe more. He did not ask her anything else about it and on the third day she sat up in a chair and they shared a glass of wine from glasses he had found in a prop box. Several times she returned a polite and serene smile and looked more like the woman he had known before.

At night he lit the candles and he pulled the chair over to the mattress. He had bought a couple of newspapers and a comic and he tried to read to her in his best French accent. He had no rhythm and mispronounced badly but she did not correct him. Only lay there and listened to him trying and she would turn on her side and rest her hand on his foot. Each time she touched him he paused. Looked around the side of whatever he was trying to read as if to make sure it was her hand and not something in the dark that he wasn't ready for. The candles burned and the sky became a navy blanket and even after she nodded off he kept reading and as he sat next to her he realized that he had been here before. With his mother, reading at her side. Dark outside. Dark inside. Past midnight and with Ella sleeping he folded the paper and set it on the floor next to the chair and he said to the attic the world repeats itself. He said it with certainty as if it was something he had always known but just now found the courage to admit. I have been here before and I will be here again. I wonder what war I will fight in next and will it be worse and who will be the enemy. What hand will I try to hold somewhere in my future that will remind me of this hand I am trying to hold now. This hand that I want to hold on to as if it were something priceless and precious and I think that it is. This sick hand but it will not be sick forever and I will make sure of that. I will try as hard as I can try no matter that I know I am at the mercy of whatever circles us around. We are here now but we will be here again and next time with the child but will it be with different faces and different sounds but the same desperate feeling? The same slipping grip on what we have made?

She was fast asleep. Her hand across the toe of his boot. He reached down and moved her hand to below her chin. She breathed in and out with a barely audible wheeze.

I will go wherever you want to go, he thought. I should have the last time and I know it. You wouldn't be sick and we would be somewhere safe like you said. I should have listened but I'm listening now. Wherever you want to go and whatever you want to do. He had three days left where the laws of war were concerned but he didn't care. All he wanted was for the morning to come and for her to wake and feel better so that he could tell her we can go. As soon as you feel like it, we can go.

Morning came. He was out when she woke. Ella sat up and rubbed her eyes. Rubbed her stomach. She leaned over and grabbed a bottle of water and drank. And then she slowly got to her feet and stood and stretched. She spotted a pack of cigarettes and matches on top of a stack of books and she took the bottle of laudanum from the chair. She removed the cap and drank a sip and then she lit the cigarette and milled around the attic with cautious steps as if the floor might collapse beneath her.

She moved until the cigarette was gone and she flicked it out of the window. Then she knelt next to her suitcase and dug around until she found the advertisement that had brought her here. Nick had placed it on the bottom beneath skirts and stockings and boots. Folded it neatly in the center. She unfolded it and placed it flat on the floor and pressed the paper with the palm of her hand to smooth the wrinkles. With the tip of her finger she slowly traced the outline of the dancing girl as if she would later have to draw it while blindfolded. She traced it once. Twice. Then she folded the ad and slid it back underneath the clothes. His pocketknife was on a plate next to the suitcase and she picked it up. Squeezed it in her hand. A door closed in the alley and she heard Nick coming up the stairs and she stuck the pocketknife into her suitcase. Then she sat in the chair with her legs crossed.

He came in holding a white bag of croissants and a bottle of milk and when he saw her sitting up he smiled and said you look better today. He moved to her and kissed her cheek. Set the bag on the floor. She then pulled him close and kissed his forehead. Cheek. Mouth.

'You are a special doctor,' she said.

'Are you hungry?'

'Yes.'

'That is good. The more you eat the better you'll feel. I think.'

He handed her a croissant from the bag. Took one for himself. He uncapped the milk and handed the bottle to her and she drank.

'Maybe after you eat we can make it down the stairs. Get some real air and some real coffee.'

'I think it is possible.'

'Good. Did you want some medicine?'

'I took some. But I do not hurt so much as before.'

'But you still hurt?'

She nodded and ate.

'If we can get outside you will feel better,' he said.

'I think when you return you should tell them to give you a white coat and put you in the hospital. Do you have hospitals?'

'Sort of.'

'Then you will become a doctor. No more gun.'

'I'm not going back,' he said. 'So there is no worry.'

'The war ends while I sleep?' she said.

'It can go on without me. I want us to go somewhere. Anywhere. As soon as you are well.'

He expected her to smile. To maybe cry. To reach for him. To give back something in the way of affirming what he had said. She only looked at the bread in her hands.

'Did you hear me?' he asked.

'We cannot do this,' she said.

'Yes. We can.'

She stood from the chair. Moved around behind him.

'I asked you to stay before,' she said. 'I do not ask this time.'

'Ella,' Nick said and he turned to her. 'I did not know. I could not have known what happened.'

'It is not that.'

'Then what is it?'

'It is only that it is different. I want you to come back. And I will be here.'

'That doesn't make sense.'

'I cannot ask you to stay.'

'You didn't ask me,' he said taking a step toward her. 'I told you I wanted to.'

'But I asked you before.'

'And I'm staying. We don't have to wait on the war or anything else.'

'I am hurting, Nick. Everywhere.'

He paused. Dropped his eyes. He waited on the silence to change her mind but it only held them.

'So am I,' he said.

He stepped toward her and she didn't move. When he was there he held out his arms and she leaned into his chest.

'I am better,' she whispered.

'Then we will go outside. Walk.'

'I want to stay here.'

'Okay.'

'Can I be alone?'

'Yes.'

She raised her head and he saw that she did not mean for a little while. Or for the day. Beneath her eyes there was no end. He let her go and stepped back. His pack was beneath the window and he walked across the attic and picked it up. A fold of franc notes and his papers were in a small pocket at the front of the pack and he took out the francs and he left them on the windowsill without her noticing. He looked at the mattress where she had been lying there thinking about it all while he sat next to her and he wished he knew what had brought her to this.

'I will return soon,' he said.

'I believe it this time,' she said. 'I will be here. I will be better.'

'And then we will go.'

'Yes. And then we will go.'

He had three more days but he walked directly to the Saint-Lazare station. He boarded the first available train and he sat by the window in an empty car. The whistle blew and the porter made the final call and then at the last second a rumble of rowdy voices spilled into the car. A gang of soldiers already drunk or still at it from the night before and they pushed and shoved and laughed as they swapped bottles. They spotted Nick and lifted him up and hugged him as if he were a lost brother. They shoved bottles at him and he nodded politely and took a swig of this and a swig of that. The soldiers stumbled over one another when the train lurched forward. A couple of the men going down in the aisle and then the others piling on top and yelling and cackling with intoxicated exuberance. And then they started singing. Songs about lanky and loose women and songs about whiskey and songs about rambling men and then more songs about women. They sang and swayed and drank and tried to wrestle Nick into their boisterous world. But he only sat still in the midst of them with his eyes on the passing landscape and for the first time he felt like he understood something about his mother as the same blackness that had governed her began to seep into him.

When the train came to a stop and he returned to camp he did not report to his battalion. He did not go and get a rifle and pistol. Instead he found his commanding officer and he volunteered to go into the tunnels.

12

IT WAS THE WAR BENEATH the war. While men and machines destroyed one another above the ground, hundreds of feet below the surface miles of tunnels twisted and weaved and were busy with men crawling on their hands and knees. Working in absolute silence. In candlelight or maybe in the pitch black. Trying to hear and kill before being heard and killed. The Germans digging one way and the Allies digging the other. Hundreds of human moles burrowing and clawing their way through the French underground.

The first tunnelers were British workers brought to France as a special unit. Experienced miners and tunnelers who knew how to dig efficiently. Understood how to work and understand one another without the need for words. They handled kick irons and spades with precision to remove clumps of dirt and clay as quietly as clumps of cotton. Because noise meant death.

The tunnels were high and wide enough to crawl through or walk through stooped at the waist. Twentyfour hour work by the steady changing shifts of men who lined the tunnels and passed the dirt and stone out piece by piece. Hand to hand. They worked under the constant fear of death. Carbon monoxide poisoning or tunnel collapse. Enemy explosion if one of their tunnels was found out. Or the crisscrossing of enemy tunnels and fighting with fists and knives in the dark and cramped spaces like blind barbarians.

This was the world that Nick entered when he returned from Paris. When he left her there because she wanted to be alone. Had to be alone. Because she said she hurt everywhere. He wanted to disappear and so he would disappear.

In the first years of the war the tunnels began as a defensive project to detonate the German land mines that mutilated and maimed the infantry. But as the war had worn on, the tunnels now turned to the offensive. As an aid to the infantry as explosives could be set that would throw great masses of earth into the air that would climb high into the sky and pause like the silhouette of a great willow tree. The massive explosions killed, distracted, opened lines for the infantry that weren't there before. With the Western front at a standstill, the Allied tunnels turned ambitious.

The trained workers were long dead and gone and the tunnels relied on men who learned the basic skill of digging and removal and silence from those buried before them. Another group handled the explosives and detonation. A select few and the most important were the listeners. Trained and tested ears who were responsible for detecting movement of the enemy. Detecting the direction of their tunnel. The proximity. A simple miscalculation meant catastrophe.

Nick joined the workers who filed down into the tunnels and passed the mounds of clay and dirt from one to another. Toward the end of the line wheeled carts sat along steel tracks and the earth was then pushed out of the tunnel by weary men with hurting backs and large pupils. He had twice seen bolts of fire shoot through a tunnel after Germans sniffed them out and set explosives, the fire rushing toward him like a fierce orange torrent and he and the others dropping flat with faces in the ground while the gust shot past. Others were dragged out on fire or suffocated and some never came out and had in an instant found their graves.

But he kept going back in. He was one of few Americans in the tunnels as most were British and French. Some of the workers were lifelong miners recruited from the coal mines of France. Men already rejected for the infantry because they were too old or too small or in possession of some other physical abnormality. But they were welcome to the tunnels and they worked with vigilance and appreciation. All that the assortment of men and nationalities meant was the men were silent in different languages. And Nick found what he wanted in the silence of the tunnels as he never felt the urge to speak. He could pass dirt and think about what he loved and what he didn't love and what he regretted and what he would say when he stood at Judgment and had to explain. Quiet and simple labor in the closest he thought he could be to hell. He thought and passed dirt all day. Or all night. There was no way to tell the difference.

As the tunnel-building kept its aggressive pace, collapses and casualties doubled. The men were given less relief and this caused less precision which caused noise. Noise captured by the German listeners. Explosions to follow. There could be no rest and new men were almost impossible to come by and soon the number of listeners had dwindled to twenty and then twelve and now ten.

During shift changes the men would wander over a hillside and sit in the shade of a grove. Some would sprawl out on their backs and fall into a dropdead sleep while others would squint at the light of day and stare across the bluewhite sky while chewing pieces of bread and sausage. Sallowfaced and hardworking men with gnarled hands and thin waists. Their numbers shrinking each time they came into the light and as Nick chewed an apple or stared up at the clouds and imagined the shapes of monsters he knew they were losing and could not figure it to be any other way. He did not want to die in the tunnels. But he sure as hell didn't want to die in the tunnels because of the mistake of another so he found the commanding officer. He was sitting on his helmet. Digging dirt out from under his fingernails with a pocketknife. He raised his head and squinted at Nick who stood there in some vague resemblance of the soldier he had once been.

'What do you want?' he asked.

'I'm a good listener,' Nick answered.

He scraped at his fingernails. Drank from a canteen.

'We're damn near out of those. You know what you're asking for?'

'Yes.'

Without another question as to what made him a good listener or why he thought he was a good listener, he was given a geophone and a tunnel map. A box of matches and a handful of candles. A compass and a canteen and several tins of sardines. He was shown on the map where he needed to be and when he asked how long he needed to stay, he was told as long as you can. Just send a report every hour and if you detect movement and believe we should set explosives then for God's sake say so. That's what we're fucking here for.

He did not disappoint. He was a good listener and to both his surprise and that of his superiors he was good at estimating distance and differences in elevation. He could sit for hours with so little movement that twice a passing worker had seen him and tapped his leg thinking he was asleep. Except for the shaking of his hand at random times he was perfectly still. He set the two geophone diaphragms on the tunnel floor and ran the tubes to his ears, a bearing between the geophone pointing in the direction of any detected sound or ground movement. It did not take much to move the bearing. The clank of shovel hitting rock. A man grunting from pain. The movement of a line of men hurrying to get where they were supposed to be. In addition to the geophone he had begun to fill an empty sardine tin with water and he set it next to the candle. Any movement in the water and he knew they were close. Maybe already on them. The skill was to detect what mattered. Where the most men congregated or the sound of German explosives being set so that you could give the signal to evacuate and then break ass getting clear.

Nick had four times ordered explosives and four times the explosion had murdered in piles. When he suspected a large group and after he quickly anticipated the distance and elevation between the two tunnels, he pointed to a spot on the tunnel wall and moments later came the fire power. Silently a hole was drilled into the earth and then a steel tube six inches in diameter was slipped into the hole. Explosives were packed into the tube and then sandbags were stacked against the back of the tube to ensure the explosion went forward and vertical.

Four successes that made him confident and only strengthened the energy he put toward the necessary concentration. He sat for six hours. Eight hours. When asked if he wanted relief he mouthed the words I will tell you when I am ready.

When attentive to the water in the tin or with the tubes in his ears, he thought of only the physical. His stomach growling or always the need to piss. Choking back a tickle in his throat or muffling a sneeze. It was the time he spent out of the tunnels, when he could see the stars at night or smell smoke or study the faces of the others mired in this war, that his thoughts chased him and he seemed to only see her. He imagined her walking around Pigalle trying to decide what to do. Saw her trying to figure out how to ask about the pills for what she needed and the rundown dance halls she moved in and out of as she talked to girl after girl who kept passing her on to someone else. You need to talk to so-and-so. She can get you some. And then he saw her finding the woman who gave her what she needed. Said it don't hurt none. Plenty girls around here done it. Wouldn't know it though cause they don't miss nary a night's work. He saw her with the pill bottle in her hand and saw her walking and walking. For days and nights as she squeezed the bottle and walked the city and wondered if he was coming back like he said. Or is he already dead and even if he is not dead and he does come back you cannot have this. You cannot feed yourself. You have no home. You have nothing. He listened to her talking to herself and he saw the placid expression of resignation once she sat down in the attic with a bottle of wine and the pills in her hand and he saw her wash them down. Down now and no decision left to be made and her thin hands holding the bottle to her mouth and drinking and drinking, trails of red down the sides of her mouth and meeting under her chin. The bottle to the floor and he saw her lying on her back and the attic light shifting to violet and then in the middle of the night he saw her starting to feel it and he saw her realize there would be much more to it. He saw her as the hours moved on and she cramped and twisted and bled and vomited. And then another day and another day of the same and when he couldn't stand it anymore he walked to the tunnel entrance and said I'm ready and he crawled under like an animal.

It had taken several weeks but they had now moved ahead and were beneath enemy lines. The Allies had planned a grand explosion on the eastern flank of the German line, a stronghold that the infantry had not been able to budge. Thousands of men lost trying. It was time for something new.

Nick's job was now to listen as defense. To make sure that the men could keep working. That the explosives could be loaded. He focused and did not leave his post for a solid eighteen hours leading up to the attack. His eyes wild and his stomach begging for something to eat but he only drank water. Only listened and watched the water and the bearing. He raised his eyes from time to time and rubbed them. Shifted his kneeling position into a sitting position. Shifted his sitting position back to a kneeling position. The tunnelers worked and they were getting close and had been given the hour of ignition. The command from above declared that we will by God be ready when that hour comes and if we are not then we'll all go to hell together. The infantry was prepared for blastoff and then it would pour into the eastern flank with every man who could walk or pull a trigger.

During that long stretch Nick did not detect a sound and it made him uneasy. Every hour he sent the report. No sound detected. Each time that he wrote the three words on the slip of paper he felt as though he had missed something. It cannot be this quiet. It never has been. He wiped his eyes and refocused and tried to relax. Tried to give himself completely to the silence as if he was an apparition that could pass through the earth and join the other side and see them doing whatever it was they were doing. It cannot be this quiet.

The explosion was set for seven a.m. and by sheer will and determination the tunnelers finished the job with an hour to spare. A shell the size of a whiskey barrel was set into the earth and filled with enough power to obliterate anything within a one hundred meter radius. An immense throwing of the earth that would then be followed by a vast sinking and the exhausted and hungry tunnelers were loaded onto trucks and cleared away. All but Nick who stayed at his post while the explosives were inserted and the charges set. Since the early hours of his post he had resigned himself to staying and he had emptied his pockets to see what he was leaving behind to this world. Some scraps of paper. The nub of a pencil. An army-issued pocket watch. Papers that gave his full name and date of birth. Some loose thread. A piece of wood from one of her frames. The contents laid out on the ground like evidence and he thought of his father and his mother. Thought of their house and the business and the things they owned and the photographs that hung on the wall in the hallway of grandparents and great grandparents and aunts and uncles. His family line and his family's permanence in his family's town and to them it all meant something. But this was all that he was leaving and he knew that it didn't matter. Leaving was leaving and it was all the same. With only thirty minutes to ignition, he took the tubes from his ears and picked up the tin can and drank the water. Then he held the piece of frame between his fingers and he began to cry for a thousand reasons and only God knew he was there.

God and the German listener who sat only thirty feet away from him and had been sitting there just as patiently as Nick. God and the German listener and the two German soldiers who packed the explosive into the dirt and pointed it in his direction. Had he not been crying he would have been wearing the tubes and he would have heard them. Had he not drunk the water he would have seen it wave in the tin. Had he not fallen sobbing face first into the dirt like a man who had found in the years of his life nothing worth salvaging then the explosion would have removed his head from his body.

13

HE HAD BEEN DUG OUT and tossed into a pit with other dead bodies when he had been unconscious. He woke and found himself sandwiched between the arms and legs of others and he heard German voices and he didn't move. Confused and reaching to remember. Pain in his head and neck and it took some time but it slowly came back to him. Waiting at his post and waiting for the big explosion and falling to his knees and then the blast above him. And then as he dug and pushed at the earth crumbling around him the grand explosion and it all moved and it all shook and the clay and stone around him flew away and hung in the air and then came crashing back down and all went black. His thoughts foggy but he tried to stay with them until he put enough of it back together.

Eventually he slit open his eyes and saw the soldiers standing at the edge of the pit smoking cigarettes and every few minutes other men in uniform would appear at the edge of the pit with a big wheelbarrow stacked with the dead. The bodies wore different flags on their sleeves but that mattered no more as the pit was a place of equality. Nick watched as more bodies were dumped and they slid down and tumbled awkwardly onto the others. He couldn't move or they would kill him and he knew he was bleeding from more than one place but his choice was to move and be shot or stay still and pray that he didn't bleed dry before he could try and climb out and into cover of night. To where, he didn't know.

He prayed. He promised God and Jesus and Mary and whoever else would listen that if someone would please save him he would give it all back and I will pray every morning and every night and I will give everything I have away and I will feed the poor and read to the sick and please let me out of this hole and please stop this bleeding and if you help me climb out of this pit please dear God let my legs work and I promise I will give it all back.

He prayed and promised and prayed and promised for two days as there seemed to be no rush by the men surrounding the pit. He tried not to sleep but he dozed in and out and there was nothing in his dreams that didn't involve the wrath of man and as soon as he woke he began to pray and promise once again as if it were synchronized with his cautious breathing. The Germans kept smoking and kept dumping bodies and then finally, after two days and two nights of playing dead, after ignoring the vermin that crawled across his face, after promising God and the saints a lifetime of service and gratitude, he heard the German word for fire and he had no choice. The sun was dropping toward the horizon and the sky bled from pink in the west to lavender in the east and he knew that once dark fell he had to move. His lips were dry and cracked and he ached for water and food and he didn't know if his arms and legs would work. After dusk he listened for the voices but they had moved away from the pit. He watched and listened and the stars appeared and flickered across an endless sky.

And then he moved.

He began by wiggling free from the dead that covered his legs and pressed against his head and chest and as he twisted and turned he had to bite the collar of his shirt to keep from screaming as a shot of pain raced down his spine. Rats and mice skittered across the dead litter as if aroused by his movement and with a clenched jaw he freed himself from the bodies. He was hurt and thankful for the dark so that he couldn't see what he looked like because he knew that would make it easier to give up.

He crawled up. Stiffened bodies and the smell of hell and eyes frozen open that envied him as he maneuvered his way to the edge of the pit. Again he listened and he heard voices but they were at a distance so he lifted his head and looked out across the land. Maybe a hundred yards away men gathered around campfires and milled around tents. There were hundreds of tents and dots of firelight orange spread out across the treeless fields but they were all away from the pit.

And then he heard a weak voice.

Help me.

He turned and looked. An arm raised from the corpses and the voice came again. Help me.

A soldier yelled something at the edge of the German campsite and he couldn't wait. He wanted to say to the voice, I can't help you. I want to but I can't and I hope that you don't remember that I was here and that you asked me but I can't and I pray that you die before they bring the fire.

He crawled out and began in the opposite direction. His legs had gone numb under the weight of the others and two days of immobility and they dragged behind as he moved on his elbows. There was nothing that he could remember about the direction of the attack or the trenches or anything. He only knew that he was crawling in the opposite direction of the men who would light the pit on fire. He groaned as he crawled across the damp and tattered earth. Darkness all around him. He came to puddles and wanted to drink but he knew the gas lingered in them and that it would burn him through. He bumped into a canteen and the cap was gone but several dirty drops fell onto his tongue and disappeared.

Several times he looked back and it seemed as if he was going nowhere so he stopped looking and only crawled and began to talk to God and though he asked for His power and strength, the notion of such a being became so vague to him that the word itself seemed as nothing more than a sound. Only another of the many sounds that filled the wartorn landscape. He began by talking to God but then began talking to himself and he didn't speak of faith or hope but he spoke of the literal world, reminding himself of the colors in a sunset or what he liked to eat for breakfast or the most efficient way to shovel snow from a sidewalk. And he talked of Paris and the way her eyes seemed to turn from green to blue in the sunshine and how when he spoke too much English she would touch the top of his hand and nod slowly as if to motion him back to their halfway point.

He talked and crawled and stopped and rested and crawled and muttered again. It took time but soon he was beyond being seen. Behind him he heard voices and he turned and saw men with torches walking toward the pit. He heard their laughter and their silhouettes staggered and he rested and watched. Two of the men circled the pit and emptied large containers of kerosene onto the bodies and the others with torches followed them to give light. To make sure that this would be a good soaking and only have to be lit one time.

Help me, the voice whispered across the darkness. Nick bowed his head. Believed that death would come for him anytime now. He slapped at his legs and told them to come on. Come on right now.

He heard the flush of fire when the first torch was tossed into the pit and a scream splintered the night. He began again and didn't look back. You can't look back and you can't think back and you had no choice. None of us have a choice. There were only so many hours until daybreak and he didn't know if he was half a mile or a hundred miles from anything that may give him cover. He struggled for hours and his elbows began to bleed and he felt himself bleeding again from other places and he no longer talked to himself or to God as he knew that better men than him were burning in the pit or would die tomorrow or the next day. The dehydration and hunger moved on him and his mind began to play about as he nudged farther. Animals moved that weren't there. A song echoed from a soprano voice. Shells exploded that hadn't been fired. Familiar faces from his boyhood appeared across the field. Ella smiled at him from across the café table. He didn't know how far he had come or how far he had to go but he knew that it was over. Exhaustion overcame him and he lay still. Cheek against the dirt. Arms outstretched. A beautiful night above.

Help me.

14

HE OPENED HIS EYES IN a barn. He lay in a scattering of hay and he wore somebody else's white shirt and overalls. His uniform hung from a clothesline outside and the holes and tears had been stitched together. A little old woman and a cow sat with him. He raised up and grimaced at the ache that pulled through the length of his body. She had bandaged a slice in his thigh and a gash in his shoulder. The little woman moved to him with a cup of water and he drank. She refilled the cup with an old pitcher next to the stool and he drank again. And again. He tried to raise his knees and his legs but they were grasped with pain and he grabbed at his thighs and whimpered. The woman helped him to lie back down and then she took his ankles and pulled and helped Nick to straighten his legs and then she massaged them until he fell back asleep.

He woke later and she was still there and now with an old man beside her. His hair white and shaggy and a badly rolled cigarette hanging between his lips. Nick nodded to them and the man said something but Nick didn't know if it was intended for him or for the wife but either way he didn't understand. He drank more water and the old man walked over to Nick and poked him in the thigh. Nick looked at him, confused. The old woman barked a quick phrase at the old man.

He poked Nick's leg again and said in French do you feel that. The words meant nothing to Nick and he sat still. After two more pokes and repeating the question, the old man finally pulled a short piece of rope from his back pocket that he used to swat the cow when she didn't do what he wanted. He gave Nick a quick and sharp thwack across his thighs and Nick sat up and yelled and slapped back at the old man. The old man threw up his hands and laughed and pointed at the old woman and then back to Nick as if to say I told you so. She stood from the stool and marched over to the old man, swiped the rope away from him, and slapped him with it while he laughed some more and then he made for the barn door. She threw the rope and hit him in the back as he walked out and then she dipped a rag in the water pitcher and wiped Nick's face and neck.

His leg hurt where the rope had lashed him and he understood what the man was trying to find out. He lay back down and tried to remember. It took a moment but he heard the rush of the flames and saw the blaze throwing light into the black night and he felt the fire on his own skin and on the skin and the hair and the uniforms of all those piled into the great hole in the earth and then he heard the voice calling for help and he pushed the woman's hand away and pressed his hands against his own mouth and tried not to scream.

15

THE SUMMER THAT NICK WAS twelve years old he was baptized in the Episcopal church. The summer he was thirteen he was baptized in the family business. He arrived with his father in the morning at eight a.m. He swept the floors and the sidewalk. Straightened stock on the shelves. Emptied garbage. The first couple of weeks his father had to make a list or point and tell him what to do but Nick soon took to his chores with a mechanical nature. At ten he took a break and ate crackers and cheese sitting on a stack of pallets in the stock room. At noon he ate a sack lunch while he sat on the bench outside the storefront. His father sat beside him and drank coffee and nodded and spoke to the passersby. At three o'clock his father set him free and told him to be good and he hopped on his bicycle and hustled to catch up with the neighborhood kids at the city pool or in the clump of woods on the backside of the neighborhood. And this was the pattern of each summer of his teenage years and though his pals moaned and groaned when he said he had to work, or laughed at him for being stuck in his old man's store, he didn't complain though he felt a sinking feeling sometimes in the quiet hours of the late night. A feeling that something was slipping past. A feeling that would not leave him but instead would follow him his entire life.

During the work his conversations with his father were

calculated and measured as Nick hung hammers in the proper rack or stacked cans of paint or learned to count and cut six feet of rope. He never said much as a toddler and his mother had worried. He never said much in elementary school and his mother had worried. And he never said much at home or as he worked in the hardware store and his father didn't seem to mind and took it as an opportunity to fill Nick with as much doctrine as he could. Give a man a firm handshake, his father told him. Every time. The one time you don't they'll remember and try to take advantage of you later. Roll your sleeves up when you work and keep a pencil handy. Speak with respect to others or you'll never get respect in return and there's nothing more important in this world. And you need to remember, Nick, not everybody has the same advantages that you have. Not everybody has a house, a family, a business to learn. So before you criticize anybody, you think about that.

He always watched, no matter what he was doing. He took notice of the mannerisms of men when bartering with his father. He took notice of the way women walked. He took notice of the way the American flag hanging from the storefront flapped in the wind near closing time each day. He took notice of the morning sun through the front windows and the change in the shadows of the store racks and shelves as the sun rose and then dipped in the sky.

He was a watcher. He was a listener. And he was quick to remember the names of his father's customers, remember which carpenter preferred which nail or which painter preferred which brush. When the bell to the door jingled, Nick could look and see who was coming in and before they reached the counter he could damn near correctly predict what it was they wanted and how much. His father made a habit out of pretending to be occupied to see how far Nick could go on his own and by the time the boy had spent one summer in the store his father had turned over running the counter. When he was sixteen he was ordering stock. In the summer before Nick's senior year of high school, when Nick no longer left at three o'clock but stayed until the end of the working day, his father wrote the boy's name on a strip of masking tape and stuck it on the office door, right under his own blacklettered name. It was an act of gratitude, of tradition, maybe even of love by his father. But it had a single impact on Nick that took him in the opposite direction.

There had been few times that he had thought of anything other than this life but seeing his name underneath his father's name on the office door seemed to present a literal future through that very door. And he began to fear it. Fear that he would go to college and meet a girl there and then work in the hardware business and then marry that girl and buy a house in the same neighborhood that he grew up in and then have children. It ended there when he thought about it. It ended with having children because he could see the clear vision of himself and a wife and two small children sitting at the kitchen table and there was no exit from that. So there was no need to consider his life any further. It was what everyone expected to happen and until he saw his name on the office door, he had expected it of himself.

He couldn't decide if there was something wrong with that vision or not. Not everyone has had the advantages you have had, his father's voice echoed. He spent the year that he was seventeen battling the guilt of feeling unsatisfied by prosperous yet predictable coming years that had no guarantee of arriving. Battling the guilt of wanting to leave. Battling the idea of his mother alone in the house with his father and what may happen to them during the blackness without his presence to balance out the sorrow. The predictable was becoming something less to rely on and more of a weight. The Midwestern life, the great American neighborhood, knowing where you are going to be every day. Forever. College was less than a year away and in a subtle attempt to change his fate he talked his parents into letting him attend school in the East.

'Why?' his father had asked. 'Chicago is closer. So is Madison. Columbus. So is most everywhere else. You can get whatever you need close enough.'

Because I have to get out of here or I am going to die, he thought to say.

'I want to go to Yale. Like you,' he had answered. Knowing the sound of it would appeal to his father's pride. And it worked. When he was accepted at New Haven, there was no hesitation. When he graduated and the war began, he did not wait to be called but instead volunteered. It was the chance to escape and he took it. And he would kill and love and bury himself over and over again.

16

DAY BY DAY HIS STRENGTH gradually returned and he joined them in their quiet life. They lived in a small brick house with flowerpots in the window and red blooms bright with the sun. In the mornings the old man milked the cow and sometimes she gave and sometimes she didn't. He fussed and admonished and berated the cow on the bad days and on the good days he brushed her ears and sang bits of songs to her in a careful and soothing tone. He pointed and asked Nick each morning if he wanted to help and Nick said no but that didn't stop the old man from directing Nick to sit next to him and then he'd show him how to do it. The French he spoke was different from the French he had heard in Paris. The vowels more extended and the accent bearing the sound of a patient life. The man complained that he once had more cows and he held up nine fingers. He once had pigs. At least that's what Nick thought he said. Three of them. Then the old man made the sound of a truck and he raised his arms as if holding an imaginary rifle and Nick figured out that the animals had been taken away by the uniforms.

Chickens ran about the yard and eggs laid about like tiny white land mines and Nick picked up the eggs each morning and took them to the back door where the woman cooked them and then they sat at a table in the yard and ate. The man told jokes that he laughed at himself and Nick smiled and nodded but the woman never laughed as if she had heard it all before.

In the midmorning Nick took walks with the woman along the dirt road that twisted down a long sloping hill. The late summer mornings wet with dew and butterflies dancing across the wildflowers and the pop of artillery fire that they both tried to ignore. She talked to him on these walks and he was never certain of what she talked about but he gathered that she had at least one son and at least one grandson fighting out there somewhere. He had picked out three names but sometimes another name fell into her conversation and then she would point out across the fields or wave her hand toward the sky as she spoke and Nick agreed with her when it seemed like that's what she wanted. But her tone was always changing and he would sense the shift into despair and anxiety one minute and then the next she would laugh a sarcastic or doubtful laugh. There was want in her hazy gray eyes and he never interrupted or tried to console. He only listened while she let it out. She said almost nothing around the house and barn except to correct or direct the old man but on the walks she let her thoughts roam.

They only ate one other time during the day and that was in the late afternoon. Nick knew they didn't have anything to spare. But they shared with him in the late empty days. There was always bread and sometimes they ate slices of apple or thin strips of sausage and Nick pretended to be full and tried to give them food back but she would not have it. And the old man would reach and shake Nick's thin arm and then make a fist and grit his teeth. I know I need to get stronger, he would answer. But so do you. You are giving me too much and I can't eat when I know you're hungry. I'd rather us all be hungry. They smiled when he spoke and then looked at one another and tried to figure out what he'd said. The old woman pushed the food back to Nick and he ate and then the night would come and they watched the flashes in the sky.

They had asked him to come and sleep inside the house but he instead stayed in the barn. He didn't want to wake them as he came and went during the night because he could not lie still when he wasn't sleeping. Underneath the open sky he would walk across the fields and trail alongside a low stone fence that rose and fell with the curve of the land. He would talk to himself about a favorite meal or about what he wanted to be when he grew up. He recited his ABCs and he counted the stones as he walked, dragging his fingers along to feel the separations. He imagined his own tiny house sitting solitary across the sprawling land and his own chickens and cows and he imagined sharing the cows with the old man but only the good ones that gave milk each time they were asked to. He imagined learning French so that he could share in the old man's jokes and better understand the grief in the old woman's monologues. In the moonlight he saw another Nick in another time and he had found in the old French couple some semblance of what it meant to be happy or to accept where you belong. He could not picture the old man and the old woman anywhere else but here and as he walked in the shadows of the moon it seemed both strange and palpable to know your place in this world.

He didn't say anything to them once he realized he was strong enough to return. He only walked out of the barn and took his uniform from the clothesline. He changed clothes in the morning light and left the shirt and overalls hanging in place of the uniform. The old woman and her husband watched him from the open door of the kitchen and then the husband went outside and hitched the horse to the wagon. His eyes were wet as he bridled the horse and adjusted the harness but he wiped them dry and gathered himself with deep sighs. He then lit a cigarette and whistled for Nick to come on. The old woman would not come outside and Nick waved to her and waited but she would not come to him. Nick asked the old man why she wouldn't say goodbye and he only shrugged and spoke several straightforward sentences that held none of the lighthearted sentiments that Nick had come to recognize in his voice. Nick walked over and climbed into the back of the wagon and he waved to her again. The old man clicked his teeth and slapped at the reins and the horse and wagon moved along the pathway that led to the road. The old woman watched and finally crossed herself and moved her lips in prayer.

17

THE WAR HAD CHANGED WHILE Nick had been lost and recovering. As the tunnelers had dug themselves beneath the enemy the Allies had been giving up ground for weeks above against the strong surge of the German offensive. An uncertainty had lingered between the men as they cleaned machine guns and rifles and shoveled out trenches and ran barbed wire. But the Allies had rooted in and held strong and waited for the tide to turn. That had come with the success of the great explosion.

In August they were told to prepare to win it or lose it. They are coming with everything they have. And they did. The attack came in three waves with dozens of divisions and thousands of shells and grenades. The earth had become nothing more than a neverending series of degrading troughs, the explosions making holes where there were already holes and the soil growing powdery from the constant barrage. Machine gun fire crisscrossed and some shot or stabbed their own out of sheer reflex and the battle stood at a standstill for weeks. They fought like tired and hungry animals because they were tired and hungry. They came with everything and the Allies withstood and then the German line began to move back in the direction from where it had come. It moved east for the first time in months. And they pushed and chased with a renewed vigor that comes only with the potential for victory.

Soon they began to cross fields and march through demolished villages that they had already crossed and demolished before. It was as if working backward through a violent and unbelievable dream. Except there were no signs of life where there had once been fleeing families, horsedrawn wagons filled with children and blankets wrapping worldly possessions, dirty and hollow faces setting out for anywhere that wasn't susceptible to the bombing and the blood and the desires of ravaged men. The crumbled stone buildings and churches lay in piles as if they had always lain in piles, man long since gone. Reason long since gone. The destruction never finished. They fought back across the ruins and the bodies and their stomachs ached and they pushed on because they were told if you push all the way and leave none of them standing then maybe one day you can lay your armor down and go home and find a pretty girl who will open her legs for you and you can have some damn babies and a lawn chair to sit your ass in and watch them grow.

He caught up with his former division in a razed village along the banks of the Somme. The unattended fields had grown high during the summer and now waved in the wind. They had been relieved two days earlier and tomorrow they would return to the front that had continued moving in their favor. The men lay sprawled along the riverbanks and Nick asked if there was anything to eat and he was told to go to the tavern.

'Which tavern?' he asked but there was only one.

He waited to see if anyone would ask him where he had been or what happened to him and when no one asked he set out for the tavern. It was in the middle of the few streets of town and he walked in to the smell of beans and bread. A record played on a gramophone, the voice and piano wobbling with the spin of the record. Men sat at tables and drank beer and played cards and on a table against the wall sat a stack of plates and a large pot of beans. Nubs of baguettes gathered in a bowl. Nick helped himself and sat down. Looked around. He may as well have been alone.

After he ate he walked outside and found the supply tent. A redheaded man with paunchy cheeks bossed around a handful of clerks and when Nick told him he needed everything the man scratched at his chin.

'Everything?' he asked.

'Yes,' Nick said.

'You sure?'

Nick held out his arms and turned around in a circle.

'You ain't got nothing?'

'I ain't got nothing. I was in the tunnels.'

'That's a lie.'

'Why is that a lie?'

'Cause I ain't never met nobody walking who said he was in the tunnels.'

'Here I am. I'd just as soon go back down.'

'Goddamn. Where you been? The tunnels can't keep up with the way we're moving now. That shit's over with.'

'Then give me a rifle.'

'You don't need a rifle. We need machine gunners.'

'Show me the way.'

'What the hell happened to you?'

'I told you already.'

'You got the look of not telling everything,' the man said. Then he told a clerk to get Nick whatever he needed and figure out which battalion could use bodies the most.

I am a soldier again, Nick thought moments later as he walked back across the village wearing a helmet. A belt around his slender waist. And before he could find a place to sit down a whistle blew. He heard the number of his battalion called through a megaphone and it was time.

18

A FTER IT WAS ALL OVER he tried again.

He sat and waited. Stared out of the café and across at Église de la Sainte-Trinité, its front lawn lined with purpleleaf trees. He got up and paced along the sidewalk, tossed bread to a family of pigeons, bit his fingernails. Nodded to those who nodded to him when they noticed his uniform. The small man swept and sang and Nick tried to ask him about her but the man only held his ear toward Nick and gave him a confused look. After a couple of hours the café crowd had thinned and Nick stared into a short glass of whiskey. Then he got up and waved to the small man and decided to go right back to the attic.

He stood and stared at the building where she had first led him through the open door. It was the same place and he recognized nothing. No more dusty windows as they had been cleaned and brown paper lined the inside of the windows and blocked his view. A deadbolt held the door shut and locked. He stepped back from the building and looked it up and down. Looked back and forth along the street. This is it, he thought. This is it.

After midnight he returned to the locked door with half of a brick and he beat the deadbolt until the lock shattered from the doorframe. He yanked and pulled until it came free and then he opened the door, stepped in, shut it behind. The room was black and he dropped the brick on the floor and struck a match. The floor had been refinished and the walls patched and painted. A stack of scrap wood sat in the corner. Nick moved along the hallway and he went out of the back of the building. He stepped into the alley. He saw the door that led to the attic and he turned the handle and pushed but the door had been locked.

But he had to see for himself. His knuckles bled from beating the lock with the brick so he kicked. The sound of his boot against the door louder each time but he didn't care and after the sixth battering the door gave in. Pitch black but he knew where the stairs were and he followed them up without striking a match as if the dark solitude were some type of punishment. When he arrived at the door to the attic he wrapped his shaking hand around the knob and turned and said please open. And the door opened.

A gracious moon gave light through the windows and Nick moved between the costumes. He crossed the attic and the mattress was still there but the costumes they had lain on top of and underneath had been returned to the racks. The lamp was knocked over and the bulb busted. The suitcase gone. He moved to the window and ran his fingers across the windowsill where she had kept her brush and cigarette butts and the scissors she used to cut frame decorations from the costumes. He knew that her hair was still there in a pile in a corner though he didn't bother to look though he wanted badly to see it and hold it in his fingers.

In the next weeks he scoured the streets without cease. Going where she had taken him. Through the Montmartre cemetery where she'd shown him her favorite crosses and headstones. Through the vegetable market at the gates of Église Saint-

Augustin. Along the river where they sat underneath Pont de l'Alma. He was a hawk on two feet, glaring and staring and tracing their faces and he found hundreds of young women but none with her gait or with her choppy hair or pushing a cart filled with frames. At a river kiosk he bought a journal, lineless white pages inside a tender leather jacket, and he made notes to himself, trying to keep track of where they had been together, at what times of the day. Any detail that might run him across her path.

She had become a ghost. Or he had. He wasn't sure. He fought to keep her clear and vivid in his mind though with each day she became a clouded image, in the way that the dead lose their clarity and slowly fall away because we know they will not return.

At an old clothing store in Odéon he bought a suit, shirt, and shoes and kept his uniform folded neatly on a chair in the corner of his small hotel room. He then walked the same streets and expected to find her. He scribbled more notes in his journal. Spent an entire afternoon and night doing nothing but riding the Métro. Getting off and getting back on again. Changing lines. Lingering in the Métro halls and waiting for her to walk by. He stood on the steps at Place du Tertre and stared out across Paris as if a ray of light or perhaps a gracious bird might give a hint as to what part of the city held her. But she was nowhere to be found. And the seasons had changed and the green of Paris had faded. The wind knifed and evening shutters closed and there were fewer and fewer tables outside the cafés. He wandered day and night beneath the changing leaves of the trees.

The transformative landscape of the city made it seem more foreign than before and he began to wonder if she had been a figment of his imagination. If his life with her and the life created with her and the days together in this place all had existed solely in his mind. Or had she been created by his desire for something safe and true, something given to him by his subconscious to relieve his fears, to settle his nerves, to remind him that there was life beyond the butchery and that one day it would once again be available to him. To all of them. He stayed out at night, sitting on park benches under the soft glow of the lamps and standing on bridges and leaning over and looking into the slowmoving waters of the Seine. Trying to decide if she existed. Knowing that she did. But finding solace in the very sliver of a chance that maybe, only maybe, she had existed solely in the imaginary world. And he had not touched her. And she had not touched him. And they had not smiled the way they smiled and neither of them had been hurt.

It had all been his creation, he decided. So he could be the one to relieve the pain.

He did this by following young women who reminded him of her, wanting to see if he could create such an experience again. The first one he chose had the same auburn hair but it was long and bunched together loosely with pins. She wore a similar gray coat though it was a darker gray and not as short. Her scarf pushed up close to her chin and she kept her head tucked to defend against the cool. Nick was sitting among the trees in Jardin du Luxembourg in the late afternoon when he noticed her walking past the fountain and she ascended the stairs and walked right past him. He gave her twenty steps and then he followed. She walked out of the garden gates and onto Boulevard Saint-Michel. She kept a brisk pace and kept her hands in her coat pockets and only looked left or right to cross a street. Nick lingered behind when she stopped. Imagining her name. Imagining her smell. She turned right on rue des Écoles, stopping once to buy bread and another time for *Le Petit Journal*. Nick wore his hat low across his eyes and blew on his hands. She arrived at her destination, a library on rue Jussieu. She unwrapped her scarf as she entered the front door.

He sat down on a bench across the street and waited.

By the time she came out an hour later, he had all he needed from her. He had been in her sixth floor apartment and she had watered the plants on the window ledge of her tiny kitchen. She had translated the headlines of *Le Petit Journal* and two of the articles he was interested in. She had made them coffee with steamed milk and hers was too hot and he swapped cups with her because she had made his first and it was cooler. They had made love in her thin, single bed, falling off once and laughing hysterically and then going to the finish on the floor. He had taken a bath in her tub and she had sat in the window and read by the last light of day and then they had gone out to a picture show and drunk a carafe of wine at the café below her apartment.

She came out of the library and he watched her walk away. A lonely but satisfied expression covered his face. I did it, he thought. And I'll do it again.

The last days that he ever spent in the city he used in this same way. Finding one to follow and then creating their relationship. Then letting her go, momentarily reassured. And then finding another and following and beginning again. In a few days, he had lived a dozen lives with them. Had made hundreds of memories. He grew brave with the proximity with which he followed, sitting next to them when they stopped in cafés or standing only steps away at the boulangerie. Once he was chased into the dark by two companions of a woman who had seen him following. But this did not deter him as he had become complacent and satisfied with what he was doing and how he was doing it.

At the end of each episode, he would write about the woman in his journal. Give her a name, write a few sentences about where they sat for their picnic or something honest she had said to him in a moment of tenderness. He described each crippling goodbye. Each long and last embrace. And on his final day in Paris, in the last hour before his departure, as he sat in Gare du Nord and waited for the train that would carry him across the French countryside and deliver him to the ship waiting to take the scarred American home, he opened the journal and ripped the pages out and tossed them in a garbage can. Vowing to bury everything he was leaving in Paris as deep down as it would go.

II

19

THE AMERICAN LANDSCAPE WAS ABLAZE in the reds and golds of autumn as the train passed through afternoon and evening and finally into night like a lumbering dream. Nick had not slept and he held his right hand with his left to keep it from shaking. He walked the quiet length of the train to keep the shaking from his mind. Or held his hand in the sink and ran warm water over it as that somehow helped. Now he sat in the window seat and stared into the black, talking to his reflection in the muted light. It didn't happen and it didn't happen and it didn't happen he whispered as he stared at himself. The rock of the train like the rock of the earth as he sat still in the tunnels and the war raged above. He spoke in low, fractured sentences, pieces of coherence that came and went as the train carried him away from the east and shoved him toward the setting of his youth. As the miles passed he felt as if there was a strong hand on the back of his neck forcing him to look at the faceless future before him. There should have been an excitement or a joy or a relief in returning to the safety of the Midwest and he looked for those emotions in the canvas of night. He thought they might be hiding in the dark.

And then first light. He watched the world change methodically and could not deny the optimism of a rising sun as the light shimmered across the frosted, silver land. Home, he thought. The man sitting next to him awoke. Scratched at his mustache and yawned. He adjusted in his seat and looked out at the passing farmland with squinted eyes.

'Where are we?' he asked.

'Getting close,' Nick said.

'Close to what?'

'Chicago.'

In the cold and early morning the train stopped in Union Station in Chicago and Nick got off to smoke a cigarette. People moved everywhere. Boarding trains and getting off trains and loading and unloading suitcases and trunks and dragging children by the hand or coat sleeve and hurrying with briefcases and sometimes bouncing off one another and apologizing and trudging on. The porter walked back and forth along the platform and announced eight minutes until departure, eight minutes until departure. Nick smoked the cigarette down and felt for another but he was out. A newspaper and magazine kiosk and coffee stand were at the end of the platform and he stuck his hand in his coat pockets and manipulated his way through the busy crowd.

He stood in line for coffee behind a handful of others and behind him a chorus of squeals broke out. A group of women, probably mother and grandmothers and aunts, mobbed a returning soldier, a palefaced young man wearing his uniform. They hugged and cried and touched his cheeks and pulled off his hat and felt his hair. He didn't fight back and allowed himself to be embraced. Nick watched them over his shoulder. He had left his uniform across the ocean, a thoughtless act he had regretted but he was now relieved. The man behind him in line grunted and said it's your turn and Nick stepped forward.

Large, rectangular windows lined the upper walls of the depot and blocks of light shined out across the trains and travelers. Wisps of smoke and dust floated in the air. Engines clamored and hissed and the wheels of baggage carts clicked across the concrete and whistles sounded and porters shouted. Nick got his coffee and he moved away from the stand and sipped. He looked around for the welcomed soldier but he and his greeters were already gone. And then he looked up at the great board listing destinations and departure times and he didn't see the list of cities and times. He saw a scramble of letters and numbers.

He was getting closer. Closer to the hard winter. Closer to the place he had thought of a thousand times since his feet had stepped onto the soil of war. Closer to the familiar faces and streets and houses and clouds in the familiar sky.

He looked back to his train and in minutes it would back out of the station. They moved all around him. The living with the places they had a reason to go to and the routine of life once they got there. The friends or lovers who were waiting for them to arrive. They darted back and forth as he seemed to be looking for someone or something to convince him he was going in the right direction. You are doing what you are supposed to do. All around him the living moved with intent and engines exhaled and Nick was held in place by a feeling he could not name.

His bag was buried in the baggage car and he felt in his coat for his wallet and journal and existing ticket and he tried to think if there was anything he had left on the seat that he needed. Then the thought crossed his mind. I don't need anything. Not a single damn thing.

He skimmed the board. His train would leave him but he did not want to be left standing in the station, wondering if he had made the right decision. So he searched not only for a new destination but also for a quick departure and he was a third of the way down the schedule when he came across New Orleans. Departure 7:12 a.m. Gate 9.

Next to the schedule board was a round clock and it read 7:06.

He surveyed the station for the ticket window and it was across a vast hallway that was covered with hundreds of crossing bodies. There wouldn't be time. But he did not panic and the cold chill seemed to fall from him as he remembered Ella saying I was in New Orleans once. As a child with my father. Nothing that I remember. He heard her voice and imagined her moving through the crowd as a small girl holding her father's hand and then he raised his eyes toward gate 9 and this time he saw himself, walking confidently and leisurely through this sea of haste, scanning the passenger cars for an empty seat, and then stepping up into the open door, pausing at the top of the steps to turn around and look back to his mirrored image, waiting for him to come forward.

20

B Y THE TIME THE TRAIN reached Memphis he couldn't take
it anymore. Everything was too close. The windows, the
seats, the people in the seats, the ceiling, the floor. It was all
too close and getting closer. He had been traveling for days
now, first on the ship across the Atlantic. Then on the train
from New York to Chicago. Crowded trains and crowded
train stations and not being able to sleep and the rhythmic
clicking that he wished would stop and now he couldn't
manage the carriage door open and it was all closing in.

He stood in the doorway as the train eased into the station
and held his hands against its window. He pressed his nose
against the glass and fogged the window with heavy and
impatient sighs. His foot tapped and sweat gathered on his
neck and the world moved slowly outside and more slowly
behind his eyes and in the cramped space he heard the shrill
of shellfire and he felt the fragments of rock rain down on his
head and his mouth was dry and dusty. His foot tapped and
then his leg began to shake and he wished he had something to
fire. A woman holding a baby stood behind him and touched
his shoulder and asked if he was all right. Nick ignored her and
squeezed his eyes tightly and grabbed his leg and mumbled.
Hold on, just hold on. It'll go away. The woman took a step back
from him just as the train finally rolled to a stop and the strain
of steel and metal groaned through his feet and heart and he

told himself that this will not last. And the train stopped and the door latch released. He shoved it open and leapt from the car as if it might explode, landing awkwardly and taking two stumbling steps before falling facedown onto the concrete.

He lay there, his face resting against the wooden slats of the platform. Passengers exited the train and stepped around him. A woman stopped and patted his shoulder. Nick rolled over on his back with his eyes past her and she then shrugged and moved along.

He rose to his feet and paced back and forth on the platform and got his air. Then he found a water fountain and drank some water. Found the bathroom and washed his hands and face in the sink. Rubbed his eyes. Pulled it together and talked to himself in the mirror and returned to his seat moments before leaving Memphis. The car that he sat in had lost passengers and there was more air and he folded his arms. Rested his head against the window.

The train moved deeper into the Southern landscape and he remembered that they would be expecting him at home. So he took out his journal and wrote a letter to his father:

I've had the great fortune of stumbling upon some friends from my days at New Haven at Union Station in Chicago. There was Timothy Bolton of the Pittsburgh Boltons, standing right there next to the newspaper stand as I stepped off the train for some fresh air. You likely remember him as he accompanied me home one Thanksgiving. Or was it Christmas? Tall with a less than daunting strip of facial hair he calls a beard. Tim and several others who managed to avoid the vacation in France were elated to find me in one piece and begged me to accompany them to New Orleans. I will not be delayed for very long but simply could not say no to old friends.

He read the explanation to himself in a whisper. Horseshit, he thought. Every word. But that is why it will work because those are all the things they want to hear. He tore the page from the journal and when the train made its stop in Jackson, Nick mailed the letter from the station. He bought a newspaper and smoked a cigarette and waited to the last second to board. No more stops before New Orleans.

When he sat down again in the train car he read the headline: U.S. SUPREME COURT TO DECIDE ON LEGALITY OF WARTIME PROHIBITION.

'Trouble,' said a voice behind Nick. A tall man leaned forward and pointed at the headline.

'What?' Nick said.

'Fight in a goddamn war and then come home to a dry country. Tell me that's a good idea,' the man said and he flopped back in his seat and pouted. Nick folded the page and read.

After nearly two years of challenges to the wartime prohibition law, the Supreme Court of the United States will be forced to decide if the law is constitutional. If upheld, the law destroys the last vestige of hope for a wet holiday season and the 'interminable drought' will have begun.

21

HE FELT WORSE WITH EVERY passing mile and every click of the rails and every shift and sway of the car and by the time Nick meandered out of Union Station in New Orleans he was someone else. Sunkeyed and deranged because he had not been in the confining train car but he had been in the muted tunnel and in the rat-infested trenches and in the attic and in the darkness of his boyhood home and in the barn where his legs would not work and he had been in a field with a bloodred sunset after a bloodsoaked day and his eyes were shadowed and his hair a mess and he had paced up and down the aisle of the train car mumbling to himself and pressing his hands against the windows and trying to ignore the storm of voices rushing through his mind, a chorus of chaos that drowned out any thoughts of normalcy. Do you want something to eat or do you want something to drink or do you want to read the newspaper, he asked himself again and again to try and settle his mind and his shaking hand and the chorus of voices answered no every time. No you don't want anything and you will listen to us and you are stuck in this car and there is not a damn thing you can do about it. He sauntered out of the train station in a stupor and he had forgotten what city he was in and only knew that he was in some unfamiliar place, carrying the punishment of having survived.

He hadn't changed clothes since Le Havre, five days before. Rough beard and the smell of the sleepless. Wrinkled suit and a loose tie. He didn't know where he was going or what he was doing and he turned in a catatonic state and watched a mother passing by with three small children at her heels. The women and children and other passengers leaving the station all seemed to be walking in the same direction so he followed.

It was as if he had bled out of one perplexing and dreamlike sequence right into another. He was surrounded by street voices. Random shouts and obscenities and sweet callings from girls in doorways and cries from grocers and howling singsong tremolos from saloons. Children in the midst of excited games talked back and forth in some strange and meshed dialect and mumbled solicitations came from lowbrowed men on corners with bottles in their coat pockets. Beyond the voices was the rhythmic clap of hooves across the streets paved with rough, square Belgian stones. An odd chicken cluck. The strained shrill of a trumpet. The clatter of plates and knives and forks. A streetcar clicking along its line. From the Mississippi River ship horns and whistles echoed through the thin streets and alleyways.

He made his way into Jackson Square. Stores and saloons flanked the square and rising above were shabby apartments with cast-iron railings and laundry hanging from sagging clotheslines. On each side of the square were the sellers – fruits, vegetables, flowers, coffee, breads, tobacco. They sat in the backs of small, makeshift wagons, hardlooking men and women and their hardlooking, skinny children, preaching you over to their stand, promising your money's worth.

The cathedral stood tall over it all. He stared up at the arched windows and the highreaching steeple with a small, simple cross sitting at its height. A group of nuns stood together in front and shared a baguette and pigeons milled beneath them picking up crumbs and he walked over and asked a nun where he was. He was hungry. Lightheaded. He wavered some and she took his arm.

'What do you mean?' she asked.

'Where am I?' he asked again.

'Jackson Square.'

'What town?'

'Frenchtown.'

'What is that?' he asked. But he did not wait for an answer. He pulled away from her. Rubbed at his eyes. He then walked into the park in the middle of the square. A fountain sparkled in the afternoon sun and a toddler leaned over and splashed his hands in the water while his mother sat on the concrete edge wrapped in a sweater and stared out toward the sky above the Mississippi as if waiting for someone to descend. Nick nodded to an elderly couple sitting on a bench, their wrinkled hands wrapped together. A man in an apron lay on his back in the grass with his hands across his face. Nick spotted a vacant bench and he sat down and the exhaustion came over him in a swoon. His head fell back. His mouth fell open. His arms fell to his sides. And he would have fallen into a deep sleep if it wasn't for the hands that went into his pockets. Pulling out his wallet and his pocket watch and he raised his head and came alive in time to grab the thin arm. He grabbed the thin arm and twisted and the boy shrieked and handed off the wallet and watch to his friend who then turned to run.

Nick rose from the bench and chased the gangly boy out of the park. Around the fruitsellers. Through a cluster of scattering pigeons. And he was heading for an alley alongside the cathedral when the nuns corralled him. Nick caught up and grabbed the young thief by the coat but one of the nuns slapped his hand away.

'Give it back,' the nun said to the child.

The boy held out a dirty hand and gave the wallet and watch back to Nick. The boy then crossed himself and rolled his eyes and turned and ran. Nick tucked his wallet and watch into his coat pocket and nodded to the nun. She looked him over. His wrinkled clothes. His slick and unkempt hair. The faraway look in his eyes.

'Do you need a place to stay?' she asked. He yawned and then nodded. She whispered something to another nun and then she raised her finger for him to follow.

She took him into the alley and opened the tall double doors of a brick building and they entered a wide room. A long table lined the back wall and on the table sat soup pots and a tray stacked with slices of salami and bologna. Several more nuns stood at the table and filled soup bowls and served plates and the room was an array of aromas. Beef broth and cigarettes and street people. Round tables filled the floor space and men and women, young and old, sat at the tables. Some heavyeyed, slurping at the soup with shaky hands. Others sleeping with their heads down and untouched plates of food at their elbows.

She handed Nick a plate of food and walked him through the room and into a tight passage that was hardly more than shoulderwidth. They passed the kitchen and came into a courtyard where large, lazy tropical trees reached over and brushed their heads as they passed across the brick patio.

They went up a staircase and then across the second floor balcony where the strange and fakelike trees draped across the railing. The nun unlocked a rough wooden door and she said you can stay here. Nick looked inside but it was black and the nun stepped in and turned on a lamp that sat on a table next to the door. A patched quilt covered a narrow bed. Next to it was a desk and a chair and a Bible lay perfectly centered on the desktop. On a table in the back corner rested a porcelain wash basin.

The nun explained that they served dinner each night and he could help if he wanted to but it wasn't required and when he left the room he was to leave the door unlocked. Mass is Sunday. You can stay here a week. Maybe more if you're quiet but not much more. He nodded as she spoke but was not listening as he stared into the dim room before him and realized there was no way to know where you would end up or what you would become and he felt both complacent and concerned for tomorrow. He didn't hear her say goodbye and he didn't respond when she touched his shoulder and he stood there with his arms by his sides and a lost, exhausted stare. And then as if summoned, he stepped inside and closed the door. He set the plate on the bed.

The impulse struck him to leave again. To go back to the station and get on a train to somewhere else. Anywhere else. But his body did not listen and his mind quickly gave in. Sit down and eat, he thought. Then sleep. You cannot run from yourself.

22

HE GATHERED BOTTLES AND STUCK candles in their necks like she had done in the theater attic and he searched for solace in the little flames in the coming nights. For days he stayed indoors. A kind of hiding. He only slept in brief intervals and in between he sat on the edge of the bed and held his hands and feet over the candles until he was able to calm his nervous breathing and trembling hand and sleep again. All through the night he heard others in the rooms around him stirring and sometimes yelling with disgust at their degenerate fate as if it were something that could be chased away with a rage.

In his segments of sleep he was battered by dreams. The gunshots rang from everywhere. They came in clusters that flew across the heads of the men in trenches and pierced the mob of men killing in the fields and all those men screamed and panicked. The shots came from rifles and machine guns and planes and then grenades exploded in whitehot blasts and arms and hands flew into the air and he was crying and fighting and desperate for escape and on some nights he was a boy again and he raced across the battlefields and through the chaos to the wide lawns of his childhood, looking for the dead bodies that he knew were there but he only ran and ran and ran until he grew into a man and his feet were again in the mudcaked boots and his hands covered in blood. He cried out in these nightmares and tussled in the small bed and several times he woke after tumbling out of the bed and onto the floor to find his palms slapping at the floorplanks and his face wet with slobber.

In another dream he was standing outside his door and the courtyard was filled with the hungry and the drunk and he heard the gunshots and he tried to get down the stairs but was blocked by a mob of bodies and he pushed and shoved and finally made his way down into the crowd. He tried to get through, to make it into the streets and escape the attack, but he was a toy among the desperate and they tossed him around as if he had no meaning to this world at all.

And still in other moments there was no war. There was no blood. There was only a large house with many rooms sitting on the hillside of a darkened countryside. And he was standing at the open door, listening to the cry of an infant. Then he would go inside and try to find the child. The cry echoing and shifting from room to room in the great house and he could never find it, wanting to see the child and hold the child and rushing through the shadows and hearing the cry and he would grow rattled and shortbreathed and the cry would begin to fade as if floating away on some soulful wind and then he would be alone in the empty house and then he would wake alone. With his arms outstretched in the dark.

23

Y OU DO NOT NEED TO stay there any longer. It is time to come home.

We need to begin discussing your future.

The telegram came from his father on his seventh day in New Orleans and Nick had not been surprised by any of the words. He imagined his father talking to his mother about where Nick was supposed to be and what he was supposed to be doing. His father shaking his head and complaining that time has been wasted. Nick tore the telegram into pieces and left it in an ashtray on a café table.

He became part of the shuffle and wail of the city as Frenchtown was an America he never knew existed. Ceramic gutters lined the streets and washed away debris and animal droppings and the air was hazy from the smoke from coal and wood fires. Everyone, even some of the children, seemed to be smoking a cigarette or cigar or pipe. Streetcar and electric and telephone lines crossed overhead in no particular pattern as if they were not of function but instead some hectic web and lamps hung from the wires like electric piñatas. Spatterings of French and Italian and English came from faces of all shapes and colors in some convoluted dialect only a native could understand. In the early morning he watched the hustle of the vendors at the market, selling live seafood and alligator meat brought in from the swamps. Then he walked the river, stopping at the warehouse which separated Jackson Square from the wharf. In the commotion of exchange men sweated and labored and sometimes fought over their cargos of bananas and cotton and coffee and farther along the river, men moved up and down the ships with the random coordination of ants on a hill.

In the night children disappeared and shop windows bolted shut. Smoke and music rolled out of the doors of the saloons and brothels. Cards hit the tables and shrieks and catcalls filled the night. The promise of a good time called from the redlipped mouths underneath the fluttering eyelashes that did nothing to conceal their specialties and those solicitations came not only in the cover of dark but they were there in the mornings and in the afternoons. The girls were always available and the liquor was always available. It was in the jar glasses in the saloons and in teacups of quaint lunch eateries and it was handed out in pint bottles to the men working at the wharf. Nick had stood at the river late at night and seen the boats and skiffs that nestled along the banks and he knew what they were unloading. He remembered the tall man on the train and his disgust with the approaching prohibition and Nick watched the preparation to keep the country wet, the trail of bootleg liquor sailing in from somewhere out in the Gulf and then being shuffled upriver and released into the heart of the country and shifted around the coastline and circling the southern tip of Florida and then up the East Coast and spreading into all the cracks and crevices of the national terrain.

He walked during the day and he walked at night because it was free of the torture of the small room filled with bad dreams and he began to end up at the same place when he was ready to sit down and have a coffee and a cigarette. A whitewashed building in the middle of Burgundy Street. He would lean against a street lamp and stare into the establishment, with its doors opened wide and piano music spilling into the street. Flames danced in a fireplace toward the back of the room, close to the staircase where the shadows fell and vague figures climbed or descended in anticipation or resolution. The rail of the brass bar shined and the chandelier sprayed little spots of light and the young women with their bare necks sauntered between tables. Sitting on laps and lighting cigarettes and smiling and playing the game with casual ease.

He watched the men drink and then drink again and sometimes reach for places they were not allowed to reach until the deal was struck and then their hands shrank back to the glass that would be filled again. There was something about this place that seemed different to Nick. As if it were a stage designed to capture the beauty of the Frenchtown decadence. The art on the walls and the china plates and crystal glasses. The longlimbed girls and their black stockings. The bottles that never seemed to run dry. And in the midst of it all was its director, the woman with the high cheekbones and thick hair gathered on the top of her head as she moved behind the bar and between the tables. The woman who the men spoke to when they came in and who the girls checked with before they took a customer toward the staircase. The confident woman with the blacklined eyes but a touch of something sad in her expression when she slipped behind the bar to pour a drink or roll a cigarette, when she paused as though she did not believe that anyone was watching her. Something fell from her in those moments. Something that Nick recognized. He leaned on the street lamp and watched this stage and he picked out the place where he would sit when he finally decided to cross the street and go inside. The stool at the end of the bar, closest to the spot where she would slip away when her eyes fell. And each time when he returned to his small and stale room he began to imagine how it would go when he finally walked in and sat down. What he would say to her. What she would say to him. Or would participating ruin it all.

24

SOME OF THE GIRLS CALLED her madam and some of them called her Miss Colette. For three days Nick came at dusk and sat down at the end of the bar next to a lit candle and for three days he drank coffee and declined offers for liquor and flesh and waited on Miss Colette to engage him in some way. But she had given him a queer look in the first moments he declined any offers of pleasure and then she regarded him not at all as he sat there with his journal and pencil and took up space. When she moved behind the bar he kept his eyes on her, waiting on her to meet his stare and offer some kind of exchange but she only poured wine or moved cash in and out of the register or hiked up her breasts or licked her lips in the mirror. All of which kept him dreaming of who she was and what she might be.

On the fourth day he went in the afternoon. Sat in the same spot. Tapped his finger on the bartop to the rhythm of the piano. Didn't even have time to turn his head when a soft hand landed in the center of his back and when the girl recognized his profile she only said it's you again before sliding her hand away and moving toward the stairs where three other girls lazed across the steps like languid felines.

Outside in the street a handful of boys and girls played stickball. Vegetable carts knocked past on the cobblestones. A watchmaker leaned in the doorway of his shop and smoked a pipe. Nick opened his journal and began to scribble, adding to the pages of scribbling he had created the previous three times he sat there. No words. Only circles and loops and crisscrosses in dulled pencil strokes. Behind the bar Miss Colette pulled a jug from beneath and poured two shots of moonshine. She picked up a shot and knocked it back. And then she slid the other shot toward Nick and said you either pay for that and drink it or get your ass up and go somewhere else. She stood and watched as he set down the pencil and journal and reached for the shot glass but then they were interrupted by a bearlike roar from the staircase followed by a rumble of heavy footfalls and the breaking of glass. The girls on the stairs came alive and moved out of the way as the shards of the champagne glass clicked to the bottom and a big man leaned heavy on the rail to hold himself upright. Then he let out a deep belch. Stroked his beard. Adjusted his suspenders. He continued on down the stairs. Apologizing for the broken glass and patting at his round belly and ending up at the end of the bar opposite of Nick where Colette was waiting on him.

'Are you done?' she asked him.

He belched again. Wiped his mouth. Pulled cash from his pocket. 'Yeah,' he said. 'I'm done. It's a shame.'

He counted three bills down onto the bartop.

'More than that,' she said.

He laid down another. She tapped her finger on the bartop. He laid down one more.

'It's a shame, all right,' he said again.

'What's a shame?'

His coat hung on a coatrack and he moved over and grabbed it and wrestled it onto his burly frame. Then he nodded to the girls and to Colette and he walked out, slapping Nick on the shoulder as he moved out into the street and began to sing in a deep and drunken voice.

Colette mumbled something to herself and then she picked up the cash and folded it. She then looked again to Nick to see if he had touched the moonshine but Nick's eyes were out into the street where the stickball game had paused and the kids all stood still, staring up into the sky.

'Hey,' Colette said.

Nick looked back to her.

'A drink or a girl or get out.'

In the street two old women and a butcher holding a knife had gathered with the kids. All of them staring above Colette's building. Nick picked up the shot glass but put it down again when Colette came from around the bar and walked outside to see what they were looking at. Nick followed her.

There was the methodical rise of smoke above the brothel roof, a lazy gray wafting that blended easily with the other trails of smoke exuding from the rooftop stovepipes. As they watched the smoke began to thicken into a deeper shade of gray and a girl with her head covered with a scarf hurried down the stairs and out of the brothel and along the street unnoticed. The smokecloud blossomed and more gathered to watch and Colette stood with her arms folded. She had taken two steps to go back inside and see what the hell was going on when there was a loud crack and the roof fell into the third floor and high streaks of yellow and orange leapt into the sky as if reaching for redemption. First there were screams and shouts and then the rumble of feet on the upper floors and down the staircase and then another crack and sparks exploded against the dustblue sky. Some streetgoers gawked as if watching an impromptu street play while others grabbed the hands of children and hustled away.

Colette ran back inside as the flames ducked into the building and stretched out of the open windows of the third floor and then more screams and men with drinks in hand danced from their barstools to the exit and looked up and saw the fire and then hastily walked away. Colette screamed up the stairs and halfdressed girls and their halfdressed customers hurried and stumbled and got up again and made it into the street where they all began pointing and yelling and then the street shook itself alive as the fire spread quickly across the third floor and fell into the second floor. The smoke rolled down the staircase and filled the bar and Colette became vague as she ducked behind the bar and grabbed cash and called out for others as horrific screams came from the second floor and a man with his pants around his knees and his hair and shirt on fire leapt out of the window and a naked girl came out after him with her burning skin and they landed on the sidewalk and twisted and wrenched and screamed as people in the street began to run for help and beat on doors of neighboring buildings.

All Nick could hear was help me help me help me and he ran into the building after Colette. Inside was entirely filled with smoke and others crashed into him as they ran blind through the smoke and then he felt someone and he grabbed the arm and began to pull and the arm jerked away and Colette's hard voice said get your goddamn hands off of me. The smoke filled his eyes and his lungs and he almost immediately dropped down to his knees. Began to crawl. The heat coming on now and the cracks and breaks of the building frame as the fire began to roar like some pitdwelling beast and in the small backrooms of the brothel opiumfilled bodies never woke and were consumed without knowledge that today was the day they would become ash.

Nick made it into the street crawling on his hands and knees. Coughing and hacking. Someone grabbed him and helped him to his feet and he hobbled to the other side of the street. Held on to the same lamppost he had held on to for days while he watched her. A panicked street and sirens as the fire quickly destroyed the upper floors. Out in the street the girls gathered, some holding bottles of whiskey and some holding clothes and photographs. They called for Miss Colette again and again until she finally appeared from the smoke, wobbly and with the bottom of her dress on fire and two girls grabbed her and took her to the ground and beat the fire from her clothes. Another body came from a third floor window, burning and writhing on the sidewalk next to the other two bodies that were now still and smoldering and some fled and some stared in horror at their burning housemates on the sidewalk and the brilliant reds and yellows and blues of the feeding fire illuminating the Frenchtown sky and now reaching to the neighboring buildings without prejudice.

Nick coughed. Wiped at his mouth and eyes. Began to move along the street and away from the spectacle and when he was a block away he stopped. Caught his breath. Looked back at the fire and felt as if there was something he should do but this fight was lost. The roar of the flames and the screams of its victims pierced the evening and Nick went down to a knee and his hand began to shake violently. He made a fist, beat it against his leg. Unfolded his fingers and clenched them and hammered once more. He heard German voices and he felt the weight of the dead against him and his hand shook and his breaths came quick and he tucked his hand under his arm and squeezed and it tremored still and he said in a hard and loud voice I can't help you. I can't help you. I can't help.

Firewatchers next to him looked when he spoke but he only got up from his knee and screamed at them. I can't help you! He jerked his hand from under his arm and held it toward them. Look at it, he screamed. Look at it! His flapping hand and his crazed eyes and he screamed there's nothing I can do and then he shoved past them all and hurried away.

25

THREE BLOCKS AWAY FROM THE fire he stopped. He told himself he was safe. He told himself he did not do anything wrong. He let himself be and his hand became still. In the distance he heard the commotion of the burning block but he ignored it and continued on in the opposite direction and that's when he came upon the crippled old man. He was hunched and struggling along with a cane, an oversized black coat draped across his shoulders. The old man stopped and let out a raw, vicious series of coughs. Nick paused and waited for the man to gather himself before he stepped around. But the cough kept on and the man seemed to coil and then he pulled out a handkerchief just as the blood spewed from his mouth. He dropped his cane and Nick reached to help him as the old man pressed the handkerchief to his mouth. Nick held him upright and he noticed the scarred neck and then he looked at the man's hands and saw the scarred hands and wrists. These were the hands and scars of others he knew, so he held on and waited.

After a minute, the man removed the handkerchief and the bleeding had stopped. He said I got it and Nick let go of his arm and bent down and picked up the cane. The man took it and nodded in thanks. He sniffed and wiped at his eyes and then he folded the bloodspotted cloth and stuck it into his coat pocket. A rubbery, quartermoon scar framed his left eye and he touched it as if to make sure it was still there. He bent over and spit and Nick asked him if he needed something. A doctor or a taxi.

He raised and was out of breath and while Nick had thought that he was helping an old man, he could see now that he wasn't. He looked closely at the man's eyes and face and saw that the man was no older than himself.

'I need you to walk me back,' he said.

'Back where?'

'My place,' he said and he fought to get himself together. Nick waited and when he said he was ready he told Nick to hold him by the arm and come on.

It was a slow, cautious three blocks. Two men passed and called the broken man Judah but he didn't reply. A grayhaired woman wrapped in a shawl walked with them for half a block with her hand on Judah's shoulder and spoke to him with concern and empathy but he never responded until she finally stopped and watched them walk on. At the corner of Bourbon and St. Philip, Judah raised his cane and pointed at the saloon.

'Here,' he said.

'This your place?'

'That's what I said.'

Judah pulled his arm away from Nick and moved toward the door.

'Come in and eat. You look hungry,' he said.

Nick glanced into the windows and the tables were filled with curious eyes. As soon as they stepped inside the saloon the barmaid called out to Judah and said somebody just ran through here talking about Colette's place and the whole block being on fire.

'What fire?' Judah said.

154

He pulled out the chair beside him and motioned for Nick to sit down.

'The fire I just told you about,' the barmaid said. 'Don't act like you don't hear me and don't act like you don't know. She's probably gonna walk in here any second and ask you what you did with the match.'

'I didn't do nothing with it,' he said. 'If her place is on fire then it deserves to be on fire. Maybe something caught up with her.'

'Where you been?'

'Walking.'

'Walking where?'

'One more question and you can go work for somebody else.'

'You ain't worth a shit at lying.'

'That don't concern me.'

'Like hell.'

26

J UDAH FINALLY SHUSHED THE BARMAID and told her to bring
them two plates of sausage and rice and bread. We'll be
in the back. Judah moved between the tables and the locals
nodded and spoke to him. In the corner of the room Judah
opened a door that led down a narrow and shadowy hallway,
dusted in light from a single small window at the top of the
wall as if put there by accident.

They entered a windowless room at the end of the hallway.
Brick walls and a brick floor. A desk and chair on one side
and on the other side another chair and a round table and
a lamp. A cigar box and a foot-long opium pipe and opium
lamp sat on the desk. Judah lowered his cane and moved to
sit on the far side of the desk.

Nick took a cigarette from his coat pocket. Judah opened
the desk drawer and took out a box of matches and slid the
box toward Nick and then Judah took a clean handkerchief
from the drawer and pressed it to his nostrils.

Nick lit the cigarette and studied the man. His hair was
parted stiffly down the middle. Hard eyes and a sallow face.
A patchy beard camouflaged the red and scarred patches of
his jawline and neck.

'Where'd you come from?' Judah asked. As if reading
Nick's mind.

'I just got back.'

'You must've been one of the last to come home.'

'Yeah. I didn't get in any hurry. But this isn't home.'

'Where is home?'

'Minnesota.'

'Why ain't you there?'

'I'm going to be. Eventually. I needed some air.'

'Your sniffer must be broke cause fresh air ain't exactly one of our best qualities.'

'Maybe air isn't the right word.'

'How'd you end up here?'

'Just luck.'

'Is it cold in Minnesota?'

'It's lots of things.'

'I cannot say that I have ever had one thought about Minnesota until right now.'

Nick nodded. Then he motioned toward Judah's hands and wrists.

'Looks like you got into it.'

Judah opened a desk drawer and took out a mason jar and a tall green bottle. He set them on the desk and then he lifted the pipe, removed the ceramic pipebowl, and with the knife he scraped away the remaining ash.

'That shit burned me up. Inside and out.'

Footsteps thundered along the hallway and then the barmaid came into the room. She set the plates on the desk. Short spirals of hair sprang from her head and she stood with her thick hip propped out.

'Well?' she said.

'Well. What?' Judah answered.

'You heard what I said about Colette?'

'Me and the deaf.'

'Did you do it?'

157

'Do what?'

'You know what. Burn down her place and everything close to it.'

'Do I look capable?'

'Hell I don't know.'

'Then there's your answer. Now go on.'

She huffed. Shifted her weight from one leg to the other. He raised his hand and pointed at the door. She gave Nick a cross look as if to make him feel included and then she left them.

'I should go,' Nick said.

'Go where?'

Nick shrugged.

'You got to eat.'

'It looks like you have some things to deal with.'

'I got plenty to deal with without worrying about burning down a goddamn whorehouse.'

Judah attached the pipebowl to the bamboo stem and then he struck a match and lit the bulb. He gazed at the singular, bluetipped flame, waiting on the warmth and he sensed that warmth inside him, through his battered lungs and along his redscarred arms and hands and creeping through the layers of flesh and muscle that had carried tiny bits of shrapnel and poisonous gas molecules home. He breathed a heavy breath and his lungs seemed to rattle, so shaken for so long by the closerange explosions, explosions that had blown helmets from their heads and lifted them from their feet and peeled their eyes and sometimes delivered them to another world and sometimes inflicted the agony of having to remain in this one. He shifted in the chair and looked at the red skin of his arms and hands and he felt the burning and saw the gas explosions and the heavy green clouds that settled into a dirty yellow haze and blistered and burned everything and everyone and fumbling with his mask and fighting one of his own when there were not enough masks and the gas crawling into his eyes and ears and brutalizing his skin and killing what was left of the land. And then once the cloud was gone the gas settled into mud puddles and drinking water and a poisonous sip or a misstep and there it was again once you thought it was gone like some nightmare that chased you all the way to the other side.

The lamp heated and he opened the cigar box and took out a folded napkin. Carefully he opened the napkin and picked up several opium seeds between his finger and thumb. He placed the seeds onto the pipebowl and he leaned to his side and guided the pipebowl over the stream of heat rising from the lamp. He rested his head close to the pipebowl and waited for the seeds to vaporize and in a moment they heated and a bluegray mist rose. He closed his eyes and inhaled and inhaled and inhaled. The vapor filled his nostrils and he sucked it into his mouth and both mind and body sensed the deadened relief that was coming. When the vapor had made its way into him he pushed the pipe and bowl to the center of the desk. Moved his hand to his face and felt the risen scar that began around his eye. He trailed his fingers along the scar line and felt the slash of the blade and he waited peacefully for the numbing.

Nick picked up the plate and fork and ate. Judah lifted the bottle and poured half a glass of whiskey.

'You know Colette?' Nick asked.

'I know her.'

'The madam.'

'Yeah. The madam.'

'What do you have to do with what happened?'

'Not a goddam thing. Like I already said.'

'Then why are you being asked about it?'

'Because she's my wife. Or she used to be. I don't know what she is now.'

Judah lifted the glass and sipped. Then he laid his head back on the chair and stared at the ceiling, his eyelids getting heavy as the drug worked through his body.

Nick tore a piece of bread and held it between his fingers. He didn't want to ask. He had heard the answer. And he was almost certain that he wouldn't believe whatever Judah told him. But he asked anyway.

'Did you do it?'

Judah raised his head. Lowered his eyes to Nick. His placid expression was blotted out by a cloud of anguish and he seemed to become something else. Something capable of anything. He glared at Nick and in a gravelly voice he said everything that has been done or will be done was set into motion by her.

27

HALF OF THE BLOCK BURNED to the ground and left a fractured, charred, smoldering ruin. The other half stood crippled and desolate. The fire had burned through the night and seemed barely affected by the efforts to drown it out and almost as if it were simply bored of the festival it had created, the fire lessened at daybreak. By midmorning the tired men and women who had struggled against it sat down on the sidewalk across the street and drank beer and ate bread with smutty hands.

Colette had watched it all night. Never sitting. Leaning against a wall half a block away. She wouldn't answer the curious sorts who walked up beside her and asked ridiculous questions about what was going on or how long had it been going on or was anybody hurt. She wouldn't even look at them, only stared ahead until they quit talking and walked away. The flames illuminated all of Frenchtown and caused great, shifting shadows and in the hot firelight her features became torchlike, flames dancing in her eyes, her hair down and spread wide across her shoulders and her cheekbones turned red and even her shadow behind her seeming to grow with her heated anger. All night she had stood there and felt the horror of the blackened bodies and felt the loss of her house and the loss of the adjoined buildings where mothers and fathers and sisters and brothers made their home and she felt the anxiety of those fighting against it, seemingly no way to win. And she felt the relief when the fire began to weaken at dawn and as she stood there in the morning light, staring at the devastated scene. She replayed it all.

This is where I came when I believed I was alone, she thought. When I believed Judah was dead and gone. This is where I came and where I worked to forget and this is where I became someone of my own and this is where I tried to bury you in that faraway grave where they told me you were buried. Because this is where I became someone new because you left me no choice. Because this is where I decided to let you go, Judah. Where I decided you were dead but I wasn't and there had to be something for me. And this is where I walked the stairway or sat at the bar or stared out of my window all hours of the night because I could not sleep because I was imagining your shadow in the doorway.

That was that.

She imagined the girls and the men and the tall bottles of absinthe on the slick bar and Leopold on the baby grand and the frivolity of exchange and all the ridiculous habits that precluded it. She thought of the power she had grasped by moving her hips the right way with the right men in the right offices and she thought how easy and bountiful it had been to please those who wanted pleasing and she had filled her days and nights surrounded by the beautiful ones, they all wanted the beautiful ones, the men and the women, and they paid and paid for the beautiful ones.

And then one day she had been sitting at the end of the bar, smoking a cigarette and sipping rye when she looked across the chandelier-lit room and again saw Judah's shadow in the doorway except that it was not the gray, murky image of him. But him. Back from the dead and staring at her not with desire or redemption of a life lost but with contempt for what he had learned she had become and what she sold and who she sold it to. And then how without a word or a gesture he had turned and walked away and through the windows she saw his broken gait as he crept with a cane and his leaning head and uneven shoulders and she had felt it all in that moment, the separation and the pain inflicted upon him and the pain inflicted upon her and the quiet space when she believed that the death which had separated them was nothing as acute as this moment of recognition.

She moved closer to the devastation. Fire hoses continued to spray and a black soot river ran down the side of the street and men and women wanted to cross over into the ruins and search for anything but policemen wouldn't let them. At the end of the street was a pile of bags that held what remained of the burned, mutilated bodies and a whitehaired priest knelt beside them with his head bowed in prayer and a Bible tucked under his arm. Here and there stood clusters of women holding their children and crying and then Colette saw one of her own girls standing alone, staring blankly at the space where her second floor window used to be.

She approached her. Flakes of ash had settled in her bobbed blond hair. Her eyes pink and swollen. She held her arms wrapped as if she were cold.

'You've been out all night?' Colette asked.

'I ain't got nowhere to go.'

'Yeah. Me neither.'

'Who all got burnt up?' the girl asked.

'I don't know.'

The girl sniffed and wiped her nose on the back of her hand.

'What am I supposed to do?'

'Whatever you want. Employment won't be a problem for you.'

'I don't wanna go nowhere else.'

'You don't have a choice.'

'Please let me go with you,' she said and she reached out and held on to the madam's arm. Colette let her hand stay there a moment and then she pulled away.

'You're gonna have to figure it out,' she said. 'I got my own problems.'

'I ain't going to the cribs, Miss Colette,' she said. Her voice becoming shaky. 'I ain't doing that.'

'That's up to you.'

'I can't do that,' the girl said again. 'Please.'

Colette looked at her. The frantic eyes and wild hair. There was youth but she saw how rapidly it was leaving her.

'Where are the others?' she asked.

The girl shrugged and said some of them is already working. Jackie said no fire was gonna keep her from a good night's work. But I don't know where they all are.

Colette took one more long look at the girl and then at the destruction. She lifted her dress and removed a stack of folded bills from her kneehigh stockings. She gave the girl some money and said go to the cribs or don't go to the cribs. I don't care.

The girl took the money and Colette knew this would be the last she saw her. Money in their hands always led them down darker roads and in two weeks' time the girl would have become a slave to someone or something else and once the girl sank lower the madam knew she would not want her. But that was of no concern as Frenchtown never ran out of the ready and willing and she would have a full stable again when she wanted. The young woman nodded and wiped her eyes and smiled at Colette and said I'll see you soon and walked away. Colette watched her until she made the corner and the tinge of sympathy disappeared. She then looked across the street and noticed a particular policeman whom she had served well and knew that he would tell her all that he knew. But she never crossed the street, never made a step, as a thick and muscular arm squeezed her around the neck and a big hand covered her mouth and the big arms snatched her and dragged her into a nearby alley as the heels of her boots skittered helplessly and she disappeared from the street like the smoke into the sky.

28

JUDAH OFFERED NICK A SMALL apartment above the saloon. He offered him a job in the saloon but Nick said no. If I need money I'll have it sent from my father. Judah gave him a long and blank stare and when Nick asked what was wrong, Judah said that's the first time I've ever heard anybody say that.

Nick knew the apartment offer was out of necessity more than kindness. Judah needed somebody close. He needed someone like him. The winter dark came early and he ate dinner with Judah in the saloon and then helped him to the backroom to smoke or up the stairs to lie down. When he held Judah's arm or touched his shoulder he felt the knob of bone and halfexpected the creak of an old door when Judah stepped or reached. And Nick had noticed that Judah talked less as the day dragged on and slipped into night, seeming to retreat into his pain and into the numbing as the moon rose in the sky.

Judah lived across the hall and Nick heard him all hours of the night, coughing and sometimes crying out from the pain or from dreams or from both. He knocked on Judah's door and asked if he needed help but the only thing Judah ever asked for was the opium pipe and seeds and Nick would hustle down into the backroom and bring it for him. Judah would crack open the door and stick out his blotchy hand

166

and take it and close the door without a word. And then Nick would sit in the hallway. Listen to him shuffling across the floor. Listen to the bump of a chair and hacks and coughs and he would wait until it died down. When he was certain Judah had smoked and made it back to the bed he would open the door and cross through the shadows and go into Judah's bedroom. Lean against the doorway and make sure he was sleeping in the bed and not down on the floor passed out or dead.

When he was in the street or in a café or anywhere he heard their names. Colette and Judah. There seemed to be no mystery as to who was involved and he had gathered that some kind of rivalry or revenge or hate or all of it and more had led to the brothel being burned to the ground and taking half a city block with it. And she got burnt up with it, some argued. Hell no, others said. She took her shit and hit the trail. Don't matter. Either way she's gone. Ain't nobody seen her since. The waiter told the cook that he wished all the brothels would burn to the damn ground and the cook said if you burned them all to the ground you might as well burn up the whole damn place and the waiter said I wouldn't give a shit if we did. In the chatter in the diner he listened to the waiter and the cook and the men sitting at the counter both condemn and laud the selling of bodies and he heard the anger over the death of those who weren't whores but who only had the misfortune of living next to them and somebody cried out that the only way to get the whores out of the neighborhood was to do just what had been done and another stood and swore that everydamnbody in here pretending to be holy as Mother Mary has spent at least one paycheck in the cathouse and the diner roared with laughter and attention returned to plates of eggs and bacon.

Nick looked for her as he moved about. His eyes up into random upper floor windows, thinking he may catch her looking down at him. Walking along the river and moving close to figures sitting on the benches with their scarves wrapped high around their necks and their hats pulled down, thinking her eyes may peek between the fabric and find his. He looked for her in the shadows of the alley and in the red lights from brothels and he imagined her as if the disappearance was some secret between them and all he had to do was step the right way at the right time and she would be there waiting for him. Waiting to divulge what had transpired between her and Judah. She's my wife, Judah had said. Or she used to be. I don't know what she is now. Not who, Nick thought. But what. What is she now?

In the middle of the night he returned to Judah's and found him sitting on the top step to the top floor. His face and hair damp with sweat. Lips smeared red from blood and wild eyes chasing ghosts.

'Judah,' Nick said.

'The river. Across the river. Run the wire across the river and then back this way. She's over there by the river.'

Nick eased up the stairs.

'Stay down,' Judah said. He raised a feeble arm and waved it slowly.

'I'm down,' Nick said softly. 'We're down. Let's go.'

'She's out there and we can't leave her. She's out there.'

'She's okay. Let's go.'

'The river's high. It won't stop raining. It won't stop and we can't drive the stakes if it won't stop raining.'

'We need to get back,' he said. 'Retreat, Judah.'

'She's out there.'

'Someone got her. She'll meet us. We have to go now.'

Judah fell over to the side and then slumped forward, almost tumbling down the stairs before Nick caught him. The man's head rolled and Nick steadied him, pushed him upright. He slid Judah's arm around his neck and lifted, then scooped him and carried the broken man to the apartment door, surprised by how light he was. Like a child. Judah's door was halfopen and Nick pushed it with his foot. He laid him down on the bed and covered him with a blanket and turned off the lamp.

He walked back into the sitting room. Judah called out for Colette and then snapped an order to a private. Then he coughed. When he was done coughing he cried. And then he finally fell silent.

Nick looked around the room. Black-and-white framed photographs on the wall. Different women with different children. Four bearded men who looked like brothers. Judah and he guessed Colette standing at the door of the saloon. A mustached man with his arms folded across the back of a chair.

A rectangle rug covered the hardwood floor and highbacked chairs sat at each corner of the rug. A mahogany coffee table in the center. Bookcases from floor to ceiling along one wall and half the shelves filled with books and the other half the home of vases, a cigar box, a silver tray and crystal wine glasses, ceramic bowls, handpainted plates. Burgundy curtains hung along the sides of the windows and brushed the floor. A room that seemed to be waiting for someone to occupy it.

A rolltop desk sat between the two windows. Nick walked over and touched the brass knob, looked over his shoulder as if Judah may be watching from the doorway. A newspaper was folded on top of the desk and he picked it up. Looked at the front page. Thanksgiving 1919.

He set the newspaper aside and raised the knob and the desk cover rolled back. A spider darted toward the back corner and disappeared. And Nick found that the desk was empty but for three items. A pocket watch. A wedding band. A small brown bottle.

Nick picked up the bottle. No label and no markings. He pulled out the cork and smelled. A faint scent of garlic. He returned the cork just as Judah rolled in his stupor and fell from the bed to the floor. Nick went back to him but let him be as Judah did not wake, only lay with his knees drawn up and arms wrapped around his neck as if protecting himself from the things that lived behind his eyes.

Why am I alive, Nick wondered. He touched Judah's scarred forearm and then he raised his own shirtsleeve. Touched his own smooth skin. Touched his own cheeks and the back of his neck. No signs and no proof that I was even there as long as I can keep my hand still and one day even that will go away.

Judah gagged and stretched his arms and legs then he recoiled. His eyes never opening. And then there in the dark Nick saw the old woman sitting by him in the barn. The smell of manure and her calm stare. The silver hair cut crooked across her forehead and in streams around her neck and the gnarled knuckles of a lifetime of work. The husband in his overalls beside her. They were here in this room with this man with bloodstained sheets and Nick saw their faces and he loved them in ways that he had never loved his own mother and father. He stood next to Judah and wished for the old couple and prayed for the old couple and he imagined them sleeping a peaceful and dreamless sleep and he wanted them to know he was alive.

Help me, the voice whispered. And the old couple disappeared at its sound. Nick turned to look for it as if it was coming from another room. Help me. He leaned down and put his ear to Judah to see if it had come from him.

Nick rose. Held by the dark. Seized into the void because he hadn't been bad enough to go to hell or good enough to ascend to heaven and he was only here. His sole accomplishment had been to survive and even that seemed like an accident. He had always imagined being alone to be the same thing as being at peace but he knew that was a lie. And the only time he had not felt alone was in the attic in Paris and even then he would not let go and let it become a part of his life. He would not leave with her. He would not do the one thing he knew he should do.

He touched his elbows where they had bled as he crawled across the night. The single shriek from the voice that had begged him for mercy. He was on his belly and his legs were useless and he bled and he did not know why he was not the one lying in the bed scarred by the gas. He wanted to leave the room but he did not want to leave the room because it would mean going across the hall where he would struggle to sleep or sleep and dream darkly. Instead he would stand here. Listening to Judah struggle for breath. Listening to the whisper for help.

29

COLETTE WAS BOUND BY THE wrists and tied to the metal bedframe and gagged with a bandana. She was unsure exactly where she was but she could tell by the bellow of the steamboats that she couldn't be more than two or three blocks from the wharf. The room was small and square with the bed the only furniture and no windows and a sour smell. The man who had brought her there and bound her kept the lights turned off when he was gone and if it was day or night she did not know. She kept thinking that she would hear the footsteps of others either above or below but there was only his heavy, plodding tread when he came or went. Slow, dragging feet. The street sounds were random and distant and she could only figure she was tucked away in some alley in a forgotten cluster of rooms and she knew that he was the only one who knew she was there. She dozed in and out but the tick tack of rat feet in the dark kept her anxious and far from sleep.

When he came into the room he never turned on a light. He would open the door and stand at the threshold and the faint light from the hallway would break into the room. He was a giant figure but she never could make out his face. The doorway filled with his form and he breathed heavy as if chasing or being chased. Behind him in the hallway sat a wooden wagon that rattled as he arrived and as he left and it was filled with something she couldn't make out. Each time he closed the door behind him and walked methodically around the room in the blackness. In the stillness. His stature seeming to grow as he panted. Snorted. Spit. She kept her eyes following his sounds. His offbeat, exasperated breathing. The sound of a bottle being uncorked. The toss of liquid as the bottle turned up. The smack of his lips and tongue and then the sometimes strange and gentle sobs that followed. But he never touched her though he would come close. He would stand right in front of her or kneel next to her and he stank of booze and the street and his smell made her gag and then he would laugh and then lower his jaw right in front of her nose and growl into her face. Is it bad? Do you hate it? Do you hate it? Because you don't know anything.

He would then fall back on the floor and sometimes cry, sometimes beat his fists against the hardwood. And then he would crawl to the door and open it and still on his knees he would reach out and grab the handle to the wagon and pull it inside. Close the door. Black again. This their world. He would lie next to the wagon with his arm draped over the side and his hand touching whatever filled the wagon and he mumbled and babbled in a faint and sinking voice as if he were speaking from the bottom of a well.

Eventually he would raise himself and leave again. When he left he took the wagon with him and she counted two other doors closing as he was on his way out of the building.

In her solitude she wondered if she had fought hard enough when he squeezed her around the neck and dragged her away. She was right there in the street. She replayed it in her mind but it had happened fast and she knew that she had kicked and slapped and punched but he was so much bigger and so much stronger and he knew where he was taking her and it had been a quick trip. When he had gotten her into the room he held her pressed against the floor, his hand around her throat, her throat so thin and fragile in his hand, and he swore he would squeeze the life out of her right then if she made a goddamn peep or if she did anything but put her hands over her head while he tied them then he said if you ever wanna see daylight again you better not so much as lick your lips. I will make you disappear and you will rot right here if you try anything. His knees straddled her body and she could tell by the sound of his voice and by the tremble in his hands that he was somewhere at the end of a line. So she did as he said. She lay still and limp and he tied her wrists and then he moved off her and slid her against the wall. Sitting her up and then binding her to the bedrail. She replayed this over and over in her waiting hours and she wanted to find a moment where she had missed an opportunity but she couldn't. And now she wondered if there would be another.

The days passed and she didn't know how many. The sleeping and waking hours had no meaning in the dark. He had fed her bread twice and poured liquor into her mouth before gagging her again, laughing and feeling her throat and telling her to swallow or else. She wondered if anyone was looking for her but she didn't know who that might even be. Not her girls. Not anyone who owed her money. And those were the only people she knew of anymore. She wondered if Judah was satisfied. Wondered if she would recognize the face of this big man if she ever had the chance to see it. Wondered what was in that wagon and why he seemed to need it. To protect it. To love it. She wondered if she would again see the streets where she had taken her first steps and ridden on her father's back or if she would shrivel up and die. Her body consumed by the dark. And she wondered if her soul would find its way to the door and slither underneath and make its way toward home or if it too would be disoriented and panicked and unable to escape. Cast forever into this silent and secret room.

30

JOHN LAFELL FIRST APPEARED AS a figure on the Frenchtown streets the day after the fire. Broad shoulders and a square jaw and heavy brown eyes. His coat was worn through at one elbow and he wore big, laced boots as he shuffled clumsily along in a sleepless and drunken roll. Behind him he pulled a wooden wagon that had once been used for visits to the market but now held a singular item – a bundle wrapped in a patchwork quilt that filled the width and length of the small wagon.

He was out all hours of the day or night. He pulled the wagon with one hand and drank whiskey from a clear bottle with the other and stumbled and fell and sometimes got up and sometimes lay there and children jumped over or danced around him and when he rose they ran away with squeals and laughter and he trudged on. No words from his mouth and the only sound he made was that of an innocent, heartbroken soul who could not contain grief and released it in random grunts and cries.

On the third day the grunts and cries stopped and he now dragged a steel pole along as he walked with the wagon. He had taken the four-foot-long pole from the wharf where he had stopped going to work. Once he had used it to wedge between pallets and lift or separate but now he dragged it across the brick streets and it tinged in a hectic pattern as he trod through Frenchtown like some ambling, hopeless portrait of the living dead.

He stopped eating and only drank and when he ran out of money the good whiskey Samaritan gave him a bottle. When he was too drunk he knelt and slept on his knees and hunched across the bundle as if to protect it. But the sleep never lasted long and he awoke in a shout or swinging his arms at an invisible enemy and he was lucky if a street animal hadn't pissed on his leg or worse. Then he would wipe the saliva from his mouth and get to his feet and trudge along, the steel pole and the wagon dragging behind.

On the seventh day his pattern changed again and what had been a mostly quiet, wandering hulk of defeat became a wailing torrent of grief. He reared back his drunk head and screamed toward the rooftops and clouded heavens in no verbal pattern but only in wolflike howls that sent the same children who had days before played around his fallen figure running into doorways and around corners in fear. He wailed and his voice carried through the streets and echoed across the open air cafés and he swung the steel pole at sign posts and street lamps and if anyone approached him or came close to the wagon he howled and his eyes filled with teary, red menace and he was approaching a state of madness strange even to this place.

In random moments of exhaustion he sat on the sidewalk and leaned against the wagon and drifted in and out of sleep. When his head nodded, the fire blazed in the blackness of his dreams and sent suncolored streaks racing back and forth between his mind and soul. He felt the heat all over his body and the torture that came from knowing you couldn't escape. He heard the screams and he reached into the flames but he couldn't get hold of the body the screams came from and he felt the voice slip down into the inferno and disintegrate and he stomped through the flames looking for a way to bring it back, shouting out apologies and regrets but it was gone and so was everything else. This was his dream. His every dream.

He would walk and rage and drag the steel pole and the wagon and he would drink what anyone would give him and his place as the tragic figure of Frenchtown was coalesced after he was seen on his hands and knees lapping at a puddle to rid his throat of the whiskey burn. Women held hands with their children and took them in the other direction. Men watched him cautiously as he approached with their hands at the ready. From barstools and café chairs they watched him with a blend of shame and fear and care. Even the girls standing in the doorways of the cribs stopped calling to him as he walked past, his once broad, hardworking figure now diminished to a slumped, filthy wraith.

On the morning of the eighth day, he found himself looking out across the river. Down below men worked and shouted and cargo moved and the clouds were low and blotted out the eastern sun. He drank and watched. Set the bottle down and adjusted the bundle in the wagon and when he raised back up he saw a man hustling up the concrete stairs that led from the wharf to the warehouse. A moment later, the man appeared from the warehouse and hurried in his direction and as the man came closer he recognized Reed.

He wore a knit hat pulled down to his eyebrows and working gloves and he was out of breath from the quick trip. Reed reached into his coat and pulled out a brown paper bag and handed it to John LaFell.

'Goddamn you look like shit,' he said and he shoved it toward John. He was bleary and didn't move and Reed reached out and took his hand and slapped the bag into it. Its contents were hard and knotted and Reed told him to take it and do what you will but you can't keep doing this shit. If you want to know he's at his place every day at lunch. You know it, corner of St. Philip and Bourbon. And you know who I'm talking about. Everygoddamnbody knows who started the damn thing. Or do something else I don't care but for God's sake you got to do something. I been carrying this thing around with me since Grace told me she saw you the other day with a pig sniffing at your ass while you was passed out. You ain't got to do nothing with it if you don't want but here it is. I got to go.

Reed glanced at the bundle in the wagon and then turned around and was gone. John stared at the brown bag in his hand and then when he looked out again he saw Reed back at work.

He let the steel pole fall and then watched it roll. He looked back at the patched quilt and the bundle it covered. He opened the brown paper bag and pulled out the pistol and he saw the bullets in the chamber. He took a long drink from the bottle and then with the whiskey still on his tongue he licked the cold pistol from the tip of the handle to the tip of the barrel.

Colette heard the ting ting tinging of the steel pole in the hallway. And then the door opened and he stood there with it by his side like a staff. A lost shepherd. He seemed taller and smelled like death.

He took two drunken steps and fell against the wall and dropped the pole. He didn't close the door behind him and it seemed like sunlight in the hallway. He went down to a knee, mumbling to himself as if trying to explain something in a language only he could understand.

'You and your trash,' he said. 'I wish you all burnt up.'

He stood again and he burped and laughed. Not the drunken, lost laugh of days past but the shrill of the sadistic and she knew that something had changed.

He gathered himself. Walked over to her. Sat down on the floor with his legs against hers. In the light she saw his face for the first time. Haggard and puffy. Bruised and bizarre. She tried to place him but couldn't.

'You and him,' he said. His head fell back against the wall and he looked up at the ceiling. 'You did it. You don't even know it but you did it. And you been thinking all this time you were gonna be in here forever but you ain't. Today is the day. You get to go see him cause I want you both together. You and him.'

He took the pistol out of his pocket and showed it to her and said I'm gonna stick this in your ear. And I'm gonna pull the trigger unless you walk a straight line. I'll pour your blood out like a piss bucket.

She nodded. He took the pistol and pressed the end of it into her ear. He pressed harder and harder until she cried out and he pulled it back in a snap and said it can hurt a helluva lot worse. You remember that.

John LaFell stood and walked into the hallway and he pulled the wagon inside the room. And then he dropped the pistol and fell to his knees and buried his face in his hands and began to cry violently, his shoulders heaving and his head bouncing and the exasperation of something having finally reached its end. She watched him and wanted to understand and then as quickly as this came on, something else came over him and he rose with a roar and grabbed her around the throat and pressed his face into hers and rubbed his forehead against her forehead. He squeezed and she grunted and choked and with his hands shaking and his eyes alive, through gritted teeth he told her again that you're coming with me and you're gonna find out what you are.

31

NICK SAT AT THE BAR of the saloon with a plate of two slices of ham and a fried egg. Large windows stretched high up the wall on each side of the doorway and a sharp midday sun warmed the smoky room. Round wooden tables and a piano against one wall. A woodburning furnace and its black pipe ran up through the ceiling and was placed oddly in the middle of the floor between several tables. Behind the bar the shelves were filled with liquor bottles. Green, brown, clear. Short, tall, skinny, fat. A size and color for everyone.

As Nick ate the saloon had gradually filled and there were few empty seats. Two barmaids who looked like mother and daughter hustled between the tables and shouted out lunch orders to the bartender who then shouted them through a swinging door back to the kitchen. Working men with windchapped faces sat at the tables closest to the furnace and men in ties and gray or black overcoats sat around the edges of the saloon with newspapers. A pot of some concoction of a hot liquor drink cooked on a small stove behind the bar and the bartender ladled the drink into mugs and set them on the counter. The barmaids delivered them to the tables without having to be asked. Judah sat alone next to the door with a deck of cards spread out on the table.

When Nick was finished he pushed the plate aside and felt in his shirt pocket for a cigarette but didn't find one. He looked around, listened to the clatter of forks and plates and the random laughter or insult.

'Drink some of that,' the bartender said and he pointed at the liquor pot.

'What is it?' Nick asked.

'Damn good. That's what it is.'

The bartender filled a mug and set it in front of Nick. Steam danced from the mug and Nick leaned over and smelled. The scent of lemon and molasses and hard grain liquor. Nick took the mug and got up from the barstool and went and sat with Judah.

One of the working men had moved over to the piano and he rolled up his sleeves and began playing something quick and choppy and the mood of the saloon rose though they all knew they had to go back to work. Some back out into the wind and some back to offices but the piano displaced the rest of the day for a moment and brought them all together. The older barmaid lifted a redfaced man from his chair and they danced between tables and the bartender whistled and others tried to clap along with the unpredictable rhythm of the piano. Shouts and whistles filled the air and some called out for whiskey and some already had it and took out bottles tucked away in socks or coat pockets. Stomping and clapping and drinking and smoking and lunch had in an instant become something else.

But then the door of the saloon opened. And the piano player stopped playing. And the barmaid and redfaced man stopped dancing. And there was no more clapping or shouting or eating or drinking. Judah looked up from the cards lying in rows across the tabletop and Nick slid forward in his chair. At the front of the quieted house was the deranged man, a familiar woman, and a wagon.

32

T HE FIRST THING JOHN LAFELL did was remove the gag
from Colette's mouth and then he shoved her to the floor.
She went face first into the back of a chair that didn't budge
with the weight of the man sitting in it. No one moved as she
slowly got herself to her feet and her hair fell in waves around
her shoulders. Her mouth was busted and blood trailed down
her chin and matched the blood from her forehead.

John LaFell, wild hair and filthy and drunk, scanned the
room with wolfish eyes. He held the pistol up for all to see
and then he knelt and picked up the pole that leaned across
the bundle. He smacked his lips and then spit on the floor
and then he tucked the pistol in the front of his pants. He
grabbed the pole at its end and he stepped to the big window
and screamed as he swung and shattered the glass. The glass
busted and crashed in chunks out onto the sidewalk and
inside the saloon and the crowd jumped at the explosion.

He turned and looked at them and then he took patient
steps across the doorway to the other window, his boots
making deep, throbbing footsteps across the wooden floor.
He lifted the pole and swung again and another crash and
more glass shattering and now the people walking by or in
shops across the street stopped and were as still as the ones
who sat inside the saloon.

When the second window was done John LaFell tossed the

steel pole out into the street. He told Colette to sit down at the table right in front of him and she did.

Then he scanned the room again until he saw Judah.

'Come here,' he said.

Judah took his cane and pushed on Nick's leg to help himself up.

'What do you want?'

'I want you to come here,' he said and he pointed the pistol at Colette.

'He don't care if you kill me or not,' Colette said. John LaFell fired at the floor next to her chair and the wood splintered and she shrieked and everyone jerked.

'I'm coming,' Judah said.

He limped carefully around the tables and made his way toward the front. When he was there, John LaFell told him to sit down at the table with Colette. Dirty plates and mugs of those who had been there before were on the table and John LaFell reached out his long arm and swiped the table clean and the white porcelain shattered and sprayed across the floor.

'You been looking for her?' he asked Judah as he pointed at Colette.

'No.'

John LaFell took one step and backhanded Judah across the face, a loud smack that sent him back and out of his chair.

'Don't nobody move,' the big man screamed and he fired another shot now into the ceiling. All watched as Judah got himself up and back into the chair.

'You been looking for her?' LaFell asked again.

Judah wiped his face with the back of his hand, blood smearing from cheek to cheek. He nodded.

'Liar,' LaFell answered. 'You're a goddamn liar. And so is

she. But I wish you were looking for her so you'd know what it's like to look for somebody that used to be there. I want you to know what that's like.'

He backed away from them and stood next to the wagon. Then he knelt and it was as though he became someone else. The anger left his face and was replaced by anguish and sorrow and he leaned over and rested his head on top of the bundle. He began to cry a silent, tearless cry and then he raised his head, slid his arms underneath the quilted bundle, and he lifted it out of the wagon. He stood and turned and faced Judah and Colette and the bundle lay across his arms and the pistol dangled from his hand and his face was covered by the fragile expression of falling apart.

He took two steps forward and he gently laid the bundle down on the table.

He told them to open it. When neither of them moved, he raised the pistol to Judah's temple. Open it he said again and his hand trembled.

Judah took one side of the quilt and Colette took the other. It was folded on top and at the ends and they carefully unfolded the layers as if it might disintegrate in their fingertips. John LaFell lowered the pistol from Judah's head.

When they came to the final fold, Colette paused and wiped the blood from her mouth and chin. Judah took hold of the quilt and opened it and he winced and turned his head away and Colette put her hand over her mouth and nose and sucked in a big breath. The others strained their necks to try and see but they wouldn't have to wait as John LaFell told Judah to open it all the way. All the way and show them what you did. What you and her did. Show them.

Judah pulled the quilt all the way back and exposed the black, shriveled body of John LaFell's child. The arms and legs nothing more than burned black sticks and the body folded in the fetal position and across the saloon the men groaned and one of the barmaids cried out to God and some hid their eyes and some wanted a better look and in the hysteria none of them noticed when the child's father stuck the pistol to the back of Judah's head. But everyone noticed when the shotgun blast came from behind the bar and exploded the father's chest.

33

FOR WHAT SEEMED A LONG time no one moved. Silenced and stalled. The scene paused with open mouths or covered eyes and a smoking shotgun and a shriveled child and a broken father. And then the silence was interrupted by the movement of the bartender. Replacing the shotgun to the hooks beneath the bartop and vanishing through the swinging door behind the bar. Then other noises. The bell of a streetcar moving along its line and a heavy piece of glass falling from the top of the window frame and crashing onto the other fragments. Then Nick stood up and walked over to John LaFell. The blood from his chest and spreading across his stomach and shoulders. The pistol fallen from his hand. Nick picked it up with a steady hand and unloaded the bullets.

Then Judah moved. He slowly pulled himself upright in the chair and then he took the edges of the quilt and began to cover the child's corpse. Colette took the other side of the quilt and their hands met in the middle and together they folded and covered the body in the way that John LaFell had covered it. Then they stared at one another, each with the expression of remorse. Around the saloon men gathered their coats and hats and began to hurry out. John LaFell lay sprawled in the doorway and the lunch crowd left hastily through the windows as if they had shared in pulling the trigger or lighting the fire. The barmaids held hands and Judah told them to disappear into the kitchen and tell the bartender to get the hell out of here if he hasn't already. I'll take care of it when the police get here.

'Look at what you've done,' Colette said.

'I didn't do a thing.'

'Wasn't just me in that house, Judah. It was my house and the houses next door and the people in them. If you wanna burn me down then burn me down right here and now.'

'If you wanna believe I give a shit about you enough to set your house on fire then go ahead.'

The blood of her busted lip filled her mouth and there was red between her teeth and dripping from her chin and she only stared at him.

'You're the one who done all this. Not me,' he said. He looked past her and out into the street where spectators multiplied.

'Done what?' she said and she took a napkin from a table and wiped herself. 'I've been tied up in a black room for I don't even know how long. I wish you'd tell me what it is you think I've done.'

Judah pointed at the quilt and then at John LaFell and said you did all that.

'You don't make any sense.'

'You did all this when you put this on my face,' he said and he touched his fingers to the crescent scar around his eye.

She laughed a little. A quiet, huffing laugh of disbelief. Then she laughed bigger and threw back her head. She let out a big breath and then she threw the wadded napkin across the room. A police siren sounded from several blocks away.

'Your world is a place unto its own,' she said. 'It is a place of its own truth and its own consequences and it is invisible to all. I know you are in there somewhere but I don't know where. I don't know why you won't come out.'

The siren came closer. Judah put his hands on the arms of the chair and pushed himself up. He took his cane and he stepped over to the fallen body of the father. His eyes frozen open as if to sneak one last glance at those he hated.

'Where is the pistol?' he asked Nick.

Nick held it out to him and he took it.

Judah stared down at John LaFell. Coughed into his handkerchief. Colette stepped back from Judah and turned to leave and with his eyes still on the dead man Judah said go back to your whores where you belong.

Colette stopped. Removed a pin from above her ear and pulled her tousled hair back. Wrapped it into a ball and replaced the pin. She then cleared her throat and leaned over and spit. She didn't look back at him. She wouldn't. She threw back her shoulders and stepped out onto the sidewalk, just as the police car turned the corner and the street crowd separated to let it through.

34

NICK WALKED ACROSS THE SALOON floor to where the quilted bundle rested on the table. Laid his hand on top and held it there, as if waiting for a rise and fall of breath.

In front of the saloon two policemen got out of the car and yelled for everyone to get back. They stepped to the sidewalk, looked in and around. Nick folded his arms. Judah's eyes were heavy and he stood hunched.

They stepped inside and removed their hats. Both wore mustaches and one held a club in his hand as if he were ready for a brawl. The one without the club looked down at the two dead and then at Judah.

'What now, Judah?' he asked.

The other pointed the club down at John and said I know that one. That's the crazy son of a bitch that's been wandering around for the last week moaning and groaning.

'He's not crazy,' Nick said.

'He's not a damn thing anymore.'

'He was a little bit off,' Judah answered. 'He had Colette holed up.'

'I thought she'd run off,' said one of the cops.

'Naw. She burned up,' the other said.

'She ain't neither,' Judah said and he pointed out of the window with his cane. 'If you walk that way like you give a

191

damn you'll catch her. Then you can ask her about him cause I don't know a thing.'

'He had his reasons,' Nick said.

The policemen and Judah turned to Nick.

'Who the hell are you?'

'It don't matter,' Judah said. 'He don't have nothing to do with it.'

'He acts like he does.'

'I only know what I see,' Nick said and he pointed at the bundle.

The cop with the club stepped over the bodies, glass crunching beneath his black boots, and closer to Nick. He touched the tip of the club to the bundle and poked and when he poked twice Nick slapped the club away. The man's eyes opened wide in surprise and this time the club came with a backhand and caught Nick across the side of the head. He staggered and fell across a chair and landed on his back and saw a blurry ceiling.

'Goddamn it,' Judah yelled and he grabbed the cop by the coat sleeve. 'I told you he don't have shit to do with none of this.'

'He slapped my damn club.'

'I don't care what he did. You poked a damned child.'

'A what?' the cop asked.

'That thing,' Judah said and he pointed at the bundle.

'It's a what?'

'You heard me. Now help him up.'

The cop without the club moved over and stuck his hands under Nick's arms and lifted him to his feet. Nick didn't stand upright but stayed doubled over until his eyes straightened. The curious faces of the street had crept closer to the saloon and the windows were crowded with peeping heads. Both policemen began to wave them away and one told the other to call for some help and the cop without the club stepped through the mess to the end of the bar and picked up the telephone.

Nick stood up straight. Buttoned his coat. Rubbed at the rising knot on the side of his head. He dragged his hand across his forehead and eyes and he looked around. The shattered, shining glass and the wagon in the doorway and those interested in the dying filling the sidewalks and the father flat on his back and standing with his cane in the middle of it all was the creator. A fragile and sometimes bleeding shell of a man. In a slow, almost hesitating motion, Judah extended his hand and touched his fingers to the edge of the quilt. His head dropped and his eyes seemed to close and his lips parted in silent words and it was not the first time that Nick had seen the tranquil standing in the midst of chaos. Trying to resolve what had been done.

Nick walked out of the saloon and turned at the first street he came to and then he turned again. Walking fast. Find her, he thought. Find her. He was no longer in Frenchtown but hustling along rue de Clichy. Hurrying to the café where they sat though he knew Ella wasn't there. Hurrying to the abandoned theater though she was there no more. Find her before I am destroyed. Find her before I destroy myself.

He walked straight and bumped into people on the street who shoved him but he only staggered and kept going and he looked in every store window. In every café. In every grocery and down each alley and in a cigar shop and in two dress shops. Each time he stepped inside an open door he was asked if he needed help or needed something but he ignored the voices and walked the aisles and circled tables and only when he was satisfied that she wasn't there did he leave without speaking or acknowledging those who glared at him.

He tromped through the Frenchtown streets looking for her and hating himself and all the other Paris girls he had used to replace her. He wandered in some of the same shops and cafés twice. He went into the open doors of buildings and up and down staircases and he climbed a magnolia tree in front of a schoolhouse and searched from a higher perspective but she was nowhere. And then he gave up but his desperation was replaced by paranoia as he felt the sensation of being followed. Of being chased. Of something coming for him. She fled his mind and he nervously looked over his shoulder. Stopped at street corners and peeked around buildings. Breathed quickly and walked faster and he felt as though he was walking around the edge of the pit, waiting to be shoved, waiting to join the others and he smelled the kerosene and saw the torch flames against the darkening horizon and he walked faster but could not escape the edge, bound to it by the invisible rope of fate and he was being pulled toward the otherworld though he slung his arms and pounded his feet and shoved those who crossed his path. He saw the black mutilated child and then he saw himself as a boy standing there at the table next to the corpse and he couldn't make out the difference between the two and the torches came closer and now he began to apologize. I couldn't help you and I can't help me and I'm sorry. I couldn't help you but it's coming for me now and it came for the child. He pulled off his coat and slung it to the ground and yanked at his shirt collar and felt the heat and smelled the searing skin. He stomped and rambled and apologized and couldn't get free and he remained part of the carnival of Frenchtown until exhaustion and then nightfall brought him to his knees.

35

THE ST. MARK'S SANCTUARY HAD been keeping a continuous vigil for two years for those lost. Open all day and all night. On the outside wall next to the front doors a sign was hung and each Monday morning names were added to the list of the deceased or wounded or missing and each Monday afternoon and night people walked from neighborhoods all over Frenchtown to come and look at the list. And then as if the casualties abroad had not been enough to suffer, the casualties at home became real as the Spanish flu had spread into the cracks and crevices of America in a fistful of hard and cruel months that took the young and the old alike. Inside, candles burned in each corner of the sanctuary. At night an organist would play. On Wednesday evenings a children's choir would sing. There was always someone on the wooden pews crying or praying or blaming God.

With so much left to mourn in the aftermath, St. Mark's had left its doors open. Misery was still to be shared. The list of names had grown so long that a chalkboard was added where people could write the names of those they knew who had not yet been reported. Eventually there were no more names to add and the church removed the list of the dead but it left the chalkboard outside and it kept the candles lit and a note taped to the chalkboard read NAME THOSE TO MOURN AND WE SHALL MOURN.

The chalkboard had since borne the names of hung criminals, family pets, dead writers, famous showgirls, baseball legends, and Billy the Kid. Still the doors remained open because in between the gimmicks came real people with real hurt who needed to sit in the dark and believe they were saying goodbye the right way.

Tonight there was only one name on the chalkboard and it read JOHN LAFELL AND SON.

Nick sat in the sanctuary alone. He had been there for an hour and the only other person to have entered the sanctuary was an old woman to exchange the candles. On a table at the front of the sanctuary was a bouquet of flowers and a name card of the father and son. The stainedglass windows were dark with night and the candlelight was soft and wavy and Nick sat with his hands folded in his lap. He thought to pray but his mind wandered as he watched the candlelight move and he listened to the clip clops passing in the street outside. He several times looked over his shoulder to see if he had missed someone. If maybe there was at least one more soul in the sacred place interested in a man like John LaFell. But there was only him.

He coughed. A slight echo into the arched ceiling. He then reached into his coat pocket and took out gloves and put them on and was getting ready to stand and leave when the door to the sanctuary opened.

He sat still. Kept his eyes ahead. Tried to look prayerful.

The footfalls moved down the aisle, small thumps of bootheels that moved closer to him and then stopped. Then from the corner of his eye he saw the figure slide into the pew across the aisle and he turned to see Colette. Her coat collar turned up high around her neck and her hair was down, long waves of brown that draped her face and trailed over her shoulders and softened her hawk eyes. She did not look at Nick but only stared ahead and Nick knew better than to talk.

They shared the silence. He sniffed and coughed again. He had thought about her so much and now that he was alone with her he could not think of one thing to say or do but he didn't have to as she finally broke the quiet and spoke first.

'I wonder what it would be like to have a child,' she said. Her voice just above a whisper. A notion of regret.

Somewhere in the high ceiling of the sanctuary Nick could see the image of Ella. Curled on the attic floor as she hemorrhaged and hurt. Alone.

'Do you know?' she said.

He was grabbed by a sudden grief and he leaned forward and put his head down on the back of the pew in front of him. He put his hands around his throat and squeezed as if to choke it all back down and thought I could have known what that was like and I should have known what that was like but I don't and I didn't and I don't want to ever remember again. He squeezed harder until he made himself grunt and then he let go. Leaned back against the pew.

'Judah will die,' he said.

She looked at him for the first time. He had leaned his head back farther now as if wary that something may fall from the shadows above.

'He's already dead,' she said.

Nick turned to her. Whatever softness he had noticed before was gone. Her eyes cutting past the strands of hair and piercing through him.

She stood from the pew and walked to the front of the sanctuary. She stopped at the bouquet and she lifted the name card. Without looking at Nick she said when he's good and gone and his name is on the sign outside there will be two less people here to mourn him than there are here right now. That's what you need to know about Judah. He tears it all down and he'll tear you down before he's done.

She then set the card down. He expected a stomp or a fist against the table but instead she held still and he thought he noticed her shoulders moving up and down in slight huffs.

'You don't have to be like this,' he said. 'Neither does he.'

She raised her eyes toward the crucifix. Shook her head. She then turned and walked back to Nick.

'What's your name?'

'Nick.'

'You were over there.'

'Yes.'

'I can think of no other reason why you and Judah would be in the same room together.'

She moved a step closer to him. Rested her hand on the end of the pew.

'Do you know who I am?' she asked.

'Yes.'

'You're a little strange. Aren't you?'

He moved his eyes from her. Looked down at his hands and pressed them together. She crept closer. Leaned to him. Her hair falling down and brushing the side of his face.

'I'll have a new place soon. When you're ready to have something more than coffee, you come and see me. I'll get your mind onto something else if you'll let me.'

She stood up and took one more long look around the sanctuary and then she moved along the aisle, pausing at the door and glancing over her shoulder to see if he was following behind. But he was slumped forward again. Head against the pew. His hands around his throat.

36

O<small>N THE FIRST DAY OF</small> December the cathedral chimes
began to play O Little Town of Bethlehem each evening
at dusk and as if summoned by the echoing, angelic tones, an
unexpected bitter cold fell across Frenchtown. Specks of ice
fell throughout the day and night and bounced on the uneven
streets and rooftops in quiet taps. Fountains froze and along
the streets trash fires burned in barrels. Children were
wrapped in layers with whatever could be found to use for
layers and saloon and brothel doors that typically remained
open and beckoning were pulled shut to hold in the warmth
of the fireplaces and coal burning stoves. Along Canal half
the businesses hung signs on their doors that read closed for
cold and even the men with the bottles disappeared from the
street corners except for a brief appearance at noon when
they sold to the workers looking for something to pour down
their throats.

No one knew what to think. The Frenchtown gossip had
decided Judah was to blame for the fire and Colette had done
nothing to squash that talk. Merchants and brothel and saloon
owners began to wonder who was next. And so did the rest of
the inhabitants of Frenchtown. Who else does he hate? The
cathedral chimes signaled the beginning of a season of hope
but an air of apprehension of the fear of smoke and fire and
burning flesh cast its pall over the neighborhood.

Twice Nick walked to the train station. Twice he bought a ticket and stood on the platform waiting for the train. Twice he could not get over the feeling that there was something here he needed to see finished. Twice he left the station before the train arrived.

37

JUDAH AND NICK SAT IN the backroom. The movement of a lunch crowd thumped from the saloon.

'I am the only honest man I know,' Judah said. Eyes heavy and gray. 'I'm sure you think the same thing.'

'I didn't ask if you were honest,' Nick said. 'I'm asking again if you did what everyone around here thinks you did.'

'Who is everyone?'

'Everyone. This whole town.'

Judah reached into his pocket and took out a penknife. He opened it and picked at his fingernails.

'There's more than one way to answer a question.'

'I don't care if you did it or didn't do it,' Nick said.

'Then why are you asking?'

'Because if you don't tell me I'm leaving.'

Judah was filled with opium vapors and he floated somewhere between the world that exists in the vast expanse of all we have known and done and seen and the world of what touches us now. He bled a little from the nose. Coughed up phlegm. He sat in his chair with his head leaned back and the thought crossed his mind that Nick might have arrived in Frenchtown solely as a kindred spirit that would allow him to confess.

So he tried.

He began by explaining the saloon had been owned first by Judah's grandfather and then his father. He had known nothing but Frenchtown his entire life until he got on a boat and traveled across the ocean to kill or be killed. On the morning he had left Colette he wouldn't let her come with him to board because he wanted to remember her in their apartment and the way that she smelled after a bath and the way she brushed her hair as she sat on the edge of the bed and the way they sat together at the table and shared coffee or a bottle of wine or plate of redfish just out of the skillet. He didn't want to remember her standing and waving with the others, their arms in long and desperate motions that couldn't comfort or save but only seemed to him like some flagging symbol of execution.

When he spoke of Colette his voice softened as if there were someone standing on the other side of the door and Judah didn't want them to hear. He told Nick that he and Colette had grown up together, that her father had owned a tobacco store at the end of the block. Their summer days were spent out in the streets while their parents worked. They ran around with a horde of other kids but she and he had always picked one another when choosing teams or hidden together during hide and seek or taken up for one another when whatever game ended up in a fight. And she was good in a fight. Bloodied more noses than I ever did. They would sneak away from the others and walk along the river or steal oranges from the market or find their ways into alleys that closed off the rest of the world and allowed them to see one another more clearly in the shadows. As he spoke of their childhood days Judah sat up to press the back of his hand to his mouth and say she was as real to me as hunger or fear and I think I was born with her in my mind.

They were Frenchtown kids who grew into Frenchtown teenagers who grew into Frenchtown lovers. And then they got married and Judah's parents died and he took over the saloon. They had lived upstairs in the apartment with a balcony where she grew basil and oregano in small ceramic pots and then he had to leave and the last thing he wanted to see was her waving goodbye. So he had gotten up the morning of his departure and gone down early to the saloon and made them eggs and bacon and brought it back up and they ate breakfast in bed and she cried between bites and he thought to try to keep her from it but couldn't figure out any goddamn reason not to let her cry because he wanted to do the same thing. And he finally did and he moved the plates of barely eaten food off the bed and they just lay there and held on and watched the time go by until he couldn't stay any longer.

His voice trailed and he paused to heat an opium seed. The smoke rose and he took it in. His breathing slowed. He unbuttoned the top buttons of his shirt and revealed his neck and shoulders. The memories of the poisonous gas spread across his body in wild, red patches. That was a dirty surprise, he said. I been trying to figure out how to think about it the right way but there ain't no right way. How do you think about it? Goddamn rats and possums are what I hated more than anybody that shot at me. Shit blowing up all around you day and night and you got your head between your legs and you look over and through the flying dirt you see some critter making off with the last crumb of anything. I couldn't take being stuck and the whole time little shits crawling all around and over us in those fucking trenches.

I thought I was going to look like some monster and maybe I do. I laid in that bed burning like hell and I promised

Colette that goddamn I'm gonna sit on our bench at the river and hold your hand and we're gonna make some little ones and I'm gonna build a big fucking house. All I wanted to do was make it home. They did everything but bury me over there and looking at it now I wish I would've let them go ahead and do just that.

Nick rose from the chair and rubbed his hands together. It was cold in the room and he moved over to the bare bulb of the lamp and held his hand over it.

'I never told anybody that,' Judah said.

'You remind me of someone I know,' Nick said.

'Who's that?'

Nick blew hot air into his cupped hands. Then he said I made my own promises when I was over there. But I made them to God. I didn't have anybody else to make them to. And I've changed my mind. I now believe you did it.

'Did what?'

'Burned down the brothel. Killed the child. Killed the father.' Judah moved some, touched the scar around his eye.

'You can believe whatever you want,' he said. 'I'm too close to being gone to tell you a fairytale.'

'I don't see the profit in lying about it.'

'I will never lie.'

'Maybe you didn't light the match but you set the fire.'

A slither of smoke remained from the opium pipe and Judah leaned over and took in the last of the vapors. He inhaled and then held his breath until he couldn't any longer. Then he pulled open a drawer and set John LaFell's pistol on the desktop.

'You start that war?' he asked Nick.

'You know I didn't.'

204

'But I know you killed. Sons. Brothers. Fathers. Maybe even somebody's daughter for all I know.'

'So.'

'So. Why?'

'I had to. Like you and everybody else.'

'You didn't start the fight but you were a part of it. Maybe indirectly I burned down Colette's. Maybe indirectly I hurt that child. I only play my part now. It ain't your fault what you had to do. Just like it ain't mine. That fire was lit before I was even born. We only drift toward what we already been set to do.'

'You had a choice,' Nick said.

'If that's what you think,' he said.

'You don't have to hurt people because they hurt you.'

'Yeah. You do.'

His voice was tired now. The words coming out between thinly parted lips. He seemed to be on the edge of unconsciousness. Nick stepped to the desk and picked up the pistol. He held it up. Examined it. Set it back down.

'But what did she do to you, Judah? To deserve any of this?'

Judah's hand raised and paused. His eyes were closed now and he held the pose of someone dreaming and reaching out in desire. Nick turned and walked to the door and as he touched the doorknob Judah asked him, his voice low and slow as if conjured from somewhere else, how would you feel if you had escaped a tomb and then by some goddamn miracle been delivered back to the one you loved only to find out that when she thought you were dead and gone she was selling herself and a houseful of others to any animal with the money to pay the fee.

'I don't know,' Nick said. 'I don't know how I'd feel.'

'There would only be two choices. Love or hate.'

'And you chose hate.'

'I didn't choose it. She did.'

'And what about your promises? The ones you made to Colette.'

Judah grinned. Void of repentance. He reached for the opium pipe and held it in his fingertips and said Colette's promises were promises to the world and those are the easiest to break. And as far as the promises we all make to God, if every person who had ever made a promise to Him went through with their end of the deal then there'd scarcely be a lost soul in this world. He knows we won't keep them but He's got to listen. He don't have a choice. And neither do we.

38

THE HOUSE WAS A DEPENDABLE den of addiction. The door always open. Always someone to provide. Always an empty space. The windows rattled with the wind and a draft weaved from room to room like a spectral thread. Floorboard slats were missing here and there and gave the floor a gaptoothed grin and the only light came from the sun or from the moon or from the burning matches that lit the burning pipes. Sheets and drapes had been hung from the ceilings to hold the smoke low, to allow the opium haze to hold you and lift you and carry you where you wanted to go. Stray cats meandered from room to room.

As he had gradually shifted into a more permanent state of pain, Judah had begun to discover solace in the strangeness of others. He lay on the floor in the backroom with his head resting on his folded coat and his body limp and at the mercy of vapors. His cane and pipe and bowl lay next to him and the tip of the cane was covered by his spotted handkerchief. His lips moved randomly in the silent, idle chatter that he shared with the creatures of his dreams. Dried blood crusted in each corner of his mouth. Across the room a man and woman, both with matted hair and both stinking of the street, lay slumped over one another. With spacious, empty eyes she stared at the sheet that hung from the ceiling and shifted with the moving air and he slept with his mouth open and his arm crossed over his brow as if he had long since seen enough.

Judah had arrived in the early night, needing to get away from the apartment and the saloon and the room below. Inhaling and going numb and sleeping and then waking hours later and doing it again. The deep clouds that had blanketed Frenchtown had begun to separate and the moon peeked through a cloudbreak and shined down into the window above Judah's body. In the moonglow the haze seemed to thicken and it shifted methodically and gracefully as if orchestrated.

The front door of the house opened and closed and there were footsteps down the hallway and then voices from another room. There was a short exchange and then more footsteps and then the new visitor found a space and settled in. A wind pushed against the house and howled through the cracks and crevices and Judah turned in his sleep.

As a boy he had taken sick one winter and his mother had been certain he was going to die. She sat by his bedside all hours of the day and night and if she slept he didn't see it. Every time he woke, she was there watching him. When he was awake she talked to him and read to him. Taught him to play poker and go fish. Sang songs her grandmother had taught her to sing. Gave him medicine at the exact intervals that the doctor had instructed her to give it. His father would come into the bedroom randomly during the day, leaving the saloon to come home and see about him and to try and get his mother to take a break. She only ate when she tried to get Judah to take some soup or nibble on some thinly sliced ham and the only time she moved her chair away from his bed was when she slid it over to the window and lifted it open and smoked a third of a cigarette from the pack she kept hidden from his father.

He wasn't going to die then and he never was in such danger but she couldn't be convinced otherwise. She had seen too many other mothers lose their children and she had lost a baby sister and there was an imminence of heartbreak that she carried with her that she had always been ready to battle. She sat at his bedside and watched him as if her eyes alone carried a healing power and when he regained his strength and came out of the bed she carried herself with the air of victory as if she had taken the black angel into the back alley and beaten it into submission with a rolling pin. Now he was a busted and bleeding thing. And he was dying this time.

The night hours passed and the moonlight disappeared and returned, disappeared and returned as the clouds pushed into different skies. Out across the Gulf the sun showed itself on the early horizon and promised a shadowfilled day. Judah lifted his head as a slit in the wall allowed a spear of light into the room and when he opened his eyes he saw the image of his mother and he lifted his hand for her to hold it. She reached for him but then she disappeared and his hand fell to the floor.

The sunlight slashed and he rolled on his side. He didn't want to hurt anymore and wondered why he was allowed to come back. Why it couldn't have ended there with his past life still something that he ached for. His head rested against the floor and the light fell across his body and that was when he saw his deliverer. The one that he believed could help him do what he wanted to do. Kneeling next to him and taking his hand. Helping him to his feet. Lifting him and carrying him out into the sunlight and forgiving him all of his sins.

39

COLETTE STOOD IN THE MIDDLE of the floor with her hand resting on the back of a chair, one of only two pieces of furniture in the bottom floor room of the building she had moved into after the fire. A round wooden table was in the corner and a bottle of pastis and a bottle of water and a short glass were in the middle of the table. Both the second and third floors were divided into four rooms. Only half the rooms had beds and the rest of the furniture, wobbly end tables and bureaus with missing drawers and one-door armoires, had been collected from the street. The plaster flaked from the walls and the ceilings sagged and there were stairs on the staircase that were better to step over.

She had eight girls before. Out of those eight, three were dead in the fire, one tried to come back and work but her arm was badly burned from the wrist to the elbow and Colette sent her away. The other four returned ready to make up for lost time but Colette told them it was over for now. I need time to do it the right way.

Outside the streets were slick with the damp and weeklong freezing and few passed. It was past midnight and her stomach growled as she waited to see if he would show up. At twilight she had given a kid a couple of coins and had him deliver a note to Judah's saloon. A note to Nick. It said *I need to talk to you* and it gave her address and she was going to give him

210

until the cathedral chime sounded one a.m. and then she was going to make the latenight visit she knew she had to make.

She moved over to the table. Sipped from the bottle of water. When she closed her eyes she saw herself bound at the wrists and tied to the bed in the darkness. She saw him close to her. Felt him breathing in her face. She saw the child in the quilted bundle and she saw John LaFell trucking the bundle around in the wagon. Crippled by grief. Behind her eyes the house blazed in a brilliant spectrum and the writhing bodies flew from the windows and landed at the foot of her subconscious in flaming piles. She realized that what had come between her and Judah had now leaked out and spilled onto others. There were times in every day when her body and mind began to shut down on their own and allow her to drift, but then images from her burning house and from her captive days would surface and she was awake again.

It was about resilience and scorn, she decided. And that was plenty to keep her warm. But it was also about money and that's where Judah had gotten her. The fire had taken everything. Just as he had planned. She sat at the table as a man in a heavy overcoat came to the window and stopped, the tip of his cigarette a red dot against his black figure. He leaned close to the window and peered in and his breath fogged the glass. He then reached for the doorknob and turned but it was locked. He stepped back. Looked up and down the building, back and forth along the street, and then walked away.

I need to talk to you.

She didn't know what she needed to talk to him about or even why she had written the note but she found herself anxious. Waiting on this man she had caught watching her for days from the street before coming into the brothel and then sitting at the end of the bar with timid and cautious eyes. As if he was afraid of what may happen to him while he was there. Eyes she understood better now after having spoken to him in the St. Mark's sanctuary. Realizing he had been over there. That's how they look, she thought. Their eyes are there but they are not there. Sunk back from their sockets and adrift in some opaque ocean of memory. Maybe that is all there is between him and Judah. Maybe that's why he is caring for him. Maybe they understand one another, she thought. But she could not help wondering if there was more to it. If she was missing something. And this was the thought crossing her mind when the single chime sounded the hour.

She stood and bundled herself and inside her coat she felt around and took out a small silver flask and she unscrewed the top and took a drink. Then there came a knock. Nick stood in the door window with the note in his hand and he held it up as if to provide proof as to why he was here. She unlocked the door and he stepped inside.

'Are you sure this note is for me?'

'It has your name on it.'

She extended the flask to him but he didn't take it.

'Where have you been?' she said.

'Deciding.'

'Deciding what?'

'If I was going to come here.'

She took a long stroll around the bar. Drank again from the flask. Nick looked down at his feet and then moved his eyes around the nearly empty room.

'I'm curious,' she said. 'When you came into my place, you didn't want anything to drink and you didn't want a girl.'

He shook his head.

'What do you want?'

'Are those the only two choices?'

She smiled a little. She had been so long dressing up and selling depravity in Frenchtown that she had forgotten there were options. She wanted to ask him again. What do you want? But she looked at him. His roaming eyes not wanting to meet hers and his hands shoved down into his coat pockets and she believed he carried the look of perpetual wonder, a childlike expression of trying to understand the complexities of all that moved around him. It was not the face of the men and women she dealt with. The faces of lust and then more lust. She wanted to ask him. What do you want? But she knew he would not have an answer.

'What are you doing with Judah?' she asked.

'You know.'

'What does he tell you?'

'How do you mean?'

'He tell you any secrets?'

'It's difficult to talk when your mouth is full of blood.'

His eyes stayed on her then and he changed. The childlike expression gone. She now saw a man who had survived. A man who was capable. He stared at her and in the empty room where she imagined there would one day be music and dancing and bottles knocking against tables and young women telling happy men what they wanted to hear there was a bottomless silence. She stared at him and he stared back and she saw herself. Alone and without a goddamn clue.

He moved toward the door and she came from around the bar and told him to stop. She wrapped her scarf up around her chin. Dropped the flask into her pocket. Moved past him and opened the door.

'Come with me,' she said.

'I thought you said you wanted to talk.'

'We did. Now we're doing something else.'

'I'm not going with you to see Judah.'

'No shit.'

'Then what?'

'I've got an errand to run.'

'It feels late for errands.'

She took him by the shoulders. Turned him around. Nudged him across the threshold and said enough of your schoolboy bullshit. You know as well as I do some things can only be done while others sleep.

40

THEY WALKED ACROSS FRENCHTOWN TO Canal Street and boarded a streetcar that was empty but for them and another who slumped and slept. The car moved through the chilled and empty night. Away from the Quarter, the city slept a deep winter's sleep. While the streetcar rocked, Colette talked to Nick and explained where they were going and why she needed him there. I'm going to walk into a room full of men with the money to fix what all I got broken. It'll look better if somebody is with me. Somebody they don't recognize. Act like you got some kind of interest in what's going on and just nod and agree with me whenever it feels right. She kept waiting on him to ask why he should do this. Why he should be out in the middle of the night with a woman he didn't know going to a place he didn't know and agreeing to do whatever she was asking him to do but he only sat with an agreeable, almost dumb expression. As if she were speaking some language he did not understand but found mildly entertaining.

She continued instructing him until it was time to warn him. You're going to find out about the real Judah. I know you don't want to. But you're going to. You can believe whatever it is you want about Judah but I'm going to stand on my side of it all and fight like I know how to fight. That's all there is to it. It might do you some good to know him better anyhow. You need to understand who you're helping keep alive.

'You need to understand who you're helping to kill,' Nick said.

'I do know.'

'You think you know. He thinks he knows. And you'll both die that way.'

The streetcar stopped at Jackson Avenue and they exited. Grand houses lined each side of the street, two and three story houses with balconies with wroughtiron railings and brick walkways leading from the sidewalk to the front steps. Magnolia and oak trees nestled together and stretched from house to house like a natural tapestry and gas lamps burned from front porches. Grainlike flecks of ice danced in the nightbreeze as they moved in the solemn dark, turning right on the next street and walking several more blocks until they came to the house on the corner of Prytania and Second. The house was painted crimson and a headhigh brick wall stretched out and closed in the backyard and a single light shined in an upstairs window. Colette opened the front gate and stepped into the yard and Nick followed. She walked to the front steps of the house, palm trees lining the walkway, and they followed the path around to the left where a heavy iron door opened and allowed them behind the brick wall.

Behind the house was a pool that had been drained for the winter. Trellises lined the walls, covered in vines that blossomed with purples and yellows in the spring but lay like a bed of skinny sleeping snakes in the dead month of December. Along the back of the yard stood the pool house. It was a small house with big windows and many small panes and a bistro table and chairs sat on a patio next to the French doors. White curtains covered the length of the windows and from behind the curtains the lights glowed and the gathering of men was right where she thought it would be.

They moved through the shadows to the pool house door and she slid her arm around his and tugged her scarf down and said remember what I told you and stand up straight. She then pulled her scarf above her nose and opened the door and she and Nick stepped inside. The men at the table looked up in alarm from their cards and cash and Scotch as the light was thrown upon them, her smart eyes catching them from above the scarf. The cigar smoke clouded the room and Colette cut her eyes across each of the four men. Then she moved her hand to her face and pulled down the scarf and there was an exhaust of relief when they recognized her and one of them said holy damn shit and another lifted his glass and drank a shot of nervous release.

William Pitot was the only one at the table still wearing a tie and he stood up and moved around the room and he held out his hand. She took it and he said get in here and shut the damn door. It's damn near too cold to drink. The others knew her, but not like William. They all nodded and greeted her and wiped the Scotch from their mustaches.

'How'd you know we were here?' William asked.

'It's the second Tuesday of the month.'

'Jesus. You remember that?'

'I remember plenty,' she said. 'This here is Nick.'

The men nodded to him and Colette took out her flask. The man to her left pushed a pack of cigarettes and matches toward her. She took one and lit it and stared at the pile of cash in the middle of the table and the stacks of cash in front of each man.

'I hope you're lady luck. I ain't doing so good,' William said. He took a handkerchief from his pocket and wiped his forehead. She noticed he had gained some weight. And his hair was farther back and his beard was thicker and grayer.

William smacked his lips and watched her with bloodshot eyes. She had only been in the pool house for minutes but she knew that the question was burning them all behind the pleasantries, that it had burned them all from the instant she opened the door and interrupted the night. What the hell is she doing here?

'I guess you know what happened,' she said.

'Which part? The part about you being stolen and tied up or the part about the fire or the part about the shooting?'

'All of it.'

William cut his eyes at Nick. Pursed his lips in an expression of trying to decide.

'He's all right,' she said. 'He wouldn't be with me if he wasn't.' He looked back to her. Smiled again.

'I figured you left town,' William said. 'Probably wouldn't be the worst thing considering all.'

'I ain't leaving town. This is my town. Always has been. You should know that. If anybody is leaving it will be Judah.'

'Why's that?'

'You know he burned down my house.'

'I don't know it. I have heard it said.'

'I know.'

'That's not the same thing as everybody else knowing it,' he answered. One of the men stood from the table and walked to the other side of the room where there was a sofa and coffee table and he stood behind the sofa smoking his cigar.

'He did it,' Colette said. 'And he didn't just do it to me. He burned up three of the women and he burned up a kid and God knows what else or who else.'

'I said I know about it all.'

'Then do something.'

'How about we deal you in and you slow down.'

'I don't need to slow down. I need you to do something.'

'What do you want me to do?'

The other two men stood and moved away from the table. William raised his cigar and pointed at Nick.

'I don't know him,' he said. 'And we're not talking about this with somebody in the room I don't know.'

'I told you he was all right,' she answered.

'You heard me.'

Colette turned to Nick and asked him to wait outside. He glanced around the room at the eyes on him. At the eyes on her. He wanted to grab her arm and say let's go but her bent brow said she wasn't leaving until she got whatever it was she wanted. He opened the door and slipped out into the cold. She closed it behind him.

She then moved closer to the table. Peeled off her gloves. Dabbed out her cigarette. Unwrapped her scarf. Dropped the flask into her pocket and took off her coat. Her hair fell down the sides of her face and neck like ribbons and she arched her back and rubbed her fingers low across her throat and they all watched with wolfeyes to see if she would keep going. Instead she sat down in a chair across from William.

'I want to make you a deal,' she said.

'We already made one. And now it's ashes.'

'A new deal.'

'I don't understand,' he said.

'I'm about to explain.'

'I mean I don't understand why you need me for this deal or any deal.'

She nodded at the cash in the middle of the table.

'Because I need some of that.'

'You should have more than I do. Your place was a goddamn goldmine.'

'Well. I don't.'

'Don't tell me that.'

'Why else would I be here?'

'Don't tell me you didn't have a safe.'

'I didn't have a safe.'

'Why the hell not?'

'Because I stuck it all in the attic. That's why.'

'Jesus Christ. The attic?'

She reached across the table and picked up his glass and drank.

'You got to have a damn safe,' he said.

'But I didn't and now I can't do nothing about it.'

'I told you to make some money and get out of it anyway. You could've done that a long time ago. And you should've quit when Judah came back anyhow.'

'It was too late to quit then. And it's too late to quit now.'

'You got a new place already?'

'Already.'

'What's it like?'

'It's a dump.'

'Then don't waste my money and get stuck in what you'll owe. If you haven't noticed Frenchtown is about run out of highfalutin brothels.'

'I'm not interested in chandeliers and brass rails this time around. You know what's coming. We all do. And we all know it doesn't matter what the law says, Frenchtown ain't gonna stop drinking.'

William drew from the cigar. The others cut their eyes back and forth across the room, their curious thoughts shuffling from one to another in open expression.

'What are you thinking?' William said.

'I have plenty of space. Got a cellar below. It'll hold plenty of bottles. Come the new year I figure I can get three or four times what a bottle is worth. Every saloon in Frenchtown is hoarding right about now but they're gonna run out soon enough. They're too busy gambling and whoring and God knows what. When they do, they'll come to me.'

'And?'

'And that's why I need money. To stockpile right now. And you can keep me free of the politicians and half the precinct has been in my burned up beds. Not to mention everyone in this room. This'll be easy and you know it.'

William leaned back in his chair. Thumped a fat ash from the end of the cigar.

'I can't,' he said.

'You can.'

'No. I can't.'

'You have the money.'

'It ain't that.'

'Then what is it?'

'Maybe I already got a deal with somebody else.'

'Then maybe you want to double what you can make.'

'That ain't exactly all there is to consider.'

'What the hell else?'

He coughed. Drew on the cigar. Lifted the bottle of Scotch from the table and drank.

'What?' she said again.

'From where I'm sitting nobody in their right mind would get in the middle of whatever you and Judah got going on. That includes me.'

'This doesn't have anything to do with Judah.'

'If it's got to do with you it's got to do with him. You don't have to turn your head around too far to see what I got to lose.'

'It didn't bother you the first time.'

'First time around I set you up because you know how to get a man all mixed up. And we all thought Judah was with the good Lord.'

'Or the devil.'

'Either way.'

'You weren't mixed up. You and everybody else in this room got plenty in return.'

'Yeah. But nothing was being burned down and there weren't any dead bodies. It was just a good time.'

'Then get him arrested. You can make one call and they'll show up tomorrow and pin this all on him and that'll be the end of it.'

'Judah didn't light the goddamn fire.'

'He paid to have it lit.'

'And that's a bigger problem. Whoever it was is out there walking around and I don't want nothing to do with him either. I figure if a man is willing to get paid to burn down a goshdamn city block then if I get on your side of things Judah will damn sure send him my way.'

'You're overestimating Judah.'

'You're underestimating him. And everything else. Cause I got news for you. Judah is in a shitload of trouble already. You can't pull that stunt and get away with it. Not even in Frenchtown. He's a damn crippled war hero and it's been hands off but that won't last. Too many people got hurt. Too many people lost. Seems like everybody is waiting on him to just die and let it take care of itself. He better hurry.'

Colette leaned back in the chair. He looks satisfied, she thought. In himself. In all that bullshit. As if it was a speech he prepared and had only been waiting for her to appear in the middle of the night and ask for his help.

She stood from the chair. Her eyes changed. The tension

falling out of them as she moved slowly around the table. She sat down in the chair next to him and gave him the look that always won. Then she reached over to his arm. She unbuttoned the cuff of his shirt and rolled up his sleeve and traced her fingers along his forearm.

'Please,' she said. 'We can do this. There's nothing to worry about. And you can have whatever you want. Whatever. Whenever. Like always.'

William put his hand on top of her fingers. He held them and said I don't know if I can this time. You got the right idea but you're a wildcard. Always have been. You and Judah should just drop it and go back to the way you were. Seems like the best thing for everybody.

She returned his patronizing smile. And then she dug her fingernails into the skin of his forearm. His eyes went big in confusion and then in pain. He tried to snatch his arm away but she had him. He shoved at her shoulder and then at her face but she wouldn't let go and he yelled out to the others who hurried across the room and dropped their drinks and cigars. Get her off me get her off me. They grabbed Colette around the waist and legs and pulled and lifted her out of the chair, her body parallel to the ground and nails still dug into the flesh of his arm as if desperately clutching a cliffside. They gave her one more good pull and she came loose. Small red halfmoons lined William's forearm and his face was blushed and his eyes glassy. He clutched his bleeding arm and screamed for them to throw her the hell out of here.

She didn't fight as they carried her out of the door. But when they dropped her on the ground she got up and took a swing that grazed the back of somebody's head. They faced her and she was heated and ready. And they slowly moved back toward the door as if wary of some wild animal, closing and locking it behind them. From inside William yelled don't ever come back here or I'll help Judah bury you.

She kicked the door and said give me my goddamn coat. Stood at the door a moment and listened to their voices and moving about. She turned around and realized Nick should be there but he was gone. She looked across the yard at the house and a light had come on downstairs. From the other side of the brick fence a neighbor's dog began to bark and then the door opened and her coat flew out onto the patio and the door slammed shut and the lock clicked. She picked up the coat and put it on. The backporch light turned on and she crossed the lawn and hurried through the gate and out onto the sidewalk.

She thought she would find Nick waiting there. Or waiting at the end of the street. But she didn't and she moved on through the dark and the feeling of being a stranger in this town came over her. As if she were walking these streets for the first time. As if she would ride the streetcar for the first time. She felt at the mercy of the world, something so light and fragile. Something weak and unacknowledged. In the cold night she was consumed by the idea that she wasn't really there. Or that maybe she had never been. Or that maybe she was no longer interesting. And maybe she no longer loved and that didn't leave much to offer.

Am I really here, she wondered. Like Judah. He is here. But he's not here.

She reached Jackson Avenue and waited for the streetcar. Her hands were deep in her coat pockets and her fingers tapped against her leg, skin and blood under her fingernails. She saw the single headlight of the streetcar moving toward her. She began to hum. She hummed and tapped her fingers and by the time the car arrived she was laughing out loud at the look on William's face when he realized she was going for it. That she could hurt him.

I'll show them, she thought.

The streetcar stopped and she climbed on. The only person riding. It bumped and then moved along the rail. She slid across the wooden seat and sat close to the window, her breath fogging the cold glass.

You and Judah should just go back to the way you were, he had said.

The way we were, she thought. Dancing at a masquerade ball and sitting at the river sipping gin and watching the sun go down and playing hide and seek between the market stands. Cheating together in school and swiping cigars from her father's store and swiping quarters from the saloon cash drawer. Arriving at the moment they had known they were coming to since childhood when they married under a magnolia tree. Arriving at the moment they had known was coming when Judah said I have to go.

Why can't you just go back?

Because I put my hardest part forward when I believed he was dead and that is what I am now. And she imagined the Judah before. Standing straight. Shoulders back. Lifting her onto the bartop in the saloon and pouring her a drink. Then she saw him as he was now. Lifting a cane. The war a part of his body. A part of his mind. His scars. She thought of Judah's face and the crescent scar he hadn't brought home and the night she gave it to him.

The rough night in the brothel, the out-of-town brothers who got what they wanted and then sat at the bar and drank and drank until they decided they didn't have to pay. They had told the girls in the room they would pay downstairs and then they had told the bartender they were done and leaving.

Colette had met them at the door and told them what they owed and they laughed at her. Told her to get her ass out of the way and she reached behind her and locked the door and they laughed harder. I'll slap a damn woman, one of them said. You and me both, said the other. The piano player stopped playing and those sitting at the window tables or at the bar all went silent and watched.

'You won't slap me,' she said to one. And then to the other.

'Saying it twice don't make it no sweeter,' one said and he slapped his brother's arm and they cackled. They both wore bushy mustaches and silver watches and shared the same sarcastic eyes.

She told them again what they owed and they again said we ain't paying and move your whore ass away from that door.

They were drunk and slow and she was quick to her boot and quick with the blade and she had sliced one across the arm and the other across the cheek before either could put together what was happening. The brothers gawked and each saw the other's blood and they went for her. She dodged them and by now the bartender had come around the bar brandishing a champagne bottle that he smacked over one head and then another, the bottle breaking neither time to the astonishment of all as it sent both brothers to their knees. Colette kicked one to the floor and she reached in his coat pocket and pulled out his cash-filled wallet and the other hit her hard in the side of the face with an all or nothing haymaker. The bartender cracked him again and this time the bottle shattered and he went limp and out.

Colette had gone to the floor. The wallet falling from her hand. The knife falling from the other. The room spinning. Men rose from their chairs and helped the bartender drag the brothers out of the door and into the street. Her girls gathered around Colette. Helped her sit up, then helped her off the floor and into a chair. A wet towel for her swelling cheek. Someone picked up the wallet and the knife and gave them to her and then the girls helped her upstairs and to her room. She drank a shot of whiskey and a glass of water and then lay down on the bed. Turned off the lamp. The wallet on the nightstand. The knife still in her hand, not ready to believe it was all over.

She had never asked Judah why he had chosen that night to come to her. Why that was the night that he let it all fall, his anger and his hurt, and limped across Frenchtown in the late night to be with his wife again. But that was the night he had chosen and he came to the front door in the deep hours. The bartender and two of the girls sat alone at the bar. When he came in, none of them spoke, only looked at him with surprise. He asked which room was hers and the bartender told him top floor at the end of the hall. He crept up the stairs like an insect, each step hurting him a little more than the one before, until he reached the top floor. He bent and gathered himself. Let the pain subside. Then he made his way to the end of the hall where he opened her door and the streetlight came in her open windows and he saw her asleep on top of the covers. She was on her side and the pale light lay draped across the curve of her body.

Judah leaned his cane against the wall and moved to the bed. Sat down carefully on the edge. He reached out with a careful and sorrowful hand to touch her, so many years since the last time he had touched her, and as he dropped the weight of his hand across her hip, she felt it and she rose panicked and fearful of this touch in the dark and with the knife that had never left her hand she swiped at the figure and he screamed and fell back and to the floor, the blood coming fast to the halfmoon slice that bent around his bewildered eyes.

She stepped down from the streetcar and minutes later she found herself standing in front of Judah's saloon. A candle left burning on a table in the corner. The window to what had been their bedroom right above her. She heard a long and winding moan. And she knew it was the kind of pain that could only belong to him.

41

Nick found himself standing at the site of the fire. A pint bottle in one hand and a letter from home in the other. He had stood at the door of the pool house with his ear pressed against the cold glass until he heard William begin to promise consequences against Judah and then he slipped off into the dark. Hurrying back to the streetcar and then hurrying to Judah where he found him facedown in the bed and wheezing for breath. He turned him over. Got him comfortable. And then on his way out he saw the letter addressed to him lying on the floor. A letter from his father.

You need to be home for Christmas, it read. Your mother expects you. There is much time to make up. You are twentyeight years old. Not a young man anymore. I will expect you.

He swigged from the pint bottle. The liquor hitting him hard and fast. I'm twentyseven, he thought. He kicked at a smutty pile of bricks and closed his eyes and tried to see what used to be there. Tried to see the ghosts of the women and their smooth and bare legs and he tried to hear the clink of the glasses and the sounds of pleasure. He swayed as the liquor burned and then he did not see the women as they teased and touched but he heard the rage of the fire and he heard the screams and saw the blazing bodies and he felt it all and his head fell back and his mouth fell open and it was as if the great sorrow of the world came together in a deepnight mist that slipped down his throat and into his soul and he opened his eyes to chase away the screams. He tossed the letter onto the blackened mess and he drank from the bottle and when he started to walk again it was with a loose and drunken gait.

He staggered along. Inside the saloons they gathered in the smoky light and along the sidewalks of the brothels they stood in dark coats that fell open and their pale legs snaked out into the cold and Nick stopped and stared. Come on over here, they said. You look lonely, they said. Don't be lonely, they said. He wobbled. Tripped but caught himself. Don't run off, they said. Come back and let me make it all right, they said. But he kept moving though he kept thinking about what it would be like to hold out his hand and let one of them take it and disappear into a room where no one cared what they were doing and if he could get himself to stop thinking then he wouldn't care either. He came to a cart on the side of the street and he sat down. Around him were the echoes of music. The echoes of laughter. He sat in the somber light of the lamppost and drank and knew he would be sick but he drank more.

That was when he saw the figure walking toward him. Coming out of a brothel at the end of the street. He couldn't tell if it was a man or woman until she was close as she wore a black fedora pulled down tightly on her forehead. A long gray coat flapped behind her. He rose from the cart, mesmerized by her lengthy strides and he pretended to almost bump into her and she gave him a sharp glance and never broke stride and the catlike glint in her eyes grabbed Nick and pulled him.

It's Ella, he thought.

He tucked the bottle in his coat pocket and kept a halfblock behind and the woman walked without turning her head as if focused on some target way off in the distance. She kept a quick pace and he hurried to keep up. His breaths in little drunken gasps. She walked along Dauphine toward Canal, a lanky figure wearing the clothes of a different gender, pants too big and flapping on her thin body and the hat down across her eyes. At each corner she stopped. Lifted the hat and looked around. Nick anticipated her stops and he was already ducking into an alley or into a doorway or behind others on the street by the time she looked in his direction. The farther along Dauphine she walked, the darker Frenchtown became as if she were traveling deeper into a well. Fewer and fewer stood on the street. No music. Footsteps echoing. Shadowlike figures hovered in doorways or on balconies and the weight of those eyes fell on the woman and the man following her.

She reached Iberville Street and turned to the right and it seemed that the farther she walked, the more Frenchtown gave up. The buildings leaned against one another as if only trying to make it through the night. Smoke crept from opium houses and smoke hung in the night air from alleyfires lit by street people who stared drunkenly or hungrily into the low flames. Her pace slowed the deeper she moved into the dark and Nick closed in on her. Nervous and curious and he began to see her now like he saw her in the candlelight of the theater attic while they lay together on a pile of costumes or like he saw her in the sunlight of the cafés and he wanted to run and grab her and hold her and say here I am.

She stopped at a street lamp and felt in her coat pockets. Felt in the trouser pockets. Took off her hat and pulled out a matchbox. Nick crept closer along the sidewalk. A donkey neighed and a man walked past leading the animal with only a scarf tied around the animal's neck. She struck a match.

Held it in front of her face. Stared until it burned down to her fingers and she dropped it. Then she walked further along the street. The sidewalks lined with shacklike cribs. Short and ramshackle rooms stacked against one another like something from a child's drawing. Behind the crib doors was the cheapest deal in town. And the most dangerous. The lamppost gave the only light and figures moved about in the sinister illumination as if slowed by the dark. Or by time. Or by resignation. A cry of hate or lust or disgust came from one of the cribs and then a door slammed. Nick turned his head at the noise and when he looked back the woman had vanished. The city block was buried in shadows and he hurried up one side of the street and then the other, looking both ways, tripping and falling over an unconscious body and he went down with a heavy grunt as the bottle fell from his pocket and rattled across the cobblestones.

He sprang to his feet like a good soldier. Backed away from the body quickly with his hands made into fists and eyes of fright. He turned around in a circle as if anticipating being ambushed and then he gathered himself. Realized the body wasn't moving and no one was reaching for him or even interested. He looked around in the dark and felt disoriented and even tricked. Wondered if she had baited him and she was no longer Ella but she was an enemy. An enemy who knew he would follow and walk into this open grave where she could make him disappear and this was not the place he wanted to disappear. He took several shaky steps backward, his arm stretched out and hand feeling in the dark for guidance. He looked for her again. Saw her nowhere. As if she had morphed with the shadows.

Then he heard a rummaging down a narrow corridor. He felt in his pocket for his own matches but he had left them in the apartment with the sleeping Judah. The sound came again, the noise of something like hungry animals searching in the night for food. He stepped into the corridor, a lean space between the back of the crib houses and the concrete wall running the length of the block behind them. The sound came again, a sound of disarray. A voice cried out and Nick froze. Turned and looked over his shoulder to see how far along he had come, wanting to make sure he could escape. Up ahead in the dark the rummaging continued and two cats screeched and Nick balled his fists again. And then he was snatched and his arm wrenched behind him and he felt the blade on his throat.

'Don't goddamn move,' the voice said.

The man bent his arm up and pressed the blade against his throat and Nick wanted to yank and turn but he knew that would slice him. The woman in the hat stepped around the man and stood in front of Nick and she kicked him in the gut and the man moved the blade just as Nick went down to his knees and he grabbed the back of Nick's hair and held him.

'Get his pockets,' he said. The woman opened Nick's coat and felt inside, taking cigarettes and a fold of dollars and his journal. She then reached around to his backside and lifted out his wallet. She raised the journal and slapped him across the face with it and then she kicked him in the ribs and he fell with his chest against the ground and then the man stomped on his back and they kicked and kicked as Nick drew himself into a ball and grunted with each blow. They paused to catch their breath and then the man delivered a hard punch to the back of Nick's head and Nick was on the edge of passing out when the woman raised her hand and told the man to leave him be. We got it all. Let's go spend some money.

The man delivered one more kick into Nick's side. The

woman counted the money and the man said give me the cigarettes and they moved along the thin corridor arm in arm.

Nick rolled over and lay on his back. Touched his throat to make sure there was no blood. He lay there for a long time. Drunk and dizzy eyes into a grayblack sky. Circles of pain where he had been kicked. The cold air drying his open mouth. He finally rolled to his side. Moved to hands and knees. Slowly got himself upright. He moved gingerly with one hand holding his side and the other against the concrete wall to guide. When he reached the end of the corridor a voice came from a balcony across the street. If you want something around here you ain't got to work so hard, she called. It don't take much more than a quarter to get what you want on this side of town.

He started walking and sat down in the first saloon he came to. Two dollars had been missed, stuck down in the deep front pocket of his trousers and he got a glass and a bottle of whiskey and sat alone at a table in the corner. A candle on the table waving and with tired eyes he stared at the candle until it hurt and then he followed the spot around the murky saloon until it disappeared. He drank two drinks quickly. A throbbing in the back of his neck. The saloon was empty but for three men sitting at the bar playing cards with the bartender. He felt as though he were sinking. Measured and certain.

The next time he tried to stand the room spun around and he fell across a chair and hit the floor. The men looked at him a moment and then returned to the game. Nick grabbed a chair and lifted himself into it. Now he heard laughter and he turned to look but the saloon was blurred. All was blurred. He put his hands on the chair arms and pushed. Stood again. Wobbled but held on. One step and he was down again and this time he was out. When he woke he had been dragged out of the saloon and he was lying on his back on the sidewalk. His pockets had been emptied for good this time and both his coat and belt were gone. He shivered and was sick and could barely keep his eyes open from the pain exploding through his head and neck. He crawled along the sidewalk. Busted and drunk and cold and he was solitary in the night and on this street and in this city and in this world.

III

42

KADE MCCRARY HAD ALWAYS BEEN the loudest guy in the room no matter the size of the place or the nature of the crowd. His boisterous temperament was matched by the bushlike, coffeebrown beard that draped his face and reached down to his shirt collar and seemed to create a hairy platform for his verbal acrobatics. He stood against the small bar in the train's dining car, a whittled down cigar pinched between his burly knuckles and a drunken grin causing his whiskers to rise. Lipstick was smeared across the shoulder of his wrinkled denim shirt and across the cheek of the woman holding on to his arm and trying to keep her feet. They had entered a dining car with its whiteclothed tables filled but after half an hour the crowd had fled the goodtiming couple and left them in the solitude of their own havoc.

'Pour me some more,' she said and she leaned back and slapped at his thick arm. He slapped her back with more force than he should have and she lost her balance and hit the floor with a cackle.

'Hell, honey. You can't have me down there. This is a public place.'

'Get your big ass down here,' she said and she reached up and grabbed him by the suspenders and pulled. He went down to a knee and she rose up and they swapped a sloppy kiss that smeared the candy apple lipstick over both their mouths. The waiter behind the bar leaned over and watched them with irritated eyes and then continued wiping the glasses he had been wiping since they had walked in.

'You have to get up off the floor,' the waiter said. He had been serving in the dining car for ten years and thought he had seen it all. But he hadn't. He ran his hand across his thin mustache and neatly cropped hair as if his own presentation might somehow affect theirs.

The woman tugged at Kade's neck and pulled him down all the way and when he fell on top of her, her small body disappeared except for her bare legs that stuck out from her short dress. She raised her legs toward the ceiling and yelled choo choo.

'Get the hell up,' the waiter said and he walked around the bar. Little grunts and snorts of laughter rose from the two as they grabbed and groped and the waiter said they had about five seconds to quit the nonsense.

'Or what?' Kade said and he rose to his feet. The smaller man's face went into the larger man's beard and it was wet with drink and slobber and the waiter stepped back and wiped his face in disgust.

'You're acting like animals except worse,' the waiter said. 'Now stop it.'

'Come on now,' the woman said and she lifted herself from the floor and straightened her dress. 'Ain't nobody in here to be bothered.'

'Not anymore,' the waiter said. 'Your carrying on took care of that already. And out walked a carload of tips with them.'

'Hell's bells,' he said and he grabbed the woman around the waist and pulled her to him. 'He wants a tip. What you got left in that little black purse?'

Her purse sat on the bartop and she picked it up and shook it.

'Nothing,' she said.

'Nothing?'

'If it's anything left then it's figured out how to rattle around without bothering to make a sound.'

He dug in his pocket and pulled out a few singles and a wadded napkin and some stray matches.

'How about a dollar?' he said and he slapped it down on the bar. 'I'd say that mustache alone is worth at least a damn dollar.'

The woman crowed and took a cigarette from a pack on the bar.

'You're incorrigible,' the waiter said.

'What's that mean, fancy pants?'

'It means you ain't corrigible,' the woman answered.

'Light this cigar again, honey,' he said and held it toward her. She struck a match and lit her cigarette and then held it to the cigar nub.

The door to the dining car opened and a woman holding a small child saw the couple at the bar and she turned around and walked out.

'You'd be more comfortable in your own seats,' the waiter told Kade.

'You might as well give up,' Kade said. 'We ain't going nowhere.'

The waiter shook his head. Draped the dishtowel over his shoulder and set a glass down on the bar. Kade slipped a pint bottle from his back pocket. He removed the cap and poured the waiter a taste. The waiter picked up the glass and held it to them and the woman clapped as if she had won something. The man took a drink from the bottle and handed it to her and she did the same.

'Here,' the waiter said and he gave her the towel. 'Wipe your mouth.'

'You look like a clown,' Kade said. 'Got lipstick damn everywhere.'

'Thanks to you,' she said. She wiped the lipstick from the sides of her mouth and cheeks. She then slapped Kade across the head with the towel before giving it back to the waiter.

Kade drank again and then the woman drank again. She then asked him how much longer until New Orleans and he said we're taking a detour. I got something I got to do in Birmingham.

'You said we were going to New Orleans.'

'We are going to New Orleans. But I said I got to make a stop.'

'You didn't say nothing about a stop before.'

'I didn't say nothing about the sun coming up tomorrow neither but it's going to.'

'Fine then,' she said and she rubbed up next to him. 'How much longer? I got the cabin fever.'

'Not long,' the waiter said and glanced at his watch. He sipped his drink and smoked now, leaning against the bar in full surrender. 'Maybe thirty minutes.'

'See?' the man said. 'Fresh air is on its way.' He slipped his hand down and slid it up under her dress.

She jumped back and said you got to wait boy.

'I ain't waiting,' he said and he crept toward her with his arms spread wide and she squealed. The waiter knew the only way to deter them from their carnal games would be another drink so he killed his and asked for another. They pawed and pulled and grabbed and the waiter knocked the glass against the bar until Kade finally took his eyes from the woman and said if you're gonna knock that goddamn glass around at least do it in rhythm but the waiter kept knocking in sporadic beats. Kade finally paused. Winked at the woman. Then he settled against the bar and poured them all another round.

The two walked arm in arm along the Birmingham platform, swaying from side to side, her drunken voice echoing across the station. The cold air chilled her bare legs and he said you need some stockings but she only kicked her feet up and said I ain't hiding these legs. They reached the end of the platform and Kade said I got to run to the can.

'So do I,' she said.

'Then let's go.'

The bathrooms were next to the ticket office and she blew him a kiss as she pushed open the bathroom door. He pushed open the door to the men's room but held it. When the door fell closed behind her he turned and walked back toward the train. A whistle blew and the porter called out for departure and he broke into a run, beard and belly bouncing and he raced along the platform and made it to the dining car just as the train door closed behind him. He bent over, wheezing and coughing. Raising his head to look out of the window and see if she was chasing after him but nothing. The train nudged and then began to slowly pull out of the station. Kade stood. Hands on hips. Big breaths. He reached a barstool and plopped down. He took off his hat and pulled out the bottle. The waiter slid his empty glass over.

43

J UDAH SAT IN A CHAIR at the rolltop desk and held the brown bottle. Then he set it down. Picked it up again and swapped it from hand to hand. All you have to do is open it and drink it and go lay down.

It had all happened as he intended except for the final step. He had found a man willing to take a payday in exchange for taking flasks filled with gasoline into Colette's house and doing his business and then lighting the house on fire. He had found a man who had agreed to light the fire and then leave town. But Judah had known Kade for years and had listened to his boorish voice and watched him start brawls in the saloon and he knew that he might agree to take the money and set the fire and leave town but that he would not leave town for good. And that was what Judah had wanted. He wanted Kade to return and drink and smoke and gamble and run his mouth and let Colette and everyone else know that Judah was the one.

He wanted to give them something to talk about and he wanted to leave Colette stuck. She would know the details and there would be nothing she could do in retaliation because he wouldn't be there. The brown bottle of arsenic had been sitting in the rolltop desk for months, waiting for Judah to find the guts to open it and drink and be done. And that time had finally arrived on the day that Kade McCrary walked into

Colette's with his pockets filled with Judah's blood money and said give me a good bottle and a good woman and the softest bed in the prettiest goddamn room you got on the top floor.

There would be no more need for the opium, no need to deaden the pain. No need for gritting his teeth when he tried to get out of a chair or walk across a room and no need for the pile of bloody towels that gathered at the foot of the bed and in the corner of the room downstairs and wherever else he sat for too long. No need of holding a cold rag against the scars and no need of pressing his hands against his chest as he coughed as if to let his own lungs know that he was doing all he could to help. No need to avoid the eyes of others as he had long grown tired of the pitied expressions and he had grown tired of the hands that reached out and tried to help as if he were some ancient and decrepit relic that may crumble in a mild wind.

There would be no more memories of Colette and no more imagining her with him sitting in the apartment sharing a newspaper. Or sharing a bottle of bourbon. Or sharing any of the random movements of life that come with the peaceful acceptance of being with someone you love. No more standing at the end of the block and watching them come and go from the brothel and wondering who was doing what and with who. No more being alone.

He had the arsenic. He had the man he needed. On the morning of the day that he and Kade had agreed to burn it down he had the two barmaids come upstairs and clean the apartment. They straightened the shelves according to his directions, wiped dust from frames and tabletops and chair arms, swept the floors, cleaned the windows of the sitting room, tied back the curtains so that the sun could give light to the crisp and clean room. When they were done he leaned against the wall, pressing on the cane to keep himself upright and knew this is how he wanted to leave it. It would take days for someone to look for him and he would leave the apartment door cracked open so that whoever came would walk inside when he didn't answer the call. He would be on the bed and at rest and then when they all came to see what happened the apartment would have the appearance of the kind of place where people had lived and loved.

It was a simple plan, he thought. Kade fills the flasks I have given him. He comes to the apartment in the afternoon. I pay him. He goes to Colette's house and takes a top floor room. I follow out later and stand and watch. I want to see the smoke. I want to see the flames. I want to see her standing in the street with her hands on her hips as she watches it burn. And then I will walk away. I will come back to the apartment. I will take the bottle into the bedroom. I will drink and then I will lay down and die and leave this world to those who belong in it.

And it had gone that way exactly. Except for the man who had seen Judah on the sidewalk as the fire burned. Bent and bleeding and hurting. And he had helped him though Judah hadn't wished for it because he knew the man was another soldier before the man could say it. It was there on his face and deep in his eyes like it was in all of their eyes. Way down where the dreams and the nightmares rise up. And now he argued with himself. You are the one who accepted his kindness and you are the one who asked him to eat at the saloon and you are the one who talked to him and kept talking to him and you are the one who went upstairs to your room later after he had gone and ignored what you had promised yourself you were going to do and now you've lost your goddamn nerve.

You won't drink it and you won't do it yourself but there are other ways. He was kind to you and you see the same things in him that you see in yourself and he will help you if you ask him. It is a big thing to ask someone who doesn't understand. But he understands. He has the eyes. He has the voice of the uncertain. He has his own secrets. And if there is one thing the lost are able to recognize it is the others who are just as wounded and wandering.

44

KADE SPILLED BACK INTO FRENCHTOWN with the gusto of a man starved for flesh and drink though he had lacked neither and paid for both in the weeks since he had walked to the station and boarded the train with the outlaw's agreement with Judah that he would never return. When he arrived back he fell out of the open door of the dining car and onto the platform, slapping away hands that tried to help him up and roaring in drunken threats to break the skull of any man who laid a dirty hand on him. He had crawled along the platform, telling himself jokes that he laughed at in thunderous, coughing laughs, pausing to sit and watch the passengers walk wide of him. Reaching out and slapping at their legs and laughing again at their frightened expressions as they sidestepped the crazy bearded man. A cop appeared with his billy club at the ready and told him to get his ass moving and though he told the cop you don't scare me one damn bit he wasn't drunk enough to argue with the hurt from the club. So he got to his feet and brushed off his pants and shirt and staggered out of the station and into Frenchtown. Eager to find others like himself.

He made his way to Rampart and into a house on the corner that had its doors flung open and the rumble of a ruckus pouring out into the street. Inside a crowd huddled around a roped-off ring and two shirtless and sweaty men

248

with wrapped fists punched and elbowed and kicked at one another while the crowd screamed and spat and smoked and shoved. One man bled from his mouth and the other from his swollen eye. A bell rang from somewhere and both men knelt and money swapped hands and more bets were made and more drinks were poured. Both fighters were handed whiskey shots and the shots went down and then the bell rang again and they were on their feet and measuring one another when a gun fired from an upstairs room. The fighters paused and the crowd paused and after a moment of silence a voice from upstairs yelled my finger slipped and then the melee carried on.

Kade fell in with the raucous crowd and its energy swept him away. Soon he had a haggard, curlyhaired woman around the waist and she was tugging at his beard and they were passing the bottle back and forth. The fighter with the busted eye knocked out the fighter with the busted mouth and from the back of the room a banjo and fiddle started up while the crowd settled the bets and lit cigars and cigarettes and bought another round. Kade found a chair and sat down with the woman on his lap and she was stout and thick in the shoulders like he was and the rickety chair wouldn't hold. It buckled and he landed hard and she landed hard on top of him and the crowd roared in laughter.

The fall knocked the breath out of him and she mistook his open, gasping mouth as lust and she pressed her mouth across his and he gagged and rolled her off right before he suffocated. She slapped at him and they wrestled around in the fragments of splintered chair until she used his beard as leverage and he hollered I give up. She helped him up and around them men and women danced to the banjo and fiddle. The crowd swayed and the room was gray with smoke and alive with lust. Voices howled and women pulled at men and men pulled at women and above it all somebody sang a loud lullaby in a throbbing bass tone that sounded more like pain than the sweet soothing of coming sleep. Soon two more men stripped off their shirts and kicked back shots and the bell rang. The music stopped and the crowd sized up the fighters and picked winner and loser and the first punch was thrown just as Kade stuck his last dollar down the woman's shirt and they moved toward the staircase and ascended.

Half an hour later Kade appeared on the staircase. He took off his shirt and tossed it out across the crowd and proclaimed to the whole house there wasn't anybody inside these damn walls that could whip his ass. The bottle then went to his mouth and liquor spilled down his beard and round, hard belly. He missed the next step down and tumbled and crashed into the railing at the foot of the stairs and the laughter soon gave way to all bets being placed on whoever made it into the ring with him.

Before he could get to his feet the haggard woman appeared at the top of the stairs and let everybody know that not only would she take the fight but I'll knock him out in two rounds. Kade held the railing and pulled himself up and she marched down the stairs with a hardworn swagger.

'I ain't fighting no damn woman,' he yelled.

'Too late big mouth,' the woman cackled. Money swapped hands and drinks were poured.

She stepped past him and slapped the back of his head hard and it was as if a sideshow had broken out in the middle of a sideshow. She wore bloomers and a bra that barely contained her breasts and her arms and calves were thick and trunklike. Other women gathered around her and toasted her coming victory and Kade staggered to the bar and looked at her with the eyes of the befuddled.

'Hey,' he called to her. 'I ain't hitting no woman I just copulated with.'

She and the others laughed harder, pointed at him. Even in his drunkenness he realized that he had become part of a ruse.

'I'm gonna get your money twice tonight,' she said. 'That is if you got anything left to bet on yourself.'

'I told you I ain't fighting no woman.'

A skinny old man with frantic white hair slid next to Kade and said we all heard it. You proclaimed nobody in these walls could whoop you. Said it right up there. The old man pointed and Kade slapped his arm down and told him to shut up.

'If I was you I'd get mad or something,' the old man said. 'Cause she's gonna make you sausage meat. Seen her do it many times.'

'Buy me a drink or give me a smoke,' Kade said.

The old man handed Kade his flask.

'Door's yonder if you wanna sneak on out,' the man said.

Kade turned up the flask and then passed it back.

'Too late,' he said. Then he used the old man for leverage and he climbed up on the bar and pointed at the woman and yelled I done paid for you once and after I knock you out I'm gonna have a free ride. Somebody threw a shot glass at him and it bounced off his chest and he lost his balance and crashed down on the old man. Arms grabbed him and pulled him up and the bell sounded.

Kade shoved through the crowd and stepped over the lowhanging rope. The banjo played a quick rhythm and he swung his arms and slapped at his belly and let out a boisterous belch. The woman took a last shot of whiskey and

251

the crowd parted. She stepped into the fighting square and cracked her knuckles. She hadn't stopped smiling and Kade told her he was gonna wipe that dumbass look off her face.

'You ain't man enough,' she said. 'I know that already.'

The bell rang again and the banjo stopped as Kade and the woman squared each other up. Moving deliberately around the ring. She put her hands in her curly hair and pulled. Kade's room was spinning and he licked his teeth as if to take a count.

She lunged at him and he swung wildly and missed, losing his balance but keeping his feet and when he turned around her square fist smacked his nose and then the side of his head. A hard combo that came and went before he could lift his hands. She danced a little and the crowd jeered and threw cigarette butts at Kade. He felt his nose and wiped his eyes.

She lunged again and he swung and missed again and another combo bounced off his head. They jeered. She laughed. He felt his nose and wiped his eyes. The old man handed him a flask and he drank. Slapped at his belly and spit across the ring at her feet.

This time when she lunged he didn't swing but snatched her by the coarse hair and spun her around and around and the crowd went into hysterics as the two turned around in a drunken circle. He let go and before she could yell that ain't fair he punched her in the mouth. She stepped back stunned and now bleeding.

'Smile now,' he said.

Her eyes grew fierce and she charged at Kade, her head into his stomach and they fell back into the crowd. She clawed at him and he clawed at her and the gamblers and drunks pulled them apart and shoved them back into the makeshift ring. Just then the bell sounded and Kade and the woman backed away from one another. Money changed hands. More bets were made. The woman wiped her mouth. Kade drank from the old man's flask.

'That was a pretty good idea,' the old man said.

'Go to hell,' Kade answered. His head throbbed. The room shifted. He knew he couldn't stand it much longer.

The bell rang.

She stepped into the middle of the floor and announced this is it. Round two and won't be no more. She then flew at him and sent an elbow into his jaw. He gave one back. They staggered and punched, giving and taking. Locked in a standoff. The crowd shouted and the smoke swirled and the two bulky bodies slapped against each other and Kade sensed her doubt and some of the shouts came his way now. He hit her hard against the side of the head and she was dazed and shaky and he went for the knockout but his big right hand skimmed off her forehead. The great punch spun him off balance but he caught himself and turned, knowing now was the chance to finish her. And that's when her bare and rocklike heel shot into his crotch and that was the beginning of the end.

45

JUDAH LAY ON THE FLOOR of the backroom. When he woke from his high Nick was sitting in a chair in the corner of the room. He held his coat over his arm and a packed bag sat on the floor beside him.

Judah came awake slowly. Taking time to differentiate between dream and reality. Legs first, stretching out with a moan. Then his arms, stretching out with a moan. He began to cough, a little cough that grew in force and Nick hurried from the chair and helped Judah sit up just as the blood rose in his throat and filled his mouth. Nick grabbed a stained towel from the floor and gave it to him and Judah covered his mouth as his eyes filled and tears trickled out and ran into the towel pressed against his face. The two men sat together on the floor until Judah had let it all out. Nick helped him into a chair and then he slid the other chair over and sat next to Judah.

Judah tossed the towel onto the floor. He looked at Nick with shaky eyes and then he looked over at the bag.

'I want to take you to a doctor,' Nick said.

'For what?'

'For help.'

'No doctor can fix me. We both know that.'

'Maybe not fix. I said help.'

'They can't do that either. You know what happened to me.

It's a miracle I'm even here. If you believe in miracles. Which I don't.'

'You never know what can be done for you, Judah.'

'What I need won't come from a doctor.'

'I'll run up and get you something to drink.'

'Don't,' Judah said. 'Just sit here.'

Nick crossed his legs. He was cleanshaven and his hair neatly combed and he propped his hat on his knee.

'So,' Judah said. 'This is it.'

'For now.'

'What's that mean?'

'It means I'll be back.'

'No. You won't. Once you get home that's it.'

'I'm not going home.'

He had already sent a telegram to his father. *I will see you in the New Year.* He regretted it the moment it was sent and he knew the commotion and heartache it would cause his family for him to delay his arrival even further but it was done.

'Why not?' Judah said. 'I bet it's a good place.'

'It is.'

'Then go if you have to go somewhere.'

'I don't want to have to answer the questions.'

Judah shifted in the chair. Coughed.

'There are only questions,' he said. 'Don't matter where you are.'

'I might go back to France,' Nick answered.

'Nah. You're not going back there.'

It was the idea he woke up with. Go back and stay in that city until you find her. And he had sent the telegram home with that intention and packed his bag with that intention though he knew it was a plan he wasn't going to carry out.

'I think you've got a secret,' Judah said. 'Since the first time I looked at you I thought you had something tucked away in there. First time and every time since.'

'I don't have any secrets.'

'Maybe not secrets. Whatever is inside us has all sorts of names. It was probably in there before you had to fight. That just darkened it.'

I try not to think about the war, he thought. Knowing it was a lie. Knowing he would never forget such things. They would always be there to think about and they would affect the way he thought about everything else and everyone he met in every decision he made forever.

'Where is he?' Nick asked.

'Where is who?'

'The man you paid to set the brothel on fire.'

'You think there is such a man?'

'You must know where he is. You better know.'

'Why is that?'

'I don't want to leave you like this. Let me find him. He can hurt you, Judah.'

'I can't be hurt no worse than I already am,' Judah said. A fit of coughing seized him and he fell forward and out of the chair. Nick reached to catch him but Judah crumpled to the floor, his mouth over his hands and the blood spewing between his fingers as he fought to let it out. Nick pushed the towel to Judah's face and held it there and held his other hand on Judah's back as he heaved.

When Judah was done, he turned on his side and lay there. Long pauses came between breaths and his forehead was damp with sweat.

'You have to help me, Nick,' Judah said.

'I'm trying. Tell me who he is.'

Judah reached for Nick and pulled himself into a sitting position. He then bowed his head. Lifted his frail arms and touched his own frail hands to his face, his knuckles rubbing slowly back and forth across the scars. His eyes shifted as if seeing something that only he could see and he seemed to almost withdraw within his own skin and bones.

Something opened inside of Nick as he sat next to this man. Something vast and infinite that was without a name but as familiar to him as his own reflection and in that moment he believed that he would never find his place. That as time moved he found fewer answers and more questions and all that was behind him was not really behind him but twisting and turning and keeping him from becoming whatever it was he wanted to become. And he didn't know what that was. Something vast and infinite opened inside of him and he drifted in that unbounded expanse like a mote of dust carried for thousands of miles and for thousands of years on the ceaseless wind that wraps the earth again and again. His face fell expressionless and his eyes became like the eyes of Judah, unfocused and open only because they had to be.

'Help me,' Judah whispered.

'I told you I would,' Nick whispered back.

'Not like that.'

'Then how?'

Judah turned his head ever so slowly and through the brick wall of the room he saw another world. He raised his hand and pointed a crooked finger and with a waning voice he said help me cross from this world. I don't want to do it myself.

Nick had seen it done. One soldier to another. Mercy when there was only mercy to be had. When the only answer was to end the insufferable pain. He had seen it done and he had felt the humanity in it.

'Judah,' he said.

'There is nothing left for me here,' Judah said. 'And all I do is bleed. And hurt. You have something in you I can't name but I recognize. I don't know why you are here. But you are here. And you can help me where no one else can. I don't want to be in this world anymore.'

A stream of pink saliva trailed from Judah's mouth and reached to the floor and then he cried out from the burning in his lungs. Nick reached into his bag and pulled out a clean shirt and he knelt beside Judah. Judah tossed the filthy towel away and held the clean shirt against his face.

'She was so damn beautiful,' he said.

'I can get her for you. You need to talk to her.'

Judah removed the shirt from his face and said it won't matter because she carries it. I carry it. We all do. All that we've done from the moment we began. All that keeps us from being what we once were and there's so much of that.

Nick tried to see how this was different. There was mercy when there was nothing else and he had it to give to the man begging for it. Judah was broken and dying and empty and he could do what Judah asked or he could go and get on a train and leave him to die a deliberate and aching and distressed death. He tried to figure how this was different from what he had witnessed one man do for another in the dirt of war and he could not. Judah's sunken cheeks and sunken eyes and sunken heart were grave ready, he thought. His body is finished. His spirit is finished. And it is his choice and if not me it will be someone else. Someone who doesn't see what he sees. What I've seen. What I know.

Judah opened the desk drawer. He fumbled around and felt the pistol and he removed it. Showed it to Nick and held it still as if it were something to read.

'Do you know who this belongs to?' Judah asked. 'You picked it off the floor the day the man came with the wagon. I know what I did to him and I wish he was here. He'd do it for me.'

Judah coughed and pressed the heels of his wrists against his lungs. He looked up with broken eyes and said your face has changed. Not that it ever said anything before.

'I need to go home,' Nick said.

'I'm home. And look at me.'

I'm not going home, Nick thought. And I won't ever say that again.

Judah set the pistol on the desktop.

'It would be beyond poetic for me to use this,' he said. 'I only want to numb myself into a stupor and then you can do whatever you think is best.'

'I don't know.'

'You do.'

'My Episcopal nature doesn't allow me to see it as clearly as you see it.'

'Then don't be Episcopal.'

'I haven't been. Not for a long time. But some things are inside of you whether you want them to be or not.'

Judah lifted the cigar box from the drawer and took out a small leather satchel of opium seeds. He fumbled with it and the seeds scattered across the floor. It is your chance to do something that matters, Nick thought. The seeds made tiny taps on the floor as if they were tiny drumbeats of revelation. Do something instead of watching others live around you. Die around you. Love and hate and bleed

and risk and redeem around you. There is something
wrong with you and if you want to be something different
then you have to do something different. If you could be
a savior wouldn't you choose to give that which would
heal?

Yes. I would.

46

THE ROPE THAT FORMED THE ring lay across the floor and puddles of beer and God knows what else gave a putrid smell that the coffee and smoke could not overcome. Redeyed men and women moved down the staircase and out of the door. The gruff woman crossed her thick legs and smoked and listened to the woman sitting with her whose thick mascara gathered in clumps beneath her bloodshot eyes. The woman had spilled over from Colette's house after the fire and she and the gruff woman had gotten in the habit of sharing all from the night before over the day's first coffee and smoke.

'It was him,' she said. 'I'm telling you. Ain't no way to mistake a man like that.'

'You were just drunk,' said the gruff woman.

'We're all just drunk. Half the shit we see and do we're all just drunk. That don't mess with me none. It was him.'

'Tell it then.'

'Oh I can damn sure tell it.'

She took a cigarette from the pack on the table. Leaned back in her chair and said I had been sitting at the end of the mahogany bar smoking a cigarette when Kade came in. Colette was sitting and tapping at the piano and he came over to her and said he wanted the prettiest girl in the house and he wanted a top floor room and a full bottle of the good stuff. Then he slapped down some money on top of the piano and acted like he was a real bigshot but he didn't look like it. Looked kinda dumb to me. Face covered in a puffy beard and I remember one of the buttons on his shirt was missing. But it was me and a few others available and Colette wouldn't never say which one was prettiest so she told him to pick and he looked at me and pointed. He then handed me some money and said something about it being a good afternoon for him and me both and one of the other girls laughed out loud. Colette told the bartender to give the man a bottle and he did and then me and him went upstairs. Third floor was where my room was. Right in the middle.

We did what we were supposed to do and he wasn't no good at it. Tried drinking the whole time like it was some magic trick but he just wasn't no good. Talked too much. I remember that. And then when we were done with that part he said he wanted to sit and drink a little while cause he had something else to do before we were done. I said I don't think you can do it again. But he just bellylaughed and said I don't mean that. Something else. And then me and him sat there and drank a couple of glasses. He got a little drunk and then he said I ain't supposed to tell you what I'm about to tell you but I am anyhow. I don't see no damn difference. You ain't nothing but a damn house dog and won't nobody believe what you say.

Then he picked up his coat off the floor and he pulled out two flasks. Big ones. He opened one up and held it over and said take a whiff. I smelled it and my eyes crossed cause it was gasoline. He laughed again and I was starting to hate him. He acted like he was gonna drink it and then he screwed the cap back on and he pulled out two more flasks from inside his coat. Four of them. All filled up with gas.

This place is about to light up like hell itself, he said. So you might wanna get your bloomers on and if you got anything else you want now is the time to get it. I've been paid a pretty penny to get this done and then Frenchtown has seen the last of this handsome mug. Best damn job I ever had. Get to play with tits and fire at damn near the same time. He then got up and started getting dressed and I did the same thing.

So when we were both dressed I told him I didn't believe he was gonna do it. Didn't believe a damn word he said. Besides why would you do this anyway? He said he'd been paid to do it and when I asked who paid him he said I ain't gonna say his name. But he's all fucked up. Then he grunted and let out a big burp and said let me get this done so I can hit the trail. Besides I ain't nothing but the messenger. I figure the sinner is the one who pays to have it done. Not the one who does it.

He took the first flask and poured the gasoline all over the bed. And then he opened the others and poured it all over the curtains and around the floor and as far as it would go. Then he tossed me the matches and said I'm gonna get a head start, little lady. I'll throw in another twenty if you'll light the match. I said forty. He burped again and then pulled out a wad and dropped two twenties on the floor. I nodded at him and picked up the money. He was the sinner now if we were playing by his rules.

I watched him go out the door and I looked out of the window until I saw him gone down the street. Then I tied my boots up tight and threw some clothes in a bag. I took in a big whiff of the gasoline and then I struck the match and tossed it on the bed. I remember that the first flames were the same color as the sky back home when the day was done and I'd lay in the grass with my hands behind my head and stare at the pale blue. A blue that was almost something else. And I felt the heat and watched the flames stretch out and dance. For a moment I thought that it was beautiful. But then there came the horror of it and that was something different.

47

At dusk the saloon door opened and Kade ambled in like a lost bear. His eyes paunchy and pink and his hair flat and slick. Flakes of something yellow dotted his beard and his coat and trousers were wrinkled and he carried a sour smell. He swayed. Looked around. Whistled at the barmaid who ignored him. He belched and rubbed his eyes.

'Where's Judah?' he asked her.

'In the back.'

'He ain't dead yet is he?'

'Not as far as I know.'

Kade lumbered across the saloon floor and then his footsteps pounded down the hallway and he threw open the door. Nick was sitting and he rose quickly from his chair with the commotion of the entrance. Kade cut a look at Nick and then settled on Judah. The redstained chin and the sickly eyes.

'You don't have to say nothing,' Kade said. 'I know what you're thinking. You're thinking what the hell is that son of a bitch doing here. You're thinking I paid him what we agreed on and he got his ass on the train and he promised he wasn't never coming back. That was the deal and that was supposed to be that. I know what you're thinking. And I'd be thinking it too if I was sitting where you're sitting.'

Kade pulled off his coat and hung it on the back of a chair.

He took a crumpled cigar from his shirt pocket and picked up the box of matches next to the opium pipe. Nick watched him and knew he had seen him before. Kade struck two matches and sucked at the cigar until it burned and he tossed the matchbox on the desk.

'But the thing is money don't go as far as it used to. You're thinking I got a good payday. You're thinking for a fellow like me that was a damn good payday. But what you asked me to do was go away forever and you and me both know it takes a helluva lot to go away forever.'

Judah put his elbows on the chair arms and sat up straight. He put his hand inside the neck of his shirt and rubbed at his scarred skin.

'I feel like considering the nature of the job and the nature of your request that I disappear, I deserve more than what I got,' he said. 'And I was a little pressed at the time when you brought it up so I took less than I should have. Didn't have time to think. To figure out if I was getting a fair shake or not. But I've been gone a few weeks and I've come to the conclusion that I sold myself short. And you let me, Judah. You knew you were getting a bargain. Didn't you? That's the way I see it.'

Judah sniffed again. Gave a little cough and he took his handkerchief from his pocket and touched it to his mouth. He looked at Kade and then let his head fall back and he stared at the bluegray haze against the ceiling.

'I want more,' Kade said. 'Or else I'll sing.'

'You won't sing,' Nick said.

Kade sucked at his teeth and picked at his beard. Ignored Nick.

He cocked his head and then reached over and lifted the pistol from the desktop.

'I want double what I got,' Kade said and he shifted the pistol from hand to hand. 'I don't know who this character is in here with us but this is straight between me and you. And you don't want me singing.'

'Quit saying that,' Nick said.

'Hey!' Kade yelled and he pointed at Nick. 'I ain't talking to you and I'll squash your head up against that wall if you say another word to me.'

'You don't know,' Judah said. His voice low and slow. Kade turned to Judah again and slammed the pistol down on the desktop.

'Don't know what?'

'You don't know what that man has done. You don't know what he can do.'

'He don't know me neither so I guess that makes us even.'

Nick stepped away from the end of the desk and moved around the room, stopping close to the door and behind Kade who turned his head and followed him and told him to stand still and shut up or get out.

'Okay,' Judah said.

Kade sucked on the cigar. Turned back to Judah.

'What you mean?'

'Okay. I'll pay you. But then you go. There won't be no more.'

'Well. You might be about dead but you ain't dumb.'

Judah leaned forward in the chair. He opened the desk drawer and reached in. His fingers moved around the drawer and he touched a nickel and then two pennies. He gathered them between his thumb and middle finger and he pulled his hand from the drawer. He lifted the coins to his eyes as if to make absolute certain that he held what he thought he held. Seven cents. And then he stretched out his arm and he set the coins on the desk. He thumped the nickel across the desk toward Kade. And then one penny and then the other.

Kade scooped up the coins and threw them against the brick wall and said I'm not gonna take this shit. You son of a bitch. I will snap your brokendown ass in half and just as quickly as his rage began it was overthrown by a new rage as Nick jumped onto his back and locked his arm around his thick throat and he rode him to the floor, knocking the desk and chairs as the two men crashed onto the brick. Kade grabbed at Nick's head and slapped at his arm but it was tight and strong and cutting his air, his red face getting redder and spitting and gasping and Nick squeezed and Judah called for him to turn him loose. But Nick was not choking a loud and threatening and foulsmelling man. He squeezed and gritted his teeth and clasped his eyes shut and felt as though he was choking the flesh and bone of regret. Judah cried out for Nick to turn him loose and Kade struggled and weakened and Nick wanted to kill it all away and just as Kade was going slack and fading and becoming a part of the things Nick would always remember he released him.

Nick rolled off him. Scooted back from Kade as he wheezed and coughed and came back to life. Nick's hand began to shake and he grabbed it with his other and then they both shook together. Quick breaths darted from between his lips and he pushed himself back into the corner and watched as Kade wiped the slobber from his mouth. Got to his hands and knees. Trying to find his air and when he did he grabbed his coat from the fallen chair. Reached for the desk and rose to his feet. Judah held the pistol now and it was pointed at Kade but he ignored it and said I'm gonna go in yonder and eat and drink. And I ain't paying for it. Don't care what your smartass barmaid has to say. So I'm gonna go eat and then

I'm gonna drink until this hangover has found its way and let you think about this. And I'll be back. Might be tomorrow. Might be the day after. You better get it straight in that fucked up head of yours that I want more and I'm gonna get it. He reached down and picked up his cigar from the floor and he snatched the matchbox from the desktop. Then he turned to Nick and said as far as you're concerned if I see you anywhere but inside the walls of this room I will kill you.

48

KADE WALKED OUT THE DOOR. They listened to him enter the saloon. Heard him shout demands for food and drink to the barmaid. Heard her yell back at him and then heard a plate crash and the shuffling of feet.

Nick stood and moved from the corner. He set a chair upright and sat down and tucked his shaking hand under his leg. Judah sat down again behind the desk.

'So,' Nick said.

'So.'

'Will he do what he says he's going to do?'

'Probably. He'll hang us both without knowing it.'

'They might hang you anyway, Judah.'

'Yeah. They might.'

'You okay?'

'Yeah. You?'

Nick only looked down. Judah then slumped in the chair and said I was ready to go that day. He went in and started the fire. I stood outside and watched. I was going to come back and be done with myself right then. Leave it all to them to sort out. And that's when me and you bumped into each other on the sidewalk. And still, I just want to go. This will be your last act of war. And it will be a gentle one. He slid the pistol across the desk toward him and then Judah jerked and slapped at his forehead when a pain jetted through his back and through his pelvis. He situated himself and he sneezed a bloody sneeze into a bloody rag. His eyes welled and he clenched his jaw and drew in his shoulders at the rattle in his lungs. Nick came around the desk. Picking up the pistol and tucking it into the back of his pants. Then he put his hand on Judah's back and held it there. He waited for Judah to settle and then he helped him to his feet. He helped him up the stairs and into the apartment and into the bedroom. He gave him a glass of water and a clean towel for his mouth and nose and he sat in a chair next to the bed and waited for Judah to fall asleep.

When he believed Judah was out Nick turned off the lamp. Stood from the chair and moved toward the doorway and through the dark a fragile voice said I hope you are able to get away from whatever it is you are trying to get away from. I hope we both do. Only do this for me, Nick. Do this for me without guilt. Without judgment. Because there is none.

49

SUNDAY MORNING. COLETTE WALKED DOWN the middle of the street in the middle of the day with the late December breeze at her back and her shadow from the high sun wrestling around her feet. Under her arm she carried a drawstring sack filled with all she pulled from Judah's safe. Every stack of money, every document, every scrap of paper, every envelope, even a handful of French franc coins that had snuck into the corner. She had it all and she felt like she had it all and she wore the pride of her escapade wide on her face as if to announce to the eyes that fell upon her that I am in control again. I am winning and no son of a bitch in this town is going to hold me down.

She walked into her place and as the door opened she could already see what it could become. A new chandelier and flowery wallpaper and knock down that old skintup bar and build a new one and stain it with a chestnut stain and then let it shine slick with several coats of clear finish and give it a brass railing. Bistro tables and chairs in the corners of the room where the sunlight falls and a black piano against the wall and flowers in tall vases at each end of the bar and maybe on each step of the staircase. A phonograph and a high stack of records and wine and champagne glasses clear like spring water and many mirrors to reflect the drops of light that will shine from the chandelier once the sun has gone and night has fallen and the women smile and the illusion fully reveals itself.

And Judah will pay for it all she thought as she set the sack down on top of the only barstool.

She then walked along Franklin Street with a determined gait, tunneling through her emotions with the hardshell focus of defiance and spite. She picked out four women and asked them if they were tired of the cribs and wanted a real place to work. None hesitated at the offer. She told them to get their coats because we are going out to get you something new to wear. One of them reminded her the shops were closed on Sundays and Colette said we're going to see Old Lady Wilson and she's going to measure you and then she's going to make all of you a couple of new dresses. We ain't buying what's hanging on a mannequin. It is a new day. The corners of her mouth fought back a smile with her proclamation as the girls rushed to grab coats and hats and whatever else they owned. As they scurried Colette looked at herself in the reflection of a window and she thought she looked younger. Her eyes piercing. Her mouth set in rejuvenation. She took two long steps out into the middle of the street and she spun around with her arms wide and she sang a dancing tune and seemed to float as she slid and turned and as if performing underneath spotlights for a packed house of starstruck admirers. The four girls returned and caught her but she didn't stop and they laughed and pointed but Colette did not care and she danced until her song was over and they applauded. She bowed and then waved her arm and they crossed the street in a line like little ducks.

The four women followed her and when they came to Colette's place she told them to wait. She took the sack filled with everything Judah had and she went upstairs to her room and stuck it between the mattresses of her bed, leaving an anthill lump of revenge. Then she hurried back down with an air of buoyancy and the women marched toward the dress shop on Royal where Colette knew she would have to beat on the door and then have to listen to Old Lady Wilson complain that it was Sunday but she didn't care.

After each woman had been measured and fabrics and cuts had been chosen and stockings and shoes and garters had been ordered to go along with the new dresses, Colette and the four women sat at an outside café and shivered as they shared two bottles of wine. By the time the second bottle was gone, the sun had fallen and a pink sky fell across the Gulf which soon transformed into a purple haze that eased into the Frenchtown streets. The women left and Colette sat alone and she smoked a cigarette and she felt herself falling. Falling forward. The only direction to fall, she thought. She sat with her legs crossed and the waiter asked her several times if she wanted to come inside where it was warm and each time she only shook her head lazily and then moved the cigarette to her lips. It was the transforming hour but she knew that she had already been transformed. That her transformation had come in the bright light of day. That she did not need shadows or the sultry gimmicks of night or sleight of hand. Judah's saloon closed on Sunday and all she needed was the key to the front door and the combination to the safe and she was both surprised and unsurprised to discover that both still worked. She loved that she had left the floorsafe open and the desk pushed to the side and she loved that Judah would know that she had done it and she loved that he couldn't do a damn thing about it. In the same way that he had burned down her house and left her helpless, she returned the gesture. A satisfaction burned inside her that shielded the winter cold. She thought of ordering another bottle of wine but it was time to see what all was in the sack.

She left money on the table and she walked toward her place. I'll need a new name, she thought. A good one. Something to remember. Something that makes you want to be there or if you don't want to be there you at least want to walk by and look in the windows. The kind of name that makes you want to find out. And I'll need to think about the girls. Two of them will have to go because they don't look like I need them to look but I won't worry with that until later. Her thoughts were clear and direct and she felt the twilight closing around her and she promised herself she would not give in. The things that chased her always on the hunt during the shifting hour and she walked with high knees and hard steps as if preparing to lower her head and crash through an emotional wall.

Her heel stuck between the cobblestones and she stumbled but caught herself. Someone inside a saloon cackled and whistled and she turned to look and a cowardly head ducked down. Colette straightened herself and reached behind her head. She pulled out hairpins and bent over and shook her head and when she raised it her hair fell in thick waves. She ran her gloved hands through it and smiled and the gloam seemed to smile back in its own undefined way.

She arrived at her place. She had told the women to go and do something tonight and the room echoed with her footsteps as she walked across the hardwood and to the bar. Underneath the bar was a whiskey bottle and half a dozen glasses. She took the bottle by the neck and took a glass and then she went upstairs. At the top of the stairs she stopped and listened and heard nothing and she knew she was alone.

In her room she poured the whiskey and set the glass and bottle on her bedside table. Turned on the lamp. She took off her coat and gloves. Untied her tallheeled boots and kicked them off and she rubbed at her stocking feet. She lifted the top mattress and removed the sack and tossed it on the bed, anxious to count the booty. Sat down on the bed and crossed her legs and she loosened the drawstring and turned the sack upside down and shook.

The sack was filled with exactly what she had expected. She separated the stacks of cash. Not a goldmine but plenty for what she needed. There was the deed to the saloon and the building. Business documents and bank documents. These she would stick into an envelope and return and she set them all aside. She grinned as she fanned the money. Tiny flitters of revenge. She stacked the money neatly at the foot of the bed and then she found things she hadn't expected.

Judah's two medals and their ribbons lay intertwined. Colette separated them, stretched out the ribbons, and pressed them with her palm. She trailed her fingers along the rainbow ribbon of the Victory Medal, touched the bronze circle and then felt the raised winged victory holding her shield and sword at the ready. She turned the medal over and read the words curved across the top – The Great War for Civilization. Then she moved her fingers to the purple ribbon of the Purple Heart. A deep purple with the thin white outline as if necessary to keep the rich color from leaking away. She picked up the heartshaped medal. Felt the smooth gold border. In its center the profile of a stoic George Washington.

She lay the Purple Heart next to the Victory Medal and stood from the bed. In the corner of her room was a short bookshelf and from the lower shelf she removed a coffee can.

She opened the can and took out a fold of letters, separated one from the others, and then returned to the bed. She held the letter that had been delivered to her when they believed he was dead, its edges worn and random words blotted out. She read it twice and then dropped it next to the medals.

There was one more envelope from the sack and she opened it. Several photographs fell out and lying face up was her own black-and-white image. A photograph of her in her wedding dress, standing in front of a blooming magnolia tree at the side of the Episcopal church. A white magnolia blossom hung at the tip of a branch right next to her smiling face. She held a bouquet of wildflowers that Judah had picked earlier in the day from random Frenchtown gardens, a flowerpicking thief creeping through the earliest morning light collecting something true and natural and symbolic for her to hold. Though the photograph was in shades of black and gray in her mind the colors shined with a spectrum's brilliance.

She set the photograph down and picked up two others. Both pictures of Judah's mother and father. One of them standing outside the saloon and an eight-year-old boy standing with them. The other photo of them sitting at the bar with a towel thrown over his father's shoulder and a tea cup held daintily in his mother's fingertips. Colette picked up her wedding picture and tried to recognize the woman who looked so happy. So unaware of what love could turn into when it was challenged and failed and decided to become something else that burned and sought deliverance. She turned the photograph in her hands and looked at herself from different angles. Tried to find a change in her expression with the shift of light. Something that suggested she had never existed with such bliss. And that's when she noticed it. In the church window to her left she saw his reflection. He was standing to the side and watching her as she posed. But he wasn't watching. He was admiring. Happily devastated. In Judah's reflection she realized there was no way that she could hold the picture to give any other interpretation than happiness.

She raised her eyes from the photograph and looked at the money. Looked at the documents. Looked at the images of his mother and father who she had loved. Her arrogance flaked away and she tossed the photograph of herself into the air and it twisted and fell facedown and she noticed the handwriting on the back. Again she picked it up and held it close and she noticed Judah's script. Written in pencil in a shaky hand.

I dont want to be in this world anymore.

Below the words was a brown smear and she knew that it was his wiped blood. She stuck the tip of her finger into her mouth and licked it and then she tried to wipe it away. But it had been there too long.

The room had grown dark. The transforming hour had come and gone. She stood from the bed and walked to the window and she lacked the courage to admit to the night sky that it still had much to teach her. She looked up hoping for a moon or a star to give a sense of wonder but from where she stood there was nothing to see. Only the vast and infinite dark. Hours earlier she had been strong and severe. But she couldn't survive the twilight.

She circled the room while shaking her head and then she picked up the bottle and drank. She thought of taking it all back. Thought of going to him. Thought of letting go. She looked over her shoulder at the money. The photograph was stuck in her hand and she read his words again. *I dont want to be in this world anymore.* She crossed her thumb over them and stared at the brown streak and imagined the bright red drop of blood as it fell. She set the photograph facedown on her pillow, unwilling to exchange looks with the eyes of the past.

She drank again and put the bottle on the nightstand. Then she reached to turn off the lamp but as her fingers touched the knob the stillness of the night was shattered by a boisterous bawl from downstairs. A booming cry that called her name and demanded her to show herself.

50

NICK WALKED THROUGH STREETS IN the falling night. He had gone into the saloon in the late afternoon to find him and Judah something to eat and he had noticed the hallway door open. In the backroom he discovered the desk pushed to the side and the safe open and empty and he knew it could only have been Kade. He went to the apartment to tell Judah but Judah was smoking and nodding and close to sleep so he kept it to himself. Waited until Judah was steady and resting and then he crossed the hall and took the pistol from the dresser drawer and set out to find Kade.

One last act of war. The only thought in his mind.

The cathedral chimes sounded, playing a hymn he recognized from years of sitting with his mother and father at the end of the pew where he had grown from a toddler into a young man and as the chimes played the song he couldn't name but could recognize he saw his mother and father sitting there right now. In the same spot on the same side of the aisle. And they had been there every Sunday for the last ten years as he went off to New Haven and then off to France and experienced a new kind of baptism.

He pulled his hat down low and his jittery eyes danced beneath the brim as he crisscrossed Frenchtown looking for Kade and he had remembered what he recognized him from. The day of the fire. Coming down the stairs of the brothel and standing at the bar and saying it's a shame before he walked past Nick and slapped his shoulder and walked out into the street.

The night stretched out and he finally sat down on a curb. In the house behind him Nick heard the voices of children playing. Shrieking and laughing and shouting to one another. Across the street an old woman with a blanket wrapped around her leaned in the doorway smoking a pipe. So still that but for the puff of smoke she might have passed as a withered mannequin. The only light came from a corner café and a saxophone played a bouncy tune and standing at the open door of the café was a thick man with a long and bushy beard. He slapped his leg with a newspaper in rhythm with the saxophone and he drank beer from a stein and when the music stopped he hollered for the son of a bitch to crank it up again.

Nick stood from the curb. Kade barked again at the saxophone player and then turned up the stein and chugged. A voice from inside the café told him to go to hell and he lowered the stein and belched. Nick tugged the hat down once more and walked past him unrecognized, wanting to make sure it was him.

Kade finished the beer and set the stein on the café steps. Then he called out, wanted to know if they had any cigars in there. Not shitty cigars but real cigars. The same voice called out again for him to go to hell but then a hand extended from the café door, holding a cigar. Kade reached into his pocket and stuck a coin in the hand and took the cigar from it. Then he told them saxophones were for sissies anyhow and besides I got more important shit to do than wait around for you to play something else. He tucked the newspaper under his arm and pulled a box of matches from his coat pocket and lit the cigar. He walked and smoked and Nick followed, creeping closer to him with each passing block. But then Nick fell back into the shadows again as he recognized the street and the building and Kade had led them to Colette.

51

J UDAH LAY ON THE FLOOR with his head resting next to the
open safe. Vacant eyes stared at the muted lamplit ceiling
as the opium haze covered the room. Blood was smeared
across his mouth and splattered into the safe as he couldn't
keep it from coming out of him now. It was there when he
smoked and when he didn't smoke and when he woke from
sleep and it was there when he ate and it was there when he
went to the bathroom or tried to walk into the saloon or
down the block. All he could do was smoke and keep himself
deadened to the pain in his lungs and legs and back and he
had seen the open and empty safe and that was that.

He had made it into the backroom and then collapsed
to his knees next to the open square in the floor. The drug
worked on him and he fell asleep and an hour later when he
woke the pain was there again. Inside and out. He got to his
knees and crawled to the desk and heated a few seeds and he
inhaled deeply and in resignation. He wiped his nose and face
and then lay back down and turned on his side, his knees and
arms tucked in fear of being alone.

52

KADE SMOKED THE CIGAR AND dropped the newspaper onto the scarred bartop. He called out again when his first cry wasn't answered and said I know damn well somebody is in here. Nobody leaves the front door of a whorehouse unlocked. He then heard movement upstairs.

'Colette. Somebody. Come on down here,' he said. 'I'm keeping my pants on. Got something better to talk about. Now come on.'

He strode behind the bar and took a bottle of gin and a glass and he poured and drank. Colette appeared at the bottom of the staircase and he said you ain't as easy to find as you used to be.

'Who are you?' she said though she recognized him. He had the kind of trailworn face and the brusque sound of intrusion that made him difficult to forget.

'You should know. Been in and out of your old place a few times.'

'So has everybody else.'

He drank again and smacked his lips.

'I always heard you was some kind of badass,' he said. 'But you don't scare me at all.'

She crossed her arms. Moved over to the bar and poured a short glass of whiskey and said you got until I'm to the bottom of this glass to tell me what you want.

He looked her up and down. Sucked on the cigar.

'Last time I was at your place there was a little fire. And that sweet little number that I went upstairs with did all the work. I told her I'd give her another twenty to pour the gasoline out of the flasks. Another twenty on top of that to drop the match. And she played right along. And I'm guessing you know who sent me.'

'You're not capable of surprising me.'

'Good. Cause I ain't here to surprise.'

'Then what are you here for?'

'I'm here cause I can put it to Judah.'

'Then put it to Judah. God knows if you walk in and give up Judah you're giving up yourself.'

'Not exactly.'

'Bullshit.'

'It's that whore's word on mine. I can say she did it. She can say I did it. But good luck finding her and getting her to talk.'

Colette turned up the whiskey and finished it. She then set the glass on the bar and she walked over to the front door and opened it. The cold night air drifted in and pushed the cigar smoke around the room.

'You think you're smart but you're really only boring,' she said.

'Naw. I ain't boring. And maybe I ain't smart. But I'll goddamn well walk in the police station and spill it. And they'll lock away Judah. I'll do all that unless somebody gives me a reason not to.'

'I don't give a damn about Judah or what happens to him.'

'You hate him. I ain't questioning that. But I'm guessing you don't want him to die locked up. And that's what he'd do. So I ain't even asking for much. I figure a few hundred and some freebies now and then.'

Colette stood next to the open door. A young man without a coat or a hat paused. Rubbed his arms and looked inside and she told him to go on. The chimes of the cathedral resonated and one man screamed at another at the end of the street. She looked at Kade and he was smoking the cigar again and waiting for her to say what he wanted her to say.

Colette closed the door. She took the long way around the room. Walking casually with her eyes on him. She twisted her hands and fingers as she made her way toward him and she stopped when she reached the end of the bar.

'Don't you get no ideas,' he said.

She reached underneath the bartop and pulled out a baseball bat. He raised the cigar to his mouth just as she swung and he leaned back in time to save his jaw but she caught his hand and sent the cigar flying, red sparks scattering across the floor. He hustled to the door and scatted out as Colette followed him onto the sidewalk and halfway down the block. She then let him walk off into the night and before she went back inside he called out. You better think about it. You got one more chance. I'm gonna wait about two more days for you to decide where you want to bury him and then he's done.

53

N ICK HAD STOOD ACROSS THE street and watched Kade and
Colette talking in Colette's place. He held his hand on
the pistol in his coat pocket and he saw her pull the bat from
beneath the bartop. Swinging and missing but sending the
cigar like a meteor across the room. When the door opened
and they came out Nick snuck around the corner and hid in
the shadows and listened to Kade threaten her once more
as he disappeared into the night. He hurried along the street
to catch him. To stay close. And in his haste he didn't notice
when the lights from Colette's place went out and Colette
came out of the door.

Kade drank and cussed and sat at the round table with the
other men who drank and cussed. Nick sat on the front stoop
of a bakery. Watching from across the street and smoking a
cigarette he had borrowed from a passing street girl who had
only moments before nabbed the cigarettes and pocket watch
from the pants of a drunk babyfaced tourist.

The December moon sat high in the Southern sky. Horses
clopped and midnight barges called their song across the
thick waters of the great slow river. The great release of steam
engines sounded across the darkness with the vast exhausts
of trade as Kade drank and grabbed at whatever pair of legs
walked past the table. The moon then disappeared and a

dense fog rolled into Frenchtown and the street lamps gave a sultry light.

The card table erupted and the players surrounding it were at each other in a whirlwind of fists and elbows and throats were grabbed and heads were butted and the barmaid and saloon girls stood back and watched and some laughed while the men crashed across the table and across the chairs. The table tumbled and money and chips scattered and the saloon girls scooped up both and shoved them into their brassieres and garters with nimble movement. Kade gave a great roar as hands buried into his beard and pulled and the pack rolled across the floor like a violent dust cloud. Fists and forearms found noses and jaws and there was no way to make out who was winning and who was losing and eventually the drunken mob exhausted itself and the men fell apart as if giant invisible arms had been holding them packed together and then let them go.

The barmaids and saloon girls disappeared through a swinging door in the back of the saloon. Down the stairs came a grizzled and gray man who wore a thin robe that was tied at the waist with a strand of rope. He surveyed the scene and when the dogtired and dogdrunk group of gamblers saw him they rose and stood at attention as if he were a scolding father. The man leaned over the banister and spit into a spittoon and then he began to point and give direction. The men staggered in beaten and drunken steps to do what he commanded. They picked up the overturned chairs and table. Gathered the scattered cards and chips and money and made neat piles of each in the table center. Picked up the spilled glasses and bottles and one of the men took a handful of rags from behind the bar and they wiped the wasted liquor from the floor. Then they used the same towels to wipe the blood and snot and saliva from their faces.

Nick tossed his cigarette and followed the trail of sparks with his eyes and that's when he noticed others across the street. Standing close against a butcher shop window. He could only make out murky figures through the fog but knew there were at least three of them as that's how many red cigarette tips he counted moving in the dark.

He turned his attention back to the saloon. The man in the robe shook his finger and made several remarks with a serious brow and then he called out and one of the women returned and joined him on the stairs. The men nodded in apology and agreement. Gathered their coats and hats. Shuffled in a broken line toward the saloon door and meandered off quietly.

Kade was the last to leave.

Nick crossed the street. Following and losing him in the fog but finding him again as he stopped once to bend over and vomit and another time to piss. He walked in the middle of the street and swayed from one side to the next and after he had followed him for several blocks he realized Kade had nowhere to go or was too drunk to find it. He talked to himself in slurred speech and then he finally sat down on a curb. Leaned against a lamppost and almost instantly his head knocked against it.

Nick stepped out of the street and onto the sidewalk to approach him from behind. And then he thought he heard footsteps and he spun around. Held his breath and peered through the fog but there was nothing but the dripping of water from a gutter or street faucet. He pulled out the pistol but was seized by the night and the eyes he felt upon him. Real or imagined. Kade grunted and belched and adjusted himself against the lamppost. Tried to get back to his feet and now he was kneeling. On both knees. Head bowed. And it was then that Nick heard him chanting or maybe praying. He raised the pistol and stepped behind the drunkard and his hand would not stop shaking so he switched the pistol to his left.

A final act of war, he thought. And he was taken by vengeance and anger and thirst for violence not induced by the colors of flags but by the simple distaste for another human being and the pistol only inches from Kade's head and this was not the way that he had killed before. This was something else and he knew if he pulled the trigger then he would become part of all he had seen and hated and survived and lost. His right hand shook and his left hand pointed the pistol and his body not in the dirt littered with the dead but on the sidewalk of a street where people lived and children walked with mothers and at least some men tried as hard as they could. He dropped the pistol and the clatter caused Kade to break from his stupor and he turned and swung and knocked Nick to the ground with a backhand fist.

And it was then that they rushed from the shadows and tackled Kade to the pavement. Three men. Two of them pinned Kade and despite his hollering and flailing they managed to get his hands roped behind his back and a gag crammed into his mouth. The other man pulled the drawstring sack that had been filled with Judah's belongings from his back pocket. He forced the empty sack over Kade's head and then pulled it tight around his neck and beard. The man then looked away and whistled. And then Colette appeared from the fog like some villainous ghost. She stopped at Kade. Grabbed his nose through the sack and twisted until he gave a muffled wail. And then she bent down to Nick and said don't just sit there. Get up and go. You don't see any of this.

54

TWO OF THE MEN HELD Kade's arms as they walked and punched the side of his head when he made a sound. The other man had found the pistol and held it next to Kade's ear and promised he would fill it up if he so much as spoke the word of God. Colette walked in front and led them through the clouded streets and she never spoke. Only pointed when it was time to make a turn. She held a Derringer in one hand and a cigarette in the other.

They arrived at the alley that John LaFell had dragged her into. It reeked of the dead and was littered with wooden crates and bags of garbage. A single light hung from the back corner of the alley and its glow filtered softly into the fog. Kade grunted and was again punched in the ear and then he began to whimper like a dog and he was punched again. Colette stepped over and around the debris and moved to a door deep in the alley. She opened it and motioned for the others to follow.

They moved across the dark threshold of the abandoned building. At the end of the hallway Colette opened the door to the room where she had been a prisoner. She lit a candle and motioned to the men holding Kade to bring him inside.

She pointed to the floor beside the bed and they sat him down in the same spot where she had been bound and gagged and threatened. Wondering if she would die and how bad it might be. The same spot where she had listened to John LaFell crying. The same spot where she had soiled herself because he didn't give her any options. And as the men sat Kade down and then pulled more rope from their pockets and tied his feet together she smelled John LaFell. His foul and liquorstained breath and his must of the street and these would be the smells that she could not help but associate with heartbreak. She had thought her abductor was the worst of our kind but then learned that he had only been a desolate father with no way to understand the suffering that the world had cast upon him. She closed her eyes and breathed in the odor of despair and asked him for forgiveness for what they had done to his child though she knew there was no such thing.

She opened her eyes. The men settled Kade and left the room, closing the door behind them. Colette dropped her cigarette on the floor and stepped on it. She knelt beside Kade and listened and he was fighting to conceal his sobbing and this was what she wanted. To hear him on the other side. To understand that he was not what he believed himself to be.

She placed the Derringer on the floor. Untied the string and lifted the knapsack over his head. His eyes were swollen and his cheeks red and Colette lifted the candle from the floor and waved it back and forth across his face. His eyes followed the light and then she held the candle still and they stared at one another. Colette picked up the Derringer and pushed it into the obnoxious beard of the obnoxious man until she felt it pressed against bone. And then she leaned close and put her lips to his ear and whispered. You don't fuck with me and you damn sure don't fuck with Judah. And you will sit here in this dark silence for as long as it takes me to decide when you will die.

55

NICK FOUND JUDAH STILL OUT on the floor next to the open and emptied safe. Winded and slobbering in a halfsleep. He looked down into the safe and then at the opium pipe and the seeds scattered on the floor. He touched Judah's shoulder and gently shook and tried to wake him but Judah only trembled.

He slid one arm under Judah's knees and the other behind his neck and lifted him. He carried him into the saloon and then up the stairs to the apartment and Nick knew that if he stayed this routine would play out over and over again until Judah found someone to help him end it. Nick opened Judah's door and carried him into the bedroom and laid him down on the bed. He took a chair from the sitting room and set it next to the bedroom window and sat down. The fog hung over the street and he wondered how long until daybreak.

Nick saw himself in a chair by a window on the third floor of a repossessed château. One leg crossed over the other. His arms crossed at the wrists and resting on his knee. He leaned forward. The château stood in the middle of a mostly remaining village and it had become a stop for soldiers going back and forth to the front. It had been rocked by shellfire in earlier days but stood proud though missing chunks of pillars and stone. Massive rooms with marble floors. Fireplaces tall enough for a man to stand in. A small theater with carvings on the ceilings. Across the château grounds a spring fed into a concrete pool with steps that led down into the clean and cold water and a small chapel stood with a hole blown in its roof along the backside of the grounds.

Across the lawns where elite families once spread blankets and enjoyed sunset dinners and where young girls once picked flowers and where babies had crawled there now stood a makeshift prison camp. A wire fence had been strung in a haggard rectangle and connected by ten-foot-high fenceposts. Barbed wire ran two laps around the top of the fence. Within the captives milled about without head cover or shelter and one corner of the camp had become the place for piss and shit and the foul odor hung in the air and moved on the breeze as if the putrid smell existed solely as a reminder. Some of the captives were without shirts and others without boots but they all shared the drawn and yellow faces that come with disease and hunger.

The first floor of the château was where the Americans cooked and ate. Officers kept to one end and the enlisted men kept to the other. The second floor housed the infirmary. The nurses and doctors stayed busy with those who had a chance to recover and three brothers from the village stayed busy with those who did not and they carried out bodies all hours of the day until a lieutenant asked them to only come at night.

The third floor was where the men slept and most stayed outside during the day. Smoking and dozing in the sun and sitting with their feet in the spring. But on this day bulking gray clouds hung low and a wind enhanced the odor so Nick sat inside and watched. The window looked out toward the prisoners.

The grass that had once been there was worn to mud and the prisoners moved about feebly. Few gathered in groups.

Most of them keeping to themselves. Nick noticed two soldiers moving close to the fence. Pointing and then talking and then pointing again. The prisoners noticed the soldiers and they began to drift toward them.

Then one of the soldiers stepped to the fence. Put his back to it and took two steps. He held a stick and he drew a line across the ground. The other soldier then opened his coat and pulled out four baguettes. He handed two to his partner and they tore them in half and then set them on the ground along the line. A hand's width apart.

They pointed again. One of the soldiers held a piece of paper and a pencil and he jotted down a few notes. And then the soldiers stepped closer to the fence and began talking to the prisoners and directing them toward the bread on the ground. While one explained the other teased the prisoners with a nub of bread, holding it just out of reach and then pretending to throw it over their heads. They turned and searched and some chased like fooled dogs and the soldiers bent over laughing. Again they pointed at the bread on the ground and then they stood back and watched.

The prisoners leered at the two soldiers. Their stomachs fighting between pride and hunger. And hunger finally won as a shirtless prisoner dropped to his knees and slid his rail thin arm through a square in the fence and he reached out for the bread, his bony fingers desperate and his face pressed against the fence. No chance to reach it. The others then gave in and did the same and the soldiers kept track of their bets. They had bet on the tall ones and bet on the ones who looked the hungriest though the tallest were easier to pick out. The prisoners fought and scrambled over one another. Getting low on the ground and trying to cut down the space between the fence and the bread. Shoving and slapping and biting and pulling at each other in an effort to reach the furthest. Wanting to survive. One piece of bread was reached and as the prisoner pulled it back he was molested and it was taken from him. Another piece of bread was reached and the winner was dragged backward by his feet before he could get the bread through the fence wire and half a dozen others scrambled for the baguette dropped at the edge of the fence.

The ruckus drew the attention of the other soldiers. Some wandered over and watched and then meandered away. Others cheered. Others pulled out whatever money they had and got into the game. Behind the fence, a great brawl of starvation.

Nick looked down at Judah. He didn't understand why this was what he thought of now and he realized that the rest of his life would be filled with such images. He hated the men who had set the bread on the ground and he hated the others who had joined in and he hated that he had sat in the chair and watched instead of going out and telling them all that they were the worst of men. That they deserved to be shot the moment they returned to the front. He had sat there and watched and he didn't know if that made him worse or better. He began to talk to the sleeping Judah and he told him of the chateau and of the prisoners who were so hungry and thin that their spines showed and how they clawed at one another over one bite of bread and that there would always be an enemy and it only took an instant for the enemy to become someone you didn't expect. He told him then about Paris and how warm it was sleeping next to her on top of the costumes and he told him of his father's store and how a minute there seemed to be longer than a minute anywhere else. He told him how he had searched the city for her and he told him about the wide pathways and carousels in Parc Monceau and about

296

the children chasing pigeons and about having something and then losing it but he admitted that Judah knew plenty about that. He told him about the way his mother sang in the kitchen when she made dinner and he told him about the tree outside his window that he had climbed onto its broad limb on many nights but he never had the nerve to climb down and explore further. He talked to Judah the rest of the night as Judah grunted and bled and moaned and he did not hold back any thought and it was as if a great wind was blowing through him and pushing him in another direction.

56

COLETTE POURED THE THREE MEN and herself whiskey shots and she told them what they already understood. Your mouths stay shut. This never happened. She then poured them another shot. Took some cash from her coat pocket and paid them. Said she would need them again and they all drank and nodded. And then she asked them to leave.

She removed her coat and laid it across the bar. Reached inside and pulled out the drawstring sack. The fog remained heavy but the night had begun to fade, the earliest light only moments away and in that hazy world of changing color she reminded herself of the conclusion she had come to the instant that Kade had made his threat. It was as if his loudmouth proclamations were keys to her own dungeon cell. Keys that she had been grasping for between rusted irons and her fingertips only able to skim the perfectly cut metal that would allow her to live and breathe and return to this world. His threats had slid into the keyhole and released her from her captivity and she had stepped out with only one thought in mind.

This life will be no more.

She lit and smoked a cigarette. Walked over to the cases of whiskey. Turned and gazed around the room and it felt strange to her. As if she was a visitor taking a tour of another life. She walked over to the bar and took the empty sack and walked upstairs.

As soon as she reached her room she fell face first into the pillow and lay across the money and medals and letters and photographs and cried with a severity with which she had never cried. A fierce sobbing decorated with indecipherable outbursts, cries of hurt and anger and emptiness that formed no concrete words but instead reached out to all that was trapped inside her with vague and gripping embraces. She awakened the sleeping house and one of the women knocked on the door and asked if she was all right and Colette screamed for her to go away. For all of them to go away and never come back. The woman moved away from the door but when Colette did not hear the rest of them she opened her door and screamed into the hallway for them all to get the hell out of here right now and never set foot in this place again. Her voice rang with such ferocity that the women darted out of their rooms and down the stairs and into the cold dawn still wearing their sleeping clothes with their arms filled with whatever they could carry, driven by the fear of being attacked by a lunatic.

When the house was empty she went from room to room. Ripping sheets from beds and tearing at them and kicking over nightstands and busting mirrors. She slammed lamps against the wall and threw books and brushes and shoes and whatever else she could lift and throw. She broke a chair leg free and then walked into the hallway and beat at both walls as she stomped along yelling and swinging and when she came to the staircase she kicked the railing over and over until it cracked and then she kicked it some more until it snapped and fell. She stood at the staircase panting and sweating and searching for something else to destroy. She stood with a tight grip on the chair leg and her heart pounding and her cheek bleeding where a flying shard of wood had sliced her face and then the thought entered her mind with a thunderous jolt.

Burn it.

She rushed from room to room and gathered sheets and furniture and pillows and piled it all in the hallway. She then ran down the stairs and took the matches and knapsack from the bar. She hustled back upstairs as if being chased and then she shredded the pages of a book and spread them across the pile in the hallway. She struck three matches together and dropped them.

The fire wavered but then caught and smoke began to fill the hallway. Colette hurried into her room and she sat on the edge of the bed and shoved everything into the knapsack. All that belonged to him and all that belonged to her and the simple joining of the relics of their lives into the same knapsack raised in her the hope of reconciliation. The smoke curled around her doorway and once she had it all gathered in the sack she covered her mouth and made for the stairs, the fire cracking and growing behind her. When she reached the bottom floor she grabbed her coat and made sure the pistol remained in the pocket. She then slung the knapsack over her shoulder and walked out of the building and left the door open behind her. The streets had awakened with the break of day as horsedrawn wagons moved goods toward the market and the workers slouched to work and cargo ships blared their horns from the wharf as if to announce that this day of transformation was here.

57

HE WAS STILL TALKING TO Judah at first light when he heard the sirens. He stood in the window and looked out but then his attention turned when the apartment door opened.

Colette stood in the doorway. And then she stepped inside and closed the door behind her. She looked into the bedroom and saw Judah. Nick moved from the window. She raised her eyes to him and looked back and forth between Nick and Judah but did not speak.

She set the drawstring sack on the floor. She shrugged out of her coat and then without looking she reached behind her and hung it on a coatrack on the back of the apartment door. She took one more look at Nick and then she picked up the sack and stepped into the sitting room. Nick moved to the bedroom door and watched her move around the room, touching her fingertips to the smooth wood of chairs and tables. Standing in front of photographs and staring at the faces staring back at her. She moved over to the shelves and let her eyes fall across each book or flower vase as if to catalogue it in her mind. She took it all in. Each step in the room. Each corner.

Each piece of furniture. Each pair of eyes captured in black and white.

She then stood at the table in the center of the rug and she opened the sack. She emptied the contents onto the table. The stacks of cash and documents. The medals and the photographs and the letter that pronounced Judah dead. She lifted the Purple Heart by the ribbon and looked around the room. Settled on the bookshelves. She took a handful of books and turned them on their sides. Lifted the top two books and slid the ribbon between and the medal hung. She did the same thing with the Victory Medal and the two medals hung and looked across the room like two offset eyes of valor.

She then picked up the photograph of Judah's parents in front of the saloon and the wedding photograph and set them aside. She lifted two frames from the wall and removed the pictures inside. She inserted the photograph of Judah's parents in one frame and returned it to the wall. Then she held the wedding photograph. Looked at the words written on the back. *I dont want to be in this world anymore.* Then she placed their picture in the frame and hung it next to Judah's parents.

The next piece of their life that she took from the table was the letter that had been handed to her by the representative of the United States Armed Forces. She crossed the room and took a box of matches from the coat hanging on the back of the door. She struck a match and held the letter out in front of her and held the flame to the paper's edge. It lit and the flame danced upward, black frills of smoke reaching through her fingers. She then carried it to the bathroom and dropped it into the sink and watched it until it was no more.

She returned from the bathroom and looked at Nick. Outside the sirens wailed across the morning and hurried to the fire that Colette had created.

'Tell Judah I couldn't do it,' he said.

'Do what?'

'Any of it. Tell him I am not the answer he's looking for. You are.'

Colette sat down. The adrenaline draining from her and she let out a heavy sigh. Nick took his coat and hat from a rack in the corner.

'Where are you going?' she asked.

He moved to the apartment door and opened it.

'What did you do with him?' he asked. Meaning Kade.

'I shut him up until we decide if it is better if he lives or dies.'

'We?'

'Yes. We.'

Nick moved into the doorway and she asked again. Where are you going? He did not answer and he closed the door behind him and later when she crossed the hallway and knocked on his door there was no response. When she went inside the apartment and called out there was no answer. The bed was made and there was nothing in the closet or the dresser drawers. In the small kitchen a knife and fork and spoon lay in a row next to the sink and the handful of plates and cups were on the shelf. An empty and wiped ashtray sat in the windowsill and the floors had been swept. It was quiet and clean and it was as if no one had been there at all.

IV

VI

58

H E HOLED UP IN A small hotel room two blocks from Union Station in Chicago and waited for Christmas to pass by, not wanting to make that day any more than it had to be. The buildings and sidewalks were dressed in bows and wreaths and a steady snow gave the sense of purity to the concrete and glass and steel. In the day he milled around Union Station and though he had been through the station many times, for the first time he stopped to admire the architecture. The arches and columns. The detailed ceilings and draft of natural light.

The crowd weaved through the station as so many hurried for home. He believed that he might recognize a familiar face through the sea of travelers but he only noticed reflections of those he knew. Names popped into his head and he had conversations with each name, safe conversations where he was the only one allowed to make inquiries about what has happened in your life. In between these conversations Nick sipped coffee and stayed out of the way and admired those who did not seem to flinch at the frantic nature of travel.

At night he walked through the snowcovered park and touched the tips of icicles hanging from tree limbs. Snowmen stood at random and some had eyes and noses and arms and had been created by careful hands while others stood as lumpy suggestions. Footprints of children crisscrossed and birds stuck their beaks into the frozen ground. As he left the park he walked along the water where the wind howled but he faced it and felt a strange solace in its bite.

He drank coffee at a diner down the street from his hotel. He read the newspapers and the word *Prohibition* littered the headlines and filled the articles and editorials. Only weeks before the crackdown on alcohol became official and despite the outcry and the predicted consequences of such legislation the politicians and lawmakers stood firm and ignored the possibility of extraordinary change that all others seemed to see so clearly. In the diner on Christmas Eve he sat with only the cook and a trio of hardluck regulars. He sat in a booth and they sat at the counter and he listened to them declare that this country is about to be something else and not in a good way. Any fool can see that. As if it hasn't changed enough already. Who the hell thinks it's a good idea to tell a whole country who just got done fighting their ass off in another land that you can't sit down and have a damn drink? Politicians, that's who. Don't think they ain't about to get rich. Along with a whole bunch of other people who got no business being that way.

Each day he walked the downtown Chicago streets and walked along the water and then he sat in his room and watched it snow. On Christmas Day the city fell silent and all was closed and he took his walk without the trouble of stepping around or between anyone else. He meandered through the heavy flakes, a solitary figure with only his eyes showing between a low hat and a scarf wrapped above his nose. At the park he snapped a frozen branch from a tree and he moved across the clean blanket and trailed the stick behind him as if making a line that would send him back to where he started in case he was lost. Later in the evening the diner lights shined and Nick ate a Christmas dinner of meatloaf and potatoes as he read yesterday's newspaper and listened to the cook sing Silent Night in an unexpected sweet tenor.

The day after Christmas he folded his clothes into his bag. He walked to Union Station and bought a ticket for home. He stood at the train car and watched others board and he stood next to the porter as he gave the final call. When Nick didn't move the porter called again and then he asked to see Nick's ticket. Nick showed it to him and the man said it's now or never and he hopped up the steps and Nick stepped in just as the door closed behind him.

59

THE FALLEN LEAVES COVERED THE ground in bunches and woolly bushes spread their shoots and vines reached out from untamed flowerbeds and stretched across the windows of the cottage. Sprigs of green grass had begun to protrude from beneath the layers of leaves and buds hung on the tips of tree limbs and promised new leaves and blossoms. It was spring and the night air chilled but offered something refreshing to Nick as he strolled across the sideyard and stared out into the waning night sky.

He had moved into the cottage earlier in the day. It was furnished with humble, dusty furniture and healthy cobwebs gathered in the corners of the ceilings and between chair legs though he had spent the day wiping windowsills and swatting webs with a broom. He only had a trunk to unpack and he situated his clothes in the dresser and closet of the small bedroom and then he had come outside to find a dog sitting on the front porch. A brown, panting thing with a weathered tail and a dry tongue. He took a pot from the pantry and gave the dog fresh water and then later shared a ham sandwich that the landlady had delivered in a welcome basket. The dog then disappeared but Nick left the pot on the porch just in case.

The cottage was situated in a quiet and upscale community on a strip of island that stretched east from New York City.

It was flanked by two mansions and Nick had the feeling on first sight of the cottage that he was moving into the servant quarters. The cab driver had asked him if he was sure this was the right place and Nick said I guess so. When he stepped onto the porch that was missing a board and then walked inside and saw a mouse dash across the floor he had more of a feeling that the cottage had been simply forgotten. The landlady said herself that she would have had it cleaned had she remembered she was in charge of this property but had been surprised when she received the phone call that asked her to come and unlock the place. A young man is moving in.

Nick tucked his hands into his pockets. He crossed the yard and passed beneath the trees and looked out at the water. Out in front of the cottage lay the Long Island Sound and the water lapped lazily against the shore. He had been anxious during the day for this first night as he wanted to stand at the water. Look at the stars. Admire the lights of the mansions across the bay. He had already done that once and then slept for a few hours. And here he was again. Only an hour of night remained and then the sun would rise.

When he had finally arrived in Minnesota there was a moment of disbelief. His own disbelief as he stood in the street and through the windows watched his mother move from one room to the next. Watched his father cross behind her. The snow had been shoveled from the walkway leading to the front steps. Smoke swirled from the chimney. The same wreath on the same front door. An American flag hung from the mailbox. It had seemed like a photograph that belonged to someone else and he knocked as a stranger and when his father had opened the door the first thing he did was take a step back. Not recognizing his own son. A moment of disbelief they shared in as his mother came to see who was at the door and the three of them traded uncertain looks until his mother grabbed him with a gasp and pulled him inside.

He had then spent the last two years of his life in what seemed like purgatory. The first few weeks of his return were filled with the gladhearted embraces of aunts and uncles and old friends, embraces that he returned and believed in yet he was eager for them to be over. He had answered their questions about the war and France with little more than nods or shrugs and they answered most of their own questions with stories they had already read about in magazines or manufactured through bits and pieces of gossip. Nick marveled at how much those at home claimed to have shared in what had happened abroad and he found ways to politely excuse himself from a room when he sensed an interrogation coming on.

His father had asked him to work for the hardware business, which during Nick's time away had morphed from retail into wholesale. A real job, his father said. Nick agreed. He only worked halfdays as the work didn't take much time or effort. He sat in an office in the back of a downtown building and tallied invoices and updated orders and managed accounts. At noon he would walk out without speaking to anyone and each evening at dinner his father would ask him if he was happy with the job or satisfied to be back in the family business and Nick appeased his mother and father with polite affirmations.

In the empty hours he had begun to write.

First of Paris. He wrote long letters to Ella and each letter held the same messages of remorse and love and grief. He wrote in long sentences and the letters were extensive and sometimes rambling and sometimes incoherent but in the words Nick felt the expulsion of loss and he clawed for truth. For the truth about himself and why he was the way he was. He tried to explain to her how he had become a man with such a lack of dreams and ambition and he lamented his inability to grab her and hold on. He fought for the truth and spilled it out onto the page but he soon realized that his truth shifted from one day to the next and then he saw the letters to her as a confession. He felt the unburdening in the slanted cursive, trying to make peace. Admitting freely that he did not know what to do when they had found one another in the park and that except for one clumsy and embarrassing event at New Haven she was his only one. He wrote long letters that he began in the light and finished in the dark and he apologized for making her a creature of his imagination and a visitor to his dreams. He apologized for following the other women along the Paris streets and giving them her characteristics and making her anything but as true as flesh and blood. He thanked her for the sentence that he carried with him. I want to see you when you wake. He asked her where she was and begged her to show herself. He asked her if the baby seemed as real to her as it did to him as he could not help but imagine the child to be out there somewhere. Crying and hungry and looking for a mother and father who had drifted into shadow. He covered page after page and he kept the letters in a pile underneath his bed, trying to remain close to her.

Then he wrote of Judah and Colette. But he did not write about them with the same emotion or personal sentiment. Instead he treated them as if they were characters he had seen in a play. He described Frenchtown and its dark alleys and crooked streets with a journalistic tone, not in the language of someone who had felt its temptations and been affected by its offerings. He recorded the conversations he had with Judah in the backroom of the saloon and on the sheets of notebook paper the conversations went on for longer and made extreme proclamations and sometimes were intruded upon by a third voice that had never been in the original conversation. He saw a friend in Judah and he recounted meeting the man and helping the man but he created Judah in the way that a nurse might create a patient. He wrote of the love and hate between Judah and Colette and he burned down not only her brothel but several more and he raised the Frenchtown paranoia and destruction to such a level of calamity that the city seemed to be engulfed in a constant cloud of firesmoke. He wrote of Colette returning to the apartment and he created the look in Judah's eyes when he opened them and saw her there and he wrote of their happy ending one day and their unhappy ending the next. He wrote of doing what Judah had asked him to do and he wrote of Colette doing it instead. The smells of the streets and the calls from the open windows of the brothels created the stage setting and he casually misremembered following the girl into the alley and being beaten and robbed and he casually misremembered being drunk and passing out along the sidewalk. He casually left out the burned child and the devastated father. He wrote of Judah both as a friend and as a favorite and pitiable character.

He did not write about the war. He did not write about his dreams about the war. He did not write about the panic of waking in the middle of the night in the middle of a scream. He brought home two empty boxes from the office and on one of the box lids he wrote Paris and on the other he wrote Judah. He slid the stacks of pages out from underneath his bed and put them in the correct box and tried to compartmentalize his memories and emotions.

The letters to Paris and the descriptions of Frenchtown gave him something to look forward to each day, away from the desk in the office and away from the smiles from familiar faces along the sidewalk and away from the resignation of returning to the bedroom of his boyhood. He discovered that as he wrote his shaking hand remained calm pushed by language and memory and eventually the hand stopped altogether. Even when he woke with a jerk from gunfire or the rush of men his hand remained still. So he had kept writing.

He pulled his hand from his pocket now. Flexed the fingers. A boat horn sounded from across the Sound and he looked out into the gloaming sky. In this moment before daybreak he at last noticed a green light on the other side of the water. Seemingly at the end of a dock. A great and intimidating and well-lit house standing behind in the distance. The light flashed in a steady rhythm and Nick counted the time. On for two seconds. Off for two seconds. On for two. Off for two.

He had read the newspaper that arrived each morning at the hardware store and he had realized the East was running over with money and that was his way out. He had told his father he wanted to go and work in the stock market and his father assured him he knew nothing about it. That is why I want to go and learn, Nick explained. And I can't do it here. I can't do anything here. That is not true, his father replied. In response Nick continued to show no interest in the hardware business or the Midwestern life that held his parents so comfortably. He began to go into the office an hour before anyone else arrived so he could leave earlier. He skipped dinner at home to go for long walks, long walks where he talked and debated with himself in an effort to rekindle an intellect. He ignored weekend invitations to dinner parties and he rejected any suggestion of meeting the daughter of so-and-so and when his father explained to him that his behavior was not very becoming of his family's position, Nick had only taken out a handkerchief and blown his nose.

His father had finally said you can go East and I will support you for one year but you won't waste it in the stock market. The bond business. Me and your uncles agree that is where the future lies. After that year you are free to be on your own or you will come back here and take over this business. That is your offer.

Nick accepted. His father had a contact from New Haven at a firm in Manhattan and he made a call and Nick had a job. Two long weeks passed and then he packed a trunk with the boxes marked Paris and Judah buried on the bottom beneath the clothes. But ten minutes before he was to leave for the train station, he opened the trunk and dug and took out the boxes. He went upstairs to his room and all that he had written over the last two years, all the words that had helped to settle his hand and settle his thoughts, he hid underneath the chest of drawers that still held some of his childhood clothes. He then lay on the floor and whispered to Paris and Judah, I am going to start again.

Nick sat down on the damp ground. Another horn echoed and the earliest birds sang through the trees. Daylight was coming as the stars began to flake away in a melting sky and Nick closed his eyes. Felt the anticipation of a new day and his heart beat faster as he thought of the vast American city that awaited him. So many faces and sights and sounds and I will be one of the millions, he thought. I will join in.

He sat leaning back on extended arms and waited for the sunrise. He watched the world awake and he looked over toward the pier of the great mansion to his right. The shifting light of night to day and the mist from the water played with his eyes but he thought he saw a figure at the end of the pier. Nick watched for movement but it remained still. A silhouette waiting for dawn. But even in silhouette

Nick thought that the figure seemed to hold some magical stature, as if a fairytale were being whispered into his ear and his mind creating the vision for it. A gaggle of ducks landed in the water and caught Nick's attention and when he looked back to the pier the figure had vanished. He dismissed it as imagination and then he stood and the first light brushed the horizon. And he raised his arms and reached out for the dawn as if to warm his hands on the rising sun.

317

ACKNOWLEDGMENTS

Many thanks to Ellen Levine, Josh Kendall, Sabrina Callahan, Yuli Masinovsky, Jason Richman, and the teams at Little, Brown, No Exit Press, and Trident Media Group. As always my utmost thanks to my wife and daughters.

NO EXIT PRESS
More than just the usual suspects

'A very smart, independent publisher delivering the finest literary crime fiction' – *Big Issue*

MEET NO EXIT PRESS, the independent publisher bringing you the best in crime and noir fiction. From classic detective novels to page-turning spy thrillers and singular writing that just grabs the attention. Our books are carefully crafted by some of the world's finest writers and delivered to you by a small, but mighty, team.

In over 30 years of business, we have published award-winning fiction and non-fiction including the work of a Pulitzer Prize winner, the British Crime Book of the Year, numerous CWA Dagger Awards, a British million copy bestselling author, the winner of the Canadian Governor General's Award for Fiction and the Scotiabank Giller Prize, to name but a few. We are the home of many crime and noir legends from the USA whose work includes iconic film adaptations and TV sensations. We pride ourselves in uncovering the most exciting new or undiscovered talents. New and not so new – you know who you are!!

We are a proactive team committed to delivering the very best, both for our authors and our readers.

Want to join the conversation and find out more about what we do?

Catch us on social media or sign up to our newsletter for all the latest news from No Exit Press HQ.

f fb.me/noexitpress 🐦 @noexitpress
noexit.co.uk/newsletter